MOLLY THYNNE
DEATH IN THE DENTIST'S CHAIR

MARY 'MOLLY' THYNNE was born in 1881, a member of the aristocracy, and related, on her mother's side, to the painter James McNeil Whistler. She grew up in Kensington and at a young age met literary figures like Rudyard Kipling and Henry James.

Her first novel, *An Uncertain Glory*, was published in 1914, but she did not turn to crime fiction until *The Draycott Murder Mystery*, the first of six golden age mysteries she wrote and published in as many years, between 1928 and 1933. The last three of these featured Dr. Constantine, chess master and amateur sleuth *par excellence*.

Molly Thynne never married. She enjoyed travelling abroad, but spent most of her life in the village of Bovey Tracey, Devon, where she was finally laid to rest in 1950.

D0826509

BY MOLLY THYNNE

The Draycott Murder Mystery

The Murder on the Enriqueta

The Case of Sir Adam Braid

The Crime at the 'Noah's Ark': A Christmas Mystery

Death in the Dentist's Chair

He Dies and Makes no Sign

MOLLY THYNNE

DEATH IN THE DENTIST'S CHAIR

With an introduction by
Curtis Evans

DEAN STREET PRESS

Published by Dean Street Press 2016

Copyright © 1932 Molly Thynne
Introduction copyright © 2016 Curtis Evans

Cover by DSP

First published in 1932 by Hutchinson as
Murder in the Dentist's Chair

ISBN 978 1 911413 59 2

www.deanstreetpress.co.uk

INTRODUCTION

ALTHOUGH British Golden Age detective novels are known for their depictions of between-the-wars aristocratic life, few British mystery writers of the era could have claimed (had they been so inclined) aristocratic lineage. There is no doubt, however, about the gilded ancestry of Mary "Molly" Harriet Thynne (1881-1950), author of a half-dozen detective novels published between 1928 and 1933. Through her father Molly Thynne was descended from a panoply of titled ancestors, including Thomas Thynne, 2nd Marquess of Bath; William Bagot, 1st Baron Bagot; George Villiers, 4th Earl of Jersey; and William Bentinck, 2nd Duke of Portland. In 1923, five years before Molly Thynne published her first detective novel, the future crime writer's lovely second cousin (once removed), Lady Mary Thynne, a daughter of the fifth Marquess of Bath and habitué of society pages in both the United Kingdom and the United States, served as one of the bridesmaids at the wedding of the Duke of York and his bride (the future King George VI and Queen Elizabeth). Longleat, the grand ancestral estate of the marquesses of Bath, remains under the ownership of the Thynne family today, although the estate has long been open to the public, complete with its famed safari park, which likely was the inspiration for the setting of *A Pride of Heroes* (1969) (in the US, *The Old English Peep-Show*), an acclaimed, whimsical detective novel by the late British author Peter Dickinson.

Molly Thynne's matrilineal descent is of note as well, for through her mother, Anne "Annie" Harriet Haden, she possessed blood ties to the English etcher Sir Francis Seymour Haden (1818-1910), her maternal grandfather, and the American artist James McNeill Whistler (1834-1903), a great-uncle, who is still renowned today for his enduringly evocative *Arrangement in Grey and Black no. 1* (aka "Whistler's Mother"). As a child Annie Haden, fourteen years younger than her brilliant Uncle James, was the subject of some of the artist's earliest etchings.

Whistler's relationship with the Hadens later ruptured when his brother-in-law Seymour Haden became critical of what he deemed the younger artist's dissolute lifestyle. (Among other things Whistler had taken an artists' model as his mistress.) The conflict between the two men culminated in Whistler knocking Haden through a plate glass window during an altercation in Paris, after which the two men never spoke to one another again.

Molly Thynne grew up in privileged circumstances in Kensington, London, where her father, Charles Edward Thynne, a grandson of the second Marquess of Bath, held the position of Assistant Solicitor to His Majesty's Customs. According to the 1901 English census the needs of the Thynne family of four--consisting of Molly, her parents and her younger brother, Roger--were attended to by a staff of five domestics: a cook, parlourmaid, housemaid, under-housemaid and lady's maid. As an adolescent Molly spent much of her time visiting her Grandfather Haden's workroom, where she met a menagerie of artistic and literary lions, including authors Rudyard Kipling and Henry James.

Molly Thynne--the current Marquess has dropped the "e" from the surname to emphasize that it is pronounced "thin"--exhibited literary leanings of her own, publishing journal articles in her twenties and a novel, *The Uncertain Glory* (1914), when she was 33. *Glory*, described in one notice as concerning the "vicissitudes and love affairs of a young artist" in London and Munich, clearly must have drawn on Molly's family background, though one reviewer reassured potentially censorious middle-class readers that the author had "not over-accentuated Bohemian atmosphere" and in fact had "very cleverly diverted" sympathy away from "the brilliant-hued coquette who holds the stage at the commencement" of the novel toward "the plain-featured girl of noble character."

Despite good reviews for *The Uncertain Glory*, Molly Thynne appears not to have published another novel until she commenced her brief crime fiction career fourteen years later in 1928. Then for a short time she followed in the footsteps of such earlier heralded British women crime writers as Agatha Christie, Dorothy L. Sayers, Margaret Cole, Annie Haynes (also reprinted by Dean Street Press), Anthony Gilbert and A. Fielding. Between 1928 and 1933 there appeared from Thynne's hand six detective novels: *The Red Dwarf* (1928: in the US, *The Draycott Murder Mystery*), *The Murder on the "Enriqueta"* (1929: in the US, *The Strangler*), *The Case of Sir Adam Braid* (1930), *The Crime at the "Noah's Ark"* (1931), *Murder in the Dentist's Chair* (1932: in the US, *Murder in the Dentist Chair*) and *He Dies and Makes No Sign* (1933).

Three of Thynne's half-dozen mystery novels were published in the United States as well as in the United Kingdom, but none of them were reprinted in paperback in either country and the books rapidly fell out of public memory after Thynne ceased writing detective fiction in 1933, despite the fact that a 1930 notice speculated that "[Molly Thynne] is perhaps the best woman-writer of detective stories we know." The highly discerning author and crime fiction reviewer Charles Williams, a friend of C.S. Lewis and J.R.R. Tolkien and editor of Oxford University Press, also held Thynne in high regard, opining that Dr. Constantine, the "chess-playing amateur detective" in the author's *Murder in the Dentist's Chair,* "deserves to be known with the Frenches and the Fortunes" (this a reference to the series detectives of two of the then most highly-esteemed British mystery writers, Freeman Wills Crofts and H.C. Bailey). For its part the magazine *Punch* drolly cast its praise for Thynne's *The Murder on the "Enriqueta"* in poetic form.

> *The Murder on the "Enriqueta"* is a recent
>   thriller by Miss Molly Thynne,
> A book I don't advise you, if you're busy, to begin.
> It opens very nicely with a strangling on a liner
> Of a shady sort of passenger, an out-bound
>   Argentiner.
> And, unless I'm much mistaken, you will find

yourself unwilling
To lay aside a yarn so crammed with situations
    thrilling.
(To say nothing of a villain with a gruesome taste
    in killing.)

There are seven more lines, but readers will get the amusing gist of the piece from the quoted excerpt. More prosaic yet no less praiseful was a review of *Enriqueta* in *The Outlook*, an American journal, which promised "excitement for the reader in this very well written detective story ... with an unusual twist to the plot which adds to the thrills."

Despite such praise, the independently wealthy Molly Thynne in 1933 published her last known detective novel (the third of three consecutive novels concerning the cases of Dr. Constantine) and appears thereupon to have retired from authorship. Having proudly dubbed herself a "spinster" in print as early as 1905, when she was but 24, Thynne never married. When not traveling in Europe (she seems to have particularly enjoyed Rome, where her brother for two decades after the First World War served as Secretary of His Majesty's Legation to the Holy See), Thynne resided at Crewys House, located in the small Devon town of Bovey Tracey, the so-called "Gateway to the Moor." She passed away in 1950 at the age of 68 and was laid to rest after services at Bovey Tracey's Catholic Church of the Holy Spirit. Now, over sixty-five years later, Molly Thynne's literary legacy happily can be enjoyed by a new generation of vintage mystery fans.

Curtis Evans

CHAPTER ONE

"RINSE, PLEASE."

The words reached the patient faintly, coming, it seemed, from an immeasurable distance. Barely conscious though he was, he experienced the mere ghost of a sense of satisfaction. He was still alive, then.

He opened his eyes. Mr. Humphrey Davenport was standing over him holding a glass full of a pinkish liquid in his hand, his long, yellow countenance wrinkled into an encouraging smile.

"Rinse, please," he repeated. This time the words came briskly and clearly.

The patient sat up and rinsed obediently. The liquid, as it left his mouth, took on a much deeper shade of red, and, at the sight of it, the full significance of this weird ritual came home to him. He made a swift exploration with his tongue and discovered a truly awful void.

"'Ou-ve thathen them au' outh!" he ejaculated faintly.

Long experience had made Mr. Davenport familiar with this form of elocution. He beamed.

"All the upper incisors," he assented cheerfully. "Eight altogether. They came out beautifully. Like to see them?"

He held out a repulsive little tray before which his victim recoiled, the full sense of his loss slowly dawning on him. His front teeth had gone and nothing in the world would bring them back. He returned to his rinsing. There seemed nothing else to do and, as he bent over his task, he heard the door close softly behind the doctor. The whole ghastly business was over.

The dentist chatted on.

"We'll give the gums time to recover and then fit you up with a temporary plate. Meanwhile, I should like to see the mouth again. Sometime tomorrow, if you can manage it."

The patient's sense of humour had never been very conspicuous and, at the moment, it was greatly in abeyance, but even he could see the irony of such an implication.

"I'm harthy lithy tho hathe athy enthathemeth," he lisped bitterly. Then, with a more acute realisation of the disaster that had befallen him. "Goo' Heatheth, I carth eveth torth dithincly!"

Once more Mr. Davenport exhibited uncanny skill in interpretation.

"You'll soon get used to that," he asserted reassuringly. "By tomorrow we shall have you talking splendidly. It's only a question of habit."

He flicked over the leaves of his engagement book.

"Three o'clock tomorrow, then," he said. "And the address? You gave it to me, I remember, but, for the moment, I have forgotten."

The patient suspended his rinsing operations.

"Therthothethy Thotheth," he volunteered painfully.

For a moment even Mr. Davenport was baffled.

"Perthoaythy Hothay," amended the patient, with an immense effort.

The dentist's face cleared.

"Of course. The Pergolese Hotel. Mr. Cattistock."

Mr. Davenport inscribed a neat little card and handed it to him. Ten minutes later he was being bowed out and when, badly shaken, morally and physically, he returned to the waiting room, a large handkerchief pressed to the lower part of his face, he presented a spectacle calculated to inspire terror in the minds of any other of Mr. Davenport's patients unfortunate enough to see him.

There was only one. Sir Richard Pomfrey, already a prey to uneasiness, gave one glance in his direction and retired behind the decayed periodical in which he had been trying to interest himself.

"Good Lord," he murmured and wished, sincerely and devoutly, that the morning was over.

A moment later his summons came and, squaring his shoulders, he strode out to meet his fate.

One ordeal still remained to Mr. Cattistock. Left to himself, he rose shakingly to his feet and, approaching the mirror over the mantelpiece, removed the handkerchief from his mouth. He gave one glance at his reflection and, with a low moan, tottered back to his seat and retired once more behind his already nauseating yashmak.

He sat huddled in his chair, slowly recovering from Mr. Davenport's ministrations. The effects had been moral rather than physical and, as his mind readjusted itself, his despair increased. Never again, he felt convinced, would he enjoy the sound of his own voice, mellow and well-modulated, faultlessly articulating the noble prose he loved so well. He realised, now that it was too late, how sinfully proud he had been of his delivery. No doubt this was a judgment, and a just one, on his vanity.

He had reached this depressing, but far from comforting, stage in his reflections when the door opened and another patient invaded his solitude. He regarded her over the edge of his handkerchief with the faint interest of the wholly miserable.

She swept in, exuding opulence and well-being, and Mr. Cattistock, who in his normal state was a kindly, tolerant person, took an instant and violent dislike to her. And for this he had some excuse, though his mental denunciations were perhaps unnecessarily acrimonious. She was too fat, he told himself viciously, too old for her ultra-fashionable and expensive clothes, and altogether too dyed, painted and powdered. He took exception to the small, scarlet, bad-tempered mouth, but, most of all, he hated her for her teeth which showed, small and white and even, between the painted lips. Mr. Cattistock was an unsophisticated person and none too observant at the best of times and he had no inkling that those teeth owed their being to the skill of Mr. Humphrey Davenport. Had he known this, a faint ray of light might have illuminated his gloom. As it was he was thrust, if possible, even more deeply into the abyss by the atrocious manners of the newcomer, who gave one glance at his now revolting handkerchief, turned away with an exaggerated shudder of disgust and, pointedly altering the position of an armchair, sat down with her back to him. Mr. Cattistock loathed her as he crouched in his corner, trying to summon up sufficient energy to go away.

From his position he could only see her hand now, fat, coarsely moulded and heavily beringed, the fingers beating an impatient tattoo on the arm of her chair. Insensibly he began appraising the rings which loaded the pudgy fingers. He possessed a love and appreciation of precious stones quite out of keeping with his circumstances and hated to see them in uncongenial surroundings. There was an emerald on her third finger that must have cost a fortune. Then she rose and, bending over the table, tossed the papers over impatiently in an attempt to find something to read. The full panoply of her regalia was now revealed to Mr. Cattistock and he gasped at the sight. For above the diamond star that heaved upon her bosom hung another emerald, the finest he had ever seen, and Mr. Cattistock, in his day, had handled some of the rarest jewels in the world.

He was still blinking at it when the door opened to the sound of voices and Sir Richard Pomfrey came in, in animated conversation with another patient he had encountered in the hall. His face showed the complacence of one whose visit to the dentist is over, but Cattistock, watching him idly, saw the satisfaction cloud for a second, as his eyes fell on the wearer of the emeralds. Then he turned away and gave all his attention to his companion. Cattistock, interested, cast a glance at the face of the stout lady and was shocked at the venom he saw there. Her lips parted, and he thought she was about to give expression to her feelings; then, before the little drama could develop further, the door opened and she was swept out of the room in the wake of Mr. Davenport's deferential manservant. Sir Richard did not seem to notice her departure, but Cattistock could have sworn that there was relief in his eyes as he bent over the lady he was addressing. Everything about her was in delightful contrast to her predecessor, and Mr. Cattistock, even in his present jaundiced state, found pleasure in looking at her. He continued to do so until she happened to glance in his direction and he surprised a look of mingled sympathy and repugnance in her eyes. He glanced at his handkerchief and realised, with a shock, that it was deeply stained with red. Feeling suddenly abominably conspicuous, he rose and left the room.

Sir Richard's relief at his departure was undisguised. He hitched his chair closer to that of his companion and took up the conversation where it had ceased on their entrance into the room. For another five minutes or so it flowed on uninterruptedly and Mrs. Vallon had almost forgotten the aching tooth that had brought her to Mr. Davenport's dread portals, when the turning of the door handle and the soft murmur of the manservant's voice gave warning of a further intrusion.

Sir Richard turned, with something approaching a scowl on his good-tempered face, and glowered at the new arrival. The latter, unperturbed, regarded him quizzically.

Sir Richard's annoyance vanished abruptly.

"Dr. Constantine!" he exclaimed. "What's brought you here?"

Constantine placed his hat and stick on the table.

"'The aching void the world can never fill,'" he quoted, with a sigh. "Only that or wild horses would drag me to Ilbeck Street. Am I really the third on the list?"

Sir Richard grinned.

"Your turn will come soon enough," he assured him. "Davenport's finished with me, thank the Lord. You know Mrs. Vallon, I think. She's for it in a minute."

Constantine bowed gravely.

"Moritorus te saluto," he murmured. "I knew your husband well, Mrs. Vallon, in the great days of the Pagoda, but I don't think we ever met. The old theatre has gone deplorably downhill since then."

He was rewarded by an appreciative glance from her fine eyes. Her late husband had been the most brilliant actor-manager of his day, but she was already beginning to learn that reputations swiftly made are, nowadays, as swiftly forgotten, and she was grateful for so genuine a tribute.

"I am glad sometimes that he did not live to see it in other hands," was all she said, but she looked on Constantine now with friendliness as well as interest.

She had heard of him, of course, but, until now, they had never met. The only son of a rich Greek merchant, he had been a notable figure in London society when she was still a girl at school, partly owing to his good looks, partly to sheer force of character. He was one of the finest chess players in England, but Society recks little of the game and had this been his only claim to distinction, he would have been unknown outside the chess columns of the daily papers. As it was, it would be difficult to define the reasons for his success. "Constantine has a flair for everything," Mrs. Vallon's shrewd old father had once said, "from cooking to Grand Opera, and his taste's hardly ever at fault." With the instinct of an acknowledged beauty she knew now that this flair extended to pretty women and that, as he faced her, his dark eyes ablaze with a vitality disconcerting in so old a man, he was appreciating her to the full. With the frankness that was part of her charm she returned the compliment. Beside Constantine's clear-cut, olive-skinned features, a trifle fine-drawn now with age, surmounted by the still thick, virile white hair, Sir Richard's florid good looks seemed blunted and coarsened. With a queer little feeling of protection she turned to the younger man, found his gaze, as usual, fixed upon her, and for reasons she could not define, liked him all the better for the clumsiness of his patent adoration.

"Richard's crowing too soon," she said. "He's only reached the temporary stopping stage, so far. His time's to come."

Constantine smiled.

"Then I've the advantage of both of you," he declared. "*My* tooth was stopped on Thursday! I've only dropped in for a final polish. Judging by the unfortunate remnant of humanity I met on the doorstep, Davenport's in a savage mood today!"

Mrs. Vallon shuddered.

"Don't!" she implored him. "Do you realise that my tooth *hurts?* Goodness knows what he may be going to do to me!"

Sir Richard moved uneasily. He was in no mood for a three-cornered conversation.

"I'll just ring my man up," he said. "Then I must be going. It takes hours to get anywhere in this beastly fog. In case you're in Davenport's clutches when I get back, good luck! I hope he'll stop it aching, anyway," he added, as he shook hands with Mrs. Vallon.

The manservant was not in the hall, but Sir Richard had used Davenport's telephone before and knew where to find it. He switched on the light and, shutting himself into the dark little cupboard under the stairs, rang up his flat.

Meanwhile Mrs. Vallon and Constantine settled down to the task of knowing each other better. They possessed a host of common acquaintances and it was due only to the fact that she still clung to the theatrical set in which she had moved during her husband's lifetime that they had not met before. With unerring instinct Constantine led the conversation to Sir Richard, whom he had known since his schooldays, and found instantaneous response. It was easy to see how things stood between these two.

The minutes passed. Mrs. Vallon's tooth, which, after the manner of aching teeth, had become steadily less painful since she had made her appointment with Mr. Davenport, had now ceased to hurt. Indeed, until Constantine alluded to it, she had forgotten all about it.

"Does Davenport know that you're in pain?" he asked. "It isn't like him to keep you waiting."

"I'm not," she answered. "It's stopped aching altogether! If he doesn't see me soon, I shall turn tail and go home! I can't keep my courage screwed up to concert pitch forever!"

Constantine looked at his watch.

"My appointment was for twelve," he said, "and it's a quarter past now. Richard must be ringing up half London."

As he spoke the door opened and Sir Richard came in.

"Couldn't get through for ages," he said. "There's no end of a fuss going on in the hall outside. Davenport can't get into his own consulting room! He's sent down for some tools, his man tells me. Doesn't look as if you were going to get your turn for some time yet."

Constantine looked up quickly.

"Has the last patient gone, then?" he asked.

Sir Richard shrugged his shoulders.

"The chap outside says he hasn't let her out. I thought I should find her in here."

Constantine rose and moved swiftly to the door.

"I say," expostulated Sir Richard, "she can't be locked in there. She'd have made an appalling shindy by this time!"

But Constantine had left the room, inspired by two motives: one, an inveterate dislike to playing gooseberry, the other, that flair for a situation that lay behind the insatiable curiosity that had led him into so many strange places in the course of his varied life.

CHAPTER TWO

CONSTANTINE PASSED quickly down the hall and joined the little group outside the consulting room door.

The dentist's mechanic who had been summoned from the workroom below was kneeling in front of it, removing the screws from the lock. Mr. Davenport, austere and priestlike in his white overall, stood over him, a worried frown on his usually imperturbable countenance.

"I can't understand it," he was saying. "I could swear the key was there when I came out. Can you get the lock off?"

The mechanic nodded.

"It's coming," he replied. "Lucky the screws are on the outside."

Davenport's eyes fell on the new arrival.

"I'm sorry to keep you waiting, Dr. Constantine," he said. "But you see what's happened. I've never known that lock to do such a thing before."

Constantine was watching the mechanic.

"The key's gone, I see," he remarked.

"It's not on the other side," answered Davenport. "You can see right through the keyhole. I'm practically certain it was on the outside as usual when I came out, but of course I wasn't looking for it. I may be wrong."

"It's lucky for you that it chose a moment between two appointments," continued Constantine. "I'm not sure that I should care to be incarcerated among your instruments of torture myself!"

The dentist's frown deepened.

"It didn't," he snapped. "There's a patient in there now, unless she slipped out while I was in the workroom downstairs."

"She's being very quiet then," said Constantine thoughtfully. "I wonder what she thinks is happening. Who is she?"

"Mrs. Miller."

Constantine raised his eyebrows.

"Not Charles Miller's wife?"

The dentist nodded.

"The last person I would have had this happen to," he murmured sombrely. "She won't forget it. One of my best patients, too."

Constantine moved nearer to the door, bent his head and listened.

"Not a sound," he said. "Yet she must know someone's at work on the door. If Mrs. Miller were inside we should have heard from her by now, if I know anything of the lady. I think you may take it that she's gone home. Probably got tired of waiting and slammed the door after her, jamming the lock. It's the sort of thing she would do."

For answer Davenport thrust his hand into his overall pocket, withdrew it and disclosed its contents.

"Not without her teeth," he asserted gloomily. "I've got them here."

Constantine's mouth twitched involuntarily, but there was no answering gleam in Davenport's sombre face. He was gazing with professional pride at the denture in his hand.

"There was a small adjustment," he continued. "I went downstairs to make it. I was counting on having them fitted and being well on with my next patient by now."

The mechanic twiddled the last screw out and dropped it into his pocket.

"Done it," he said, as he helped the lock away from the door with the screw driver. "It was locked all right. No wonder we couldn't open it."

He rose to his feet, stood back while Davenport pushed past him into the room, then collected his tools and departed to his lair in the basement.

Constantine lingered. He had no earthly excuse to go in, but for the life of him he could not resist waiting to overhear Mrs. Miller's reception of Davenport.

To his surprise there was not a sound from inside the room. Unconsciously he moved nearer to the door. Davenport was a taciturn creature, but surely even he would hardly go quietly about his business without a word of explanation to a notoriously temperamental patient? Mrs. Miller's silence was more easily accounted for. Constantine's lips twitched again as he reflected on the various means dentists have at their disposal should they wish to restrict any undue flow of language on the part of their patients. He knew Mrs. Miller well by sight and had even overheard her give vent to exasperation, and the vision of her deftly gagged, say, with a little tray of plaster of Paris, was an alluring one.

He was startled into alertness by the sound of his own name.

"Dr. Constantine, are you there?"

Davenport's voice was low-pitched and even as usual, but there was an unnatural note of restraint about it that Constantine's sharp ears were quick to detect and which brought him over the threshold before his own reply had left his lips.

At the first glance there seemed nothing unusual in the scene before him. Mrs. Miller was undoubtedly there, seated in the dentist's chair, facing the window, her back to the door. He could see the top of her head and one pudgy, over-jewelled hand that was resting on the arm of the chair. On the other side of the chair stood Davenport. Constantine's brain had time to register two impressions: one, the unwonted quietness of Mrs. Miller, the other, the hue of Davenport's face, which now exactly matched the spotless white of the surgical overall he wore, before the dentist spoke again in that toneless voice that, but for the most rigid self-control, would have been a shout.

"Will you shut the door, please, and look at this?"

Constantine closed the door. Owing to the absence of a lock he could not latch it. Then he crossed the room to the dentist's chair.

Davenport's voice came again, repeating, parrot-like:

"Just look at this!"

Constantine looked.

There was a long silence before he spoke.

"What a fiendish business," he whispered at last. Then: "Poor, poor soul!"

Mrs. Miller's head lay tilted back against the head-rest of the chair, her mouth slightly open, as though awaiting Davenport's ministrations. But where the fat white roll of flesh underneath her chin should have been was now a larger and more gaping travesty of the toothless mouth above, a dark gash in which the blood that had now ceased to spurt still frothed and bubbled.

Involuntarily Constantine closed his eyes, in a futile attempt to shut out the horror, only to find himself confronted with a worse assault upon his senses, for the darkness became filled with the hot, sweet reek of blood. With a shudder, he opened them again, keeping them resolutely away from the chair and its burden. But there was blood everywhere, even on the glass of the window pane, where a little trickle had already reached the white woodwork.

Davenport was speaking mechanically, with stiff, dry lips.

"Right through the jugular," he said. "God, what a mess."

He stared at the denture in his hand with mild surprise, as though he were seeing it for the first time, and made a movement to put it down on the table by his side. But the table was in no fit state to receive it and his hand shot back as though it had been stung. With an air of concentration that would have been absurd in other circumstances he crossed to the mantelpiece and carefully deposited the denture on it. He stood gazing at it, his back to the room.

"I'd better get onto the police," he said, at last.

Constantine nodded. He had been watching Davenport and, oddly enough, in doing so, had regained his own nerve. The passionate desire to know, stronger than any idle curiosity, that had lured him down so many odd bye-paths in the course of his life and had kept him young and full of zest in spite of his years, had asserted itself, and in contemplating Davenport's reactions to the shock, he had insensibly shaken himself free from the mists of pity and disgust that had obscured his vision. He stepped back from the body and took the scene in, in detail, for the first time.

The result was a low exclamation that brought the dentist to his side. His eyes followed Constantine's pointing finger.

"Don't touch it," Constantine warned him. "That's what it was done with, though."

Lying on the floor, to the left of the dentist's chair, was a knife, not unlike a butcher's carver in shape, but with a somewhat broader blade, its handle half covered by the sleeve of a garment of some kind that had been flung down beside it.

"Looks like one of my overalls," said Davenport, bending over it. "There was one hanging in the work room. ..."

His voice trailed off as he raised himself with a little shiver of disgust. The thing was drenched with blood.

"I can't stand this," he said suddenly. "The place is a shambles. Besides, we must do something."

Constantine laid a hand on his shoulder.

"Steady," he said. "Where's your telephone?"

"In the hall, under the stairs."

"Get onto the police, then, and tell them to bring a surgeon. I'll keep watch on the door here and see that no one comes in."

He did not follow Davenport out of the room, however, but stood brooding, his keen eyes taking in every detail of the scene before him. When at last he did move it was to step carefully to the window and stand peering down onto the leads that formed the roof of the kitchen underneath.

When Davenport returned from the telephone he found him in the hall, just closing the door of the consulting room behind him.

"I've found the key," he said.

Davenport stared at him.

"The key?" he repeated stupidly.

"Of this room, presumably. It's on the leads outside the window there. It looks as if whoever attacked Mrs. Miller made his exit that way after locking the door."

Davenport assented absently. His mind was on other things.

"That's a matter for the police," he said. "They're on their way here now. What's bothering me is, those people in the waiting room. My brain's gone, but there should be a couple of patients there. What am I to do? Get rid of them, or wait till the police come?"

"There was only one when I left. Mrs. Vallon. Sir Richard Pomfrey's there, but I gather that he's seen you."

Davenport frowned irritably.

"What's he hanging about for?" he snapped. "My patients don't usually cling to the premises after I've done with them!"

"Done for them, you mean," countered Constantine unkindly.

But his eyes were friendly and a little anxious. Davenport, he knew, had spent three years of the war in a German prison camp and his nerves were none too good. He was badly rattled now and had a long and troublesome interview with the police before him. Constantine detached his mind for a moment from the tragedy.

"Got anything to drink in the house?" he asked.

"Yes. I lunch here, you know. Can I get you something?"

Constantine placed a hand on his shoulder and pushed him gently in the direction of the stairs.

"Nothing for me, I can think better without it. Get yourself a stiff drink and take things quietly for a minute or two. You've time before the police get here."

Davenport hesitated, then ran swiftly up the stairs. Constantine stood thoughtfully regarding the waiting room door. The mask had dropped from his face now and he looked an old man, tired and apprehensive. His usual clarity of vision had deserted him and his mind was fumbling. He was trying to remember how long he had sat by the fire talking to Mrs. Vallon while Sir Richard was out of the room, trying to recall Sir Richard's face and the tone of his voice when he rejoined them, and all the time hearing again Davenport's fretful comments: "What was he hanging about for?" He had known Richard Pomfrey all his life and the thing was ridiculous on the face of it, but Constantine had lived long enough to know that nothing is too absurd to be true. He moved uncertainly towards the door and found the manservant at his elbow.

"Is anything the matter, sir?" he asked.

Constantine jerked his thoughts back to the present. The man looked honest and dependable and, in any case, he would have to know the truth soon.

"There has been a tragedy, I'm afraid," he said. "Mr. Davenport's last patient, Mrs. Miller, has died suddenly."

"In the consulting room, sir?"

The man's shocked voice suggested that Mrs. Miller had taken an unpardonable liberty.

"Unfortunately, yes," answered Constantine. "Mr. Davenport has sent for the police. Meanwhile, no one is to go into that room until they arrive. You had better turn away any patients who may come. Here is Mr. Davenport. He will tell you what to say to them."

As Davenport rejoined them the door bell rang. Constantine watched the man open it, caught a glimpse of blue uniforms on the step outside, and slipped quietly through the door into the waiting room, closing it behind him.

Sir Richard Pomfrey was in the act of settling himself into his overcoat before picking up his hat and gloves from the table. Perhaps Constantine's perceptions were abnormally acute, but it seemed to him that there was a touch of apprehension in his hasty turn towards the opening door. Mrs. Vallon was standing by the mantelpiece, staring down into the fire. She looked up as Constantine entered.

"Hullo," was Sir Richard's greeting. "I'm off. Mrs. Vallon has just been accusing you of pinching her appointment!"

Constantine, watching him closely, came to the conclusion that he had been mistaken. Sir Richard's blue eyes were as frank and carefree as usual and it was difficult to believe that he had any premonition of the news that the old man had determined to be the first to impart. He realised suddenly that if he intended to forestall the police it behooved him to get on with his job.

"I'm afraid Mrs. Vallon's appointment is postponed for the present," he said soberly, his eyes on Sir Richard's face. But he learned nothing there.

"Why? What's the matter with Davenport?" was his only comment.

Briefly, and with due regard to Mrs. Vallon's nerves, Constantine broke the news that Mrs. Miller was dead.

Sir Richard stared at him.

"Dead? Did she die under gas, or what? Poor old Davenport must be in a state!"

"I'm afraid it wasn't gas," said Constantine deliberately. "It looks like murder. The police are in the house now."

A gasp from Mrs. Vallon made him turn. At the sight of her face he hurried towards her, but Sir Richard forestalled him. His arm round her waist, he drew her gently towards a chair.

"It's all right," Constantine heard him murmur, as she sank into it.

She looked up at him and, as she did so, the colour slowly flooded back into her cheeks.

"I'm sorry," she said, with a valiant effort at self-control. Then her eyes met Constantine's.

"But I don't see ..." she continued. She paused to collect her thoughts. "Was that the woman who went out as we came in?" she asked.

Sir Richard nodded.

"Davenport's man came for her," he agreed. "I say, we must have been sitting here, just next door, when it happened. Pretty gruesome, what?"

Again that flickering doubt crossed Constantine's mind. Sir Richard's tone was sympathetic, but that was all. He showed none of the horrified pity that might be expected from one who, as Constantine knew, had once been at least an acquaintance of the dead woman.

Mrs. Vallon covered her eyes for a moment with her hand.

"How horrible," she whispered. "But how could she have been killed? Mr. Davenport was with her, surely? It wasn't. ..."

Constantine shook his head.

"It wasn't Davenport," he assured her. "He was downstairs in his work room. That's the extraordinary part of it. He couldn't have left her for more than a few minutes, but somebody knew and took advantage of his absence. When he got back he found her sitting in the chair, dead!"

Sir Richard was staring at the gloves he held, smoothing them with his hand. It seemed as though realisation were coming to him slowly.

"Poor soul," he said, at last. "It's a pretty beastly end, isn't it?"

"You knew her, didn't you?" asked Constantine.

Sir Richard nodded.

"We all knew her in those days," he answered. "She was one of a crowd. She'd altered a lot, though. I shouldn't have known her if I'd come on her suddenly. I fancy that marriage wasn't much of a success."

There was pity in his voice now and Constantine reflected with an inward smile that, after all, he was only acting true to type. His nerves had always been of the kind that go with beef and muscle and he had never suffered from an over-developed imagination. Mrs. Vallon was less shock proof.

"It's horrible," she repeated. "Can't we go away? I don't feel as if I could ever go into that room or sit in that chair again."

Constantine was about to reply when the door opened. A police inspector, solid and imperturbable, stood in the opening.

Sir Richard immediately took charge of the situation. As a confirmed motorist, he considered that he had acquired a technique in dealing with the police.

"Dr. Constantine has been telling us what has happened," he said. "This lady, Mrs. Vallon, would like to get away. I suppose there's nothing to keep us, is there, officer?"

The inspector consulted his note book.

"Sir Richard Pomfrey?" he demanded.

Sir Richard nodded. His tactics did not seem to be meeting with their usual success.

"I must ask for your address and those of this lady and gentleman."

It was not until he had entered them in his book that he answered Sir Richard's question.

"I'm afraid I shall have to ask you to remain here until the detective inspector from the Yard arrives. It will only be a matter of minutes now. If you'd stay in this room, please."

He turned and, before they could expostulate, the door had closed behind him.

Sir Richard glared at Constantine.

"The thing's absurd!" he declared angrily. "He can't keep Mrs. Vallon here against her will!"

"He can and will," said Constantine. "Let's make the best of it till Scotland Yard takes over. How's the tooth, Mrs. Vallon?"

Mrs. Vallon stared at him blankly.

"The tooth?" she repeated. "Oh, I'd forgotten it. It isn't hurting at all now. This awful business. ..."

"Is an efficient but drastic way of curing toothache," pursued Constantine imperturbably. "Unfortunately one could hardly set up as a dentist on those lines!"

Ignoring Sir Richard's still simmering wrath he strolled to the window and stood looking out into the fog-bound street. He had no intention of allowing his choleric friend to put himself in the wrong with the police at this stage of the affair. "I was wondering about the movements of that rather battered little person I met as I was coming in," he continued. "Was he here when you arrived?"

Mrs. Vallon looked up quickly, her interest aroused.

"Yes, he was," she answered. "Surely you don't think he had anything to do with it? He looked such a poor little creature."

"I was thinking more of the questions we are likely to be asked," said Constantine. "We may as well get our facts straight now. What, exactly, did happen?"

"When I arrived? Well, I met Richard in the hall and we came in here together."

"I'd just come out of the consulting room," put in Sir Richard grudgingly. "The fellow's appointment was immediately before mine. He came in here, looking pretty gruesome, a couple of minutes before Davenport sent for me."

"Who was here when you came back with Mrs. Vallon?"

"The little man and a fat woman, smothered with jewels, who I suppose was Mrs. Miller," answered Mrs. Vallon.

"Which of them left the room first?"

Mrs. Vallon hesitated, but Sir Richard cut in quickly.

"Mrs. Miller. She went to take her appointment and I stayed on, keeping Mrs. Vallon company until her turn came. The little chap went out about ten minutes later."

"How long was that before I arrived?"

"Directly, I should think. You must have met him in the hall."

Sir Richard had a distinct impression that, until Constantine left them to investigate the commotion in the hall, he and Mrs. Vallon had not had three consecutive minutes alone together that morning, but it would seem he was mistaken.

"Oh, no," expostulated Mrs. Vallon. "He left at least five minutes, nearer ten, I should say, before Dr. Constantine got here. I know, because I had my eye more or less on the clock. Davenport kept me waiting three quarters of an hour last time I came and I meant to expostulate with him if he did it again. You see, I'd sent in word that my tooth was aching."

Constantine's interest quickened.

"You're sure of that?" he asked sharply.

She nodded.

"Quite."

"And yet I met him on the doorstep when I arrived. Where was he in the interval?" he said slowly.

"Probably washing his face in the lavatory," suggested Sir Richard. "The poor little chap was in the deuce of a mess. Looked as if Davenport had been extracting with a vengeance."

Constantine turned once more to Mrs. Vallon.

"Have you any idea what time it was when Richard got back from the telephone?" he asked.

She reflected for a moment. Her eyes met his and he knew that, though she realised the danger of the question, she had determined to be frank with him.

"Let me see," she said. "I know I looked at the clock then because I was beginning to get annoyed with Mr. Davenport. It was close on ten minutes past twelve. I'd meant to go to my hairdresser's before lunch and I came definitely to the conclusion then that I shouldn't have time, even if I got my appointment at once."

"And I arrived at twelve, to the minute. Davenport must have been fiddling with that door for at least five minutes before I joined him. It looks as if the door was already locked when I met that man on the doorstep."

His eyes were once more on the street and, as he spoke, he saw the figures he had been waiting for loom through the fog and mount the steps. He swung round and went swiftly to the door.

"Stay where you are. I think release is at hand," was all he vouchsafed to them as he left the room.

He reached the hall in time to meet the new arrivals. One of them, an enormous man, wrapped in a voluminous frieze overcoat, greeted him with surprised cordiality not unmixed with amusement.

"On the spot again, Dr. Constantine," he chuckled, as he shook hands. "How much have you got up your sleeve this time?"

Constantine laughed. He and Detective Inspector Arkwright had cemented their friendship since their first meeting at the Noah's Ark Inn and this was one of several standing jokes between them.

"I'm fumbling," he admitted. "In any case, you'll know as much as I do in ten minutes. Meanwhile, I've got a request to make."

He drew him aside and laid the case of Sir Richard and Mrs. Vallon before him, with the result that, five minutes later, he was seeing them off from the front door.

He watched their taxi disappear into the mist, then made his way back into the house. Arkwright and his minions were in the consulting room and Constantine, as he passed the door, felt no desire to join them there. His course carried him on and through a door situated at the end of the passage, behind the stairs.

It was ten minutes before he emerged, rubbing a pair of hands black with grime on a once spotless handkerchief, satisfaction written on his countenance. He had cause for elation, for he had almost, if not quite, laid the spectre that had been haunting him ever since the discovery of the tragedy.

As he crossed the hall Arkwright came out of the telephone box.

"Been ringing up the ambulance," he said. "The photographer's at work in there now. Nasty mess, isn't it?"

He surveyed Constantine, his lips expanding into a slow smile.

"Have you got a line on anything, sir?" he asked. "If you have, it looks rather as if it had taken you up the chimney!"

Constantine tucked away his handkerchief.

"I hate dirty hands," he said, "and the trouble is that, as things stand, I can't wash them."

Arkwright looked puzzled, then leaped to his meaning.

"The lavatory!" he exclaimed. "Have you found anything there?"

Constantine led him down the hall and into the lavatory. The reason why he had been unable to use the basin was immediately apparent. The water had been allowed to run out, but a small, pinkish residue still remained and there was a smear of blood on the china rim of the basin. The towel, flung carelessly on a chair, was mottled with bloodstains.

"Washed his hands here before making his get-away," commented Arkwright.

"And this is where he went," added Constantine, as he crossed to the window and opened it.

Arkwright peered out, then, supporting himself on his hands, raised himself until he was seated on the sill, his head outside the window.

"Across the leads and in at the window next door," he substantiated. "He's left his tracks plainly enough in the soot. You didn't get out there?"

Constantine eyed him reproachfully.

"At my age?" he answered. "No, those tracks are not mine. I collected all my soot from the window-sill, which, by the way, bore no traces except a smear made, I imagine, by our friend's leg when he climbed out."

Arkwright let himself down into die room.

"I noticed that before I sat on it," he said, with a touch of amusement. "We'll follow this up. Anything else, sir?"

"A question, first. You've got a list of the patients out of Davenport, I suppose. Who was the little man whose appointment was just before Mrs. Miller's?"

Arkwright thrust a grimy hand into his pocket and produced a note book.

"Name of Cattistock," he read out. "Address, Pergolese Hotel."

CHAPTER THREE

"THAT'S AS FAR as I have got up to the present," Constantine concluded. Rising to his feet, he produced tobacco from his pocket and began filling his pipe. Arkwright extracted a match box and held it out to him.

"You did some useful spade-work before I arrived," he admitted ungrudgingly. "Funny about that little chap, Cattistock. It doesn't sound as if he'd got the temperament or the physique for a job of that sort. And yet Davenport knows nothing about him, except that he came on the recommendation of an old patient, the manager of the hotel he's staying at. From Davenport's account he must have been feeling genuinely groggy when he came out of the consulting room. He says he gave him no end of a gruelling. Doesn't think he'd be fit for much for several hours to come. In spite of which he hasn't got back to his hotel yet and they've heard nothing of him."

"He may have been taken ill on his way there," suggested Constantine, hoping devoutly that this was not the explanation.

His mind had been more at ease since the discovery of the marks on the leads outside the lavatory window, but there still remained a persistent pin-prick, that time to be accounted for when Sir Richard was presumably trying to get onto his rooms on the telephone. He was hoping it wasn't pricking Arkwright, too, when, almost as though he had been following his train of thought, the detective spoke.

"I shall have to see Mrs. Vallon and Sir Richard Pomfrey," he said. "Your account satisfies me all right, but I must get their statements direct. Meanwhile, I'll just verify the times as I've got them here."

The two men were in Davenport's waiting room. Mrs. Miller's body had been removed and the consulting room sealed. Arkwright had taken the statements of the dentist, his mechanic and Betts, the manservant, and had made his way along the leads and in at the window of the house next door. The house had been standing empty for some time and everything was thick with dust. This had been sufficiently displaced to show that someone had passed through the ground floor room that gave onto the leads, indeed the window the intruder had used had been left open. But the tracks were too blurred and indistinct to show whether the person had been coming or going, and, beyond verifying the murderer's means of entry or exit, Arkwright had discovered nothing. The detective had then adjourned to the dentist's waiting room, where he and Constantine had been pooling the information they had gathered.

Arkwright turned to his note book which lay open on the table.

"According to the dentist," he said, "Cattistock's appointment was for eleven and he arrived on time. The next on the list was Sir Richard Pomfrey, and Betts, the manservant, states that he arrived sometime between eleven fifteen and eleven thirty. Sir Richard told you that he was in the waiting room when Cattistock entered after the dentist had finished the extractions and that he left him there when he went to the consulting room. Betts then showed in Mrs. Miller, whose appointment was for eleven thirty. He was aware of this and noticed that she was about ten minutes late, so we may take it that she arrived about eleven forty. Betts saw Cattistock in the waiting room when he showed her in. He was also there when Sir Richard came back with Mrs. Vallon about five minutes later. Betts, who opened the door to Mrs. Vallon, can only give the time approximately, but there is no reason to think he is far wrong. Immediately after they had entered, Mrs. Miller went into the consulting room and, according to what Sir Richard and Mrs. Vallon told you, Cattistock, some five minutes later, left the waiting room. Therefore, if we include the dentist, five people knew that Mrs. Miller was in the consulting room from, say, approximately, eleven forty-five onwards."

Constantine nodded.

"They knew, certainly," he admitted, "but I can see no evidence that any of them went prowling on the leads. Isn't this rather waste of time?"

Arkwright shrugged his shoulders.

"It's ordinary routine work. In nine cases out of ten it leads nowhere, and in the tenth it goes all the way. Where had we got to? Eleven forty-five. From now onwards the times become more important and it's a nuisance that that ass, Betts, should have taken the opportunity to stand on the doorstep and gossip with the doctor's man from number thirty-eight just then! He's created a nice little alibi for himself, but, as a result, he never saw Cattistock leave the waiting room, nor did he see Sir Richard when he went to the telephone, though he noticed him crossing the hall from the telephone box while they were trying to get the consulting room door open. He says he was only on the doorstep for ten minutes, but I should put it at nearer a quarter of an hour myself. Anyway, he vouches for it that no one left the house, via the front door, until you arrived at twelve and met Cattistock going out. According to your account, which tallies with Mr. Davenport's, the times are as follows. Eleven forty-five, approximately, Mrs. Miller goes into the consulting room, leaving Sir Richard Pomfrey, Mrs. Vallon and this man, Cattistock, in the waiting room; eleven fifty Cattistock leaves the waiting room; twelve o'clock you arrive, meeting Cattistock on the doorstep, and Sir Richard, immediately afterwards, goes to the telephone. Meanwhile, Davenport, according to his account, leaves Mrs. Miller in the consulting room and goes to his workroom in the basement at a few minutes to twelve. At twelve five he returns and finds the door locked, and at twelve ten Sir Richard goes back to the waiting room. We may therefore take it that the murder occurred in the short interval between, say, eleven forty-eight, when the dentist left his patient and twelve five when he returned and found the door locked. That leaves the murderer eight minutes in which to do a job which he timed with amazing exactness."

Constantine glanced at him.

"Meaning that he must have been on the premises, waiting his opportunity."

"Precisely. He must, into the bargain, not only have known the hour of Mrs. Miller's appointment, but been aware of the nature of the work Davenport was doing for her, work that would take him to his workroom in the basement and necessitate his leaving her alone in the consulting room. So long as Davenport was with her he could not hope to act."

"That is sound enough," agreed Constantine. "Though, if it weren't for the knife, one might include the possibility of the crime being unpremeditated and take it that the man had merely taken advantage of a heaven-sent opportunity. Where the weapon has been brought in from outside, however, one may safely go on the assumption that the thing was planned in advance."

"It was planned all right," Arkwright's tone was grim. "That overall wasn't Davenport's, you know."

"Do you mean that the murderer brought it with him?"

"Must have. The moment Davenport got a chance to examine it he saw that it wasn't a make that had ever been used in this house. We found a pair of rubber gloves underneath it. Did you know that? They were badly stained and don't belong to anyone on the premises. It was a clever move, that overall, when you come to think of it. The chap had to get across the hall from the lavatory and, with all the precautions in the world, he couldn't count on no one's seeing him. If Betts had been in his usual place he would probably have thought nothing of it if he noticed a man dressed in an overall cross the hall. It's a sight he's accustomed to and he'd have taken it for granted that he was Davenport or one of his assistants and never given him a second glance. That's the meaning of the overall."

Constantine looked up quickly.

"And Mrs. Miller, seeing a man in an overall come into the room, would have suspected nothing," he said, in a hushed voice.

Arkwright nodded.

"Pretty grim, isn't it?" he agreed. "The chances are that he stood behind her and, bringing his left hand round from the back, tilted her head back, holding the knife in his right hand. Until he actually used violence there would be nothing abnormal in his movements. She may even have put her head back herself and opened her mouth as he came towards her. It is quite a common thing for patients to do when the dentist approaches them. By the way, you know the husband's on his way here?"

"I understood you were sending for him. Does he know?"

Arkwright looked slightly uncomfortable.

"No, I didn't tell him. He rang up from his office about twelve fifteen, while Davenport was trying to get that door open, to ask if his wife had had her appointment, as he proposed to pick her up in the car. Betts answered the phone and, being under the impression that the consulting room was empty, told him she had gone. Betts is an ass. He admits now that he never saw her leave and that she invariably asked for a taxi if she'd sent her car away as she did today. Anyway, Mr. Miller rang off and went round to his club for lunch. We've only just managed to trace him. He thinks his wife is ill and is on his way to fetch her."

Constantine frowned.

"And what, may I enquire, is the idea?" he asked. "The thing seems to my unsophisticated brain unnecessarily heartless."

Arkwright gave him a meaning look.

"There's been a certain amount of gossip about the Millers, I'm thinking," he said. "What have you heard, sir?"

"Nothing definite against either of them, though they were hardly an attractive couple, by all accounts. I've known her by sight for a long time, but I've never seen the husband. I've always understood that he was a rich jeweller and, I believe, has quite a good name in Hatton Garden. She was Lottie Belmer, an undistinguished ornament of the musical comedy stage, before she married him. Rumour has it that they were a rather ill-assorted pair."

"That tallies with my information," agreed Arkwright, "and I can add to it, owing to a rather curious coincidence. I was going through our files the other day with reference to a burglary in North London and I came across Miller's name. He landed in England from Cape Town in nineteen twenty-six, when we received a warning from the Cape Town police to keep an eye on him. It appears that he had been arrested there as a receiver of stolen goods but was discharged owing to lack of evidence. The stuff was traced to his manager, who was convicted, but there was no actual proof that Miller was aware of what was going on. We acted on the information received, but found no cause for suspicion. All the same, at the risk of seeming heartless, I'd prefer to spring this on him, before he has time to collect his thoughts. We're looking for a motive and he may be in a position to help us."

"You're sure nothing was taken?"

Arkwright shrugged his shoulders.

"How can we be? She was literally covered with stones, all of them valuable, but something may have been taken. That's one of the things her husband ought to be able to tell us. Do you want to be present at the interview, sir? He should be here at any moment now."

Constantine glared at him.

"I don't. I detest your inhuman methods."

Arkwright's smile was disarming.

"But you won't disdain to profit by them," he suggested. "I confess I should like to report to you and hear your opinion."

Constantine rose to his feet.

"I dine at eight," he said, with a severity that was not very convincing. "At the Club. You will find me at our usual table."

"If I can get away, sir," answered Arkwright.

As he was about to leave Constantine made a suggestion. His tone was casual, but there was an impish gleam in his eyes.

"You might take this opportunity of finding out whether the Millers have any connection with China or America," he murmured thoughtfully.

Arkwright permitted himself a chuckle of pure glee.

"I wondered whether you'd be able to resist that, sir," he retorted. "It was I who brought Meekins to see you, you remember and I was there when he showed you the knife."

Constantine, who was never slow to appreciate a joke at his own expense, laughed.

"I might have guessed you'd notice the resemblance," he said. "Of course I haven't handled it and, in any case, my knowledge of such things is negligible, but the knife we found beside Mrs. Miller's body looks uncommonly like the one Meekins got from that Chinese knife-man in San Francisco."

Arkwright nodded.

"We shall know soon enough," he answered. "By this time it will be in the hands of our man at the Yard. I'll report to you this evening."

The fog was still thick enough to delay locomotion and it was past eight when Arkwright arrived at the small, bohemian club at which Constantine entertained those of his friends capable of appreciating the efforts of one of the best chefs in London. He had put up Arkwright for it soon after their first meeting at The Noah's Ark and the detective had fallen into the habit of dining there whenever he could get away early enough from the Yard.* Constantine was awaiting him and brushed away his apologies with one short word of enquiry.

"Well?" he demanded, as he led the way into the dining room.

"A hard day and precious little to show for it," was Arkwright's pessimistic rejoinder. "Taking things in their order," he began, as he unfolded his napkin, "there's Miller. He can't help us. I showed him the knife and he has never seen one like it. Says he knows of no one with a grudge against Mrs. Miller or himself, for the matter of that. Nothing was said about the Cape Town episode by either of us, so he probably thinks that we are not aware of it. He has never been either to America or China and has had no dealings with any Chinese at any time in his life. That's his account, of course. We may be able to check it, up to a point, later. The knife, by the way, is Chinese and of the type used by knife-men imported by the Chinese Tongs in Chicago and San Francisco. To go back to Miller, he took the news of his wife's death normally. It appeared to come as a complete surprise to him and he was just about as shocked and horrified as one would have expected. He gave me the impression of being more than a little scared as well. As regards his wife's jewellery, he does not know if anything is missing, but will get a complete list of what she was wearing from her maid. I am going on to his house from here tonight to get it, when I shall see the maid and may get a line on something from her. I don't imagine it to be the kind of house in which the servants are likely to be close-mouthed. So much for Miller, though I've a feeling that he's holding something back on us."

"Any news of Cattistock?"

Arkwright cast a significant glance in his direction.

"None," he said shortly.

"None? Do you mean to say that the man has never reached his hotel? Why, he was hardly fit to be about when I saw him!"

"All the same, he's vanished. They've neither seen nor heard anything of him since he left the hotel to go to the dentist in the morning. His luggage is there, unpacked, and he said nothing to them about leaving. The hospitals and police stations have been canvassed, but, so far, there's no trace of his having met with any kind of accident."

"Did you dig up anything about him?"

"Very little. I've just been down there myself, interviewing the manager of the hotel, but I got very little more than he had told our man earlier in the day. Cattistock arrived on November the twelfth, two days ago. Last night he asked the manager if he could recommend a good dentist, mentioning that he had spent the greater part of his life abroad and was now living in the country and that the man he had been to there was not satisfactory. The manager, who describes him as a quiet, rather serious gentleman, very pleasant in his manner, gave him the name of his own dentist, Davenport. Says he believes he rang him up early next morning and made an appointment. This tallies with Davenport's account. Beyond that, nothing is known of him."

"He didn't mention in what part of the country he was living."

"No. I questioned all the likely and unlikely people. His luggage consists of a couple of suitcases, unlabelled, and, if he wrote any letters, he posted them himself."

"What about his clothes?"

"We ran into a blind alley there. There were three suits, all from the same tailor, an old-established, inexpensive firm in the city, and, on enquiry, we found that they were made for him about a year ago and sent to the Euston Hotel, where he was staying at the time. The tailors were given the impression that he had only just arrived in England, but, beyond the fact that he paid his bill promptly, they know nothing about him. His shirts and underclothes bear various manufacturers' labels and are all well known lines that are turned out by the thousand. The same may be said of his socks, ties, gloves, etc., and the three pairs of ready-made shoes we found. Any papers he possessed, he must have carried on him."

"No books? A man usually reads something in the train or in bed."

"A pocket Bible by his bed, with the name 'Cattistock' scrawled in pencil inside the cover, and a cheap reprint of 'Esmond' on the writing table. He has covered his tracks pretty thoroughly."

"But not necessarily purposely," pointed out Constantine. "In these days of ready-made clothing there is nothing unusual in such an outfit. It's only what you would find in nine out of ten of the rooms in an inexpensive hotel. So much for Cattistock. Anything further?"

"There's Davenport, of course. But I confess I find it difficult to imagine why an old-established and eminently respectable dental surgeon should cut the throat of one of his most profitable patients! Apart from the fact that he did it in the way most calculated to draw attention to himself!"

"The wiliest of all the devices employed by criminals in fiction, you must remember," Constantine reminded him wickedly. "'No murderer would be such an ass as that,' boomed Inspector Muttonhead, rolling his little pig's eyes, etc., etc. Congratulations, Arkwright, you did it beautifully!"

Arkwright chuckled, but his face grew a shade redder.

"Oh, I'm not disregarding him, by any means," he asserted, "but you must admit that though it comes off all right in books it's a fairly dangerous game to play in real life! Still, he undoubtedly had the time and the opportunity."

"To which, in my role of gifted amateur, I am prepared to add that Davenport, to my knowledge, is the last man in the world to cut one of his patient's throats for any reason whatsoever. I've even known him to exhibit genuine compunction when he hurt me, which shows an almost mawkish sentimentality on the part of a dentist. I haven't got the official mind so I'm quite ready to give him a clean bill of health."

"If I could do the same I should no doubt save myself any amount of time and trouble," admitted Arkwright ruefully.

"Failing Davenport, there remain Mrs. Vallon and Sir Richard Pomfrey. I took their statements this afternoon."

"If Mrs. Vallon is a suspect, so am I," retorted Constantine. "I was with her from twelve o'clock until after the discovery of the locked door."

"All the same, if my times are correct, Davenport left Mrs. Miller three or four minutes before you arrived," Arkwright reminded him, with mock solemnity.

"Do you suggest that, in the course of those four minutes, Mrs. Vallon, with incredible swiftness, dressed herself in an overall, which she was no doubt carrying in her very small hand bag, dashed into the consulting room, killed Mrs. Miller, whom she did not even know by sight, removed the overall and returned to her seat by the fire? And all this unperceived by Richard Pomfrey?"

Arkwright's guffaw so startled an old gentleman at the next table that he swallowed his soup the wrong way and spent the rest of the meal in endeavouring to wither the detective with a streaming and indignant eye.

"I'll grant you Mrs. Vallon," conceded the delinquent. "After all, as you point out, her alibi is practically as good as your own. But you can't say the same for Sir Richard Pomfrey. From twelve o'clock till twelve ten, he was out of the waiting room. Betts was on the doorstep, gossiping, and no one can check Sir Richard's movements during that ten minutes."

"The telephone call?"

"The call to Sir Richard's rooms was put through, we've traced it," admitted Arkwright, "but he only said a couple of words to his man. As for the delay he complained of, such a thing cannot occur in the annals of the telephone service! We never expected to trace that! He *could* have committed the murder and still have had time to telephone on his way back to the waiting room."

"It would leave him very little margin," objected Constantine.

"Whoever did the thing *had* very little margin," retorted Arkwright. "Come to that, the actual stabbing would only have taken a second."

"And the motive?"

Constantine was fighting a losing battle and he knew it. Arkwright eyed him narrowly.

"Did you know, sir, that Sir Richard saw a good deal of Mrs. Miller when she was Lottie Belmer?" he asked.

"I knew that he frequented the set she moved in and, I believe, was acquainted with her, but this was a very long time ago. I'm sure he never knew her in any intimate sense and he told me he had seen nothing of her for years."

"He told me that, too. But he admits that they were acquainted in the past."

"Which seems hardly a motive for killing her now," retorted Constantine. "I never moved in that set myself. My wild oats were sown years before and I have even forgotten most of the current gossip, but I do remember that Sir Richard's name was associated with a very different lady, one of the principals at the Pagoda, and that, at the time, Lottie Belmer was definitely supposed to be the property of someone else whose name I can't recall. Sir Richard's affair ended with the marriage of the lady in question and it is years since his name has been connected in any way with the Pagoda girls."

"That was in Arthur Vallon's day, I suppose?" said Arkwright.

Constantine nodded.

"Vallon owned the theatre in those days," he answered. "Rightly or wrongly his name was coupled with several girls in succession. I can't remember whether Lottie Belmer was one of them. Of one thing I can assure you. She was never, at any time, of the type to appeal to Richard Pomfrey, even in his most callow days."

Arkwright glanced at him.

"You're sure you're not a bit prejudiced in his favour?" he queried demurely.

Constantine's eyes blazed suddenly.

"Of course I'm prejudiced," he snapped, with a little burst of temper. "His father was one of my oldest friends and I've known Richard all his life. He might kill a man with his fists, in a moment of temper, but he's incapable of cutting a dog's throat, much less that of a human being!"

"As his father's friend you would say that even if you didn't think it," Arkwright reminded him.

"I've no doubt I should," admitted the old man, "but the point is that, in this instance, I believe it."

"Well, I'm keeping an open mind," said Arkwright. "We don't even know yet whether robbery wasn't the motive. This man, Cattistock, was with her in the waiting room and no doubt had a good look at all that stuff she was wearing, and Cattistock's missing. That's all to the good from your friend Sir Richard's point of view."

It was late when they finished dinner and Arkwright had only time for coffee and a cigar before leaving to keep his appointment with Charles Miller.

The jeweller's house was in one of those decorously opulent Squares that lie between Piccadilly and Oxford Street. Arkwright was to learn later that Miller, who dabbled in house property, had bought it as a speculation from the executors of a deceased law lord and had only decided to live in it owing to his wife's insistence. A butler, flanked by a spectacular footman, opened the door, but, in spite of the pomp and circumstance with which he was ushered into the library, there was a lack of polish about both servants that made Arkwright suspect that their wages were not on a par with the footman's ornate livery.

Miller was taking his ease in a huge leather-covered armchair by the fire. He waved his cigar in the direction of a formidable pile of letters on the writing table.

"See that those are taken to the post," he said to the butler. Then, with a glance at the hideous marble clock on the mantelpiece: "Take a seat, Inspector. I have to meet the boat train at Victoria, but I can give you twenty minutes."

As he sat down Arkwright took stock of the jeweller for the second time that day and liked him even less than when he had first met him. Under the first staggering shock of his bereavement he had achieved a certain dignity and it had been difficult not to feel sorry for him. Now, in the ugly, over-furnished room into which he fitted so admirably, he had become a definitely unpleasing object. The small, cunning eyes, watchful behind the thick lenses of his glasses, the long, predatory nose, drooping over moist, fleshy lips that showed deeply red against the dry, yellow skin of his heavily lined face, and the white, gesticulative hands marked him as the type of man who is distrusted by his business associates and loathed by his dependants. Without rising from his chair he craned towards a table and picked up a sheet of paper.

"Here is a list of the jewellery my poor wife was wearing," he said, in a voice so unexpectedly soft and mellow that, coming from so inharmonious a personality, it startled, rather than attracted those hearing it for the first time. "My secretary typed it at the dictation of her maid. As the things are still in your possession I cannot check it."

His English was perfect, but he spoke with a precision that betrayed his foreign origin.

Arkwright took the list and studied it, stroking his chin with his large, capable fingers. At one point his eyes narrowed, but he went stolidly on to the end. Then he looked up.

"You told the servants to be on hand, as I requested?" he demanded.

Miller stared at him.

"Certainly," he said. "But I can vouch for the correctness of that list. My wife's maid was positive as to the things she was wearing."

Arkwright gathered himself to his feet.

"All the same, I should like to see her," he said slowly. "Unless she has made a mistake, Mrs. Miller's jewels are intact, with the exception of one piece."

Miller snatched the cigar from his mouth and leaned forward eagerly.

"Then it was robbery," he exclaimed, his voice quivering with excitement. "I knew it! What has been taken?"

Arkwright consulted the list once more.

"A platinum chain with a small diamond and emerald clasp," he read out, "supporting a large oval emerald in a platinum and diamond setting."

CHAPTER FOUR

ARKWRIGHT WAS standing before the grate in a small room opening off the hall in Miller's house. The office desk, typewriting table and filing cabinet proclaimed it for what it was, the lair of Miller's secretary. A bright fire burned in the grate and a large leather covered armchair was drawn up to the hearth. Altogether the room exhibited more comfort than Arkwright would have expected the little chap to bestow upon a dependant, though the extremely capable looking individual who had been at work there when Miller's butler ushered him into the room had struck him as unlikely to stay long in any situation that did not please him. Arkwright, in the course of the few words he had exchanged with him before he gathered up his papers and left the room, had summed him up as belonging to the ruthlessly efficient type, which uses a secretaryship merely as a stepping-stone to something more ambitious. He was of a very different class, mentally and physically, from his employer who, when Arkwright left the library, was already engaged in drafting a letter to the Company with which he had insured his wife's jewels.

"If you wish to conduct your inquiry in private, the secretary's room is at your disposal," he had vouchsafed, as he unscrewed the cap of an enormous fountain pen. "I have to go out myself, in any case."

Arkwright's interview with Mrs. Miller's maid had proved more entertaining than instructive. Instead of the rather flashy foreign *soubrette* he had expected to see he had been confronted with an amazing and bedizened lady of uncertain age, whose garrulous speech betrayed her Cockney origin and who informed him that her name was Mrs. Snipe; that she had been "Miss Lottie's" dresser before she married and that he need only ask any of the stage hands at the Pagoda if they remembered "Snipey" to receive an unsolicited testimonial as to her many sterling qualities both as friend and employee. Arkwright let her talk, knowing from experience the pearls that may be garnered from just such meaningless outpourings, and learned that she had loved and cherished Miss Lottie more than life itself and that: "Where her poor lamb would have been without her, that husband of hers grudging her every penny as he did, she did *not* know. Time after time as she'd had to sit up all night with the poor lamb after one of them bills had come in and she wouldn't forget the fuss there was over that there emerald pendant, not if she lived to be a hundred. As if her pore lamb couldn't have had a dozen like it and better, in the days before she tied herself to a stinking little miser!"

At this point, seeing that Mrs. Snipe was beginning to grow incoherent in her excitement, Arkwright brought her firmly back to the matter in hand. As regards the pendant, she was unshakable. Her mistress had been wearing it when she left the house to go to the dentist's. There had even been some argument over it as, according to Mrs. Snipe, the clasp was notoriously unsafe and she had been trying to get her mistress to have it seen to for some time. But Miss Lottie was that fond of that pendant that she couldn't bear it out of her sight, not even for a day or two. Arkwright, with the skill born of long practice, stemmed the flood of eloquence once more and elicited the information that Miss Lottie, bless her dear heart, hadn't never had no enemies. How could anyone wish her any harm? As for that Miller, she couldn't say. If it had been him as had been killed now!

With some difficulty Arkwright shepherded her tactfully out of the room and sent for the butler. From him he got a comprehensive account of the movements of the household that morning.

Mr. Miller had gone to Hatton Garden as usual at nine thirty and Mrs. Miller had left the house at eleven thirty. He was positive as to the time because he had given the order to the chauffeur for that hour. Immediately afterwards Mr. Bloomfield, the secretary, had gone into the Square with the Pekinese dog, an animal, Arkwright gathered, cordially detested by the household staff. He had remained in the Square until shortly after twelve fifteen, when he had returned to the house. The servants had been in the house all the morning. As a matter of routine Miller's movements had already been checked earlier in the day. He had undoubtedly been at his office at the time of the murder and had rung up Davenport's house from there, in the presence of his typist. Before leaving Arkwright telephoned to the Yard, only to find that nothing had yet been heard of Cattistock. If he had collapsed in the street it seemed fairly certain by now that he had not been taken to any of the London hospitals and it was beginning to look more and more as if his disappearance was voluntary. Having given instructions for the circularisation of the description of the missing pendant, Arkwright groped his way through the fog to bed.

But, in the meantime, as though gathering a speedy harvest before the stifling grey blanket of the fog lifted, murder had stalked once more through the streets of London.

Big Ben had just boomed the half hour. High above Parliament Square the hands of the clock showed half past ten, but, owing to the shrouding mist, they were invisible to the few misguided pedestrians who groped their way below. The chime, curiously dead and muffled, reached the ears of the constable on patrol as he turned into Eccleston Square. It was so faint that, had he not been exceptionally keen of hearing, he would have missed the familiar sound altogether. As it was, he halted to listen, rubbing his hand across his stinging eyes, then resumed his monotonous beat, past the interminable, cavernous porticoes, each with its stretch of area railing, that loomed, grey and mysterious, through the fog. The light of his bull's-eye lantern, flickering like some absurd and inadequate will o' the wisp on locks and window catches, marked his progress and he was half-way down the southeast side of the Square before anything occurred to break the dreary monotony of his vigil.

And then it was only the sight of a woman, a tramp or flower-seller, probably, sitting huddled on the steps under one of porticoes, that arrested his attention. Pimlico fringes the borders of a much less reputable neighbourhood and it was no uncommon occurrence for drunks to stray into its squares and dream their happy dreams on its prim, Victorian doorsteps.

The constable bent over the sleeping woman. She was sitting, crouched together, her knees drawn up and her head bowed over her folded arms, obviously deep in oblivion. He placed a hand on her shoulder.

"Wake up, mother," he said. "You'll have to move on from 'ere, you know."

There was no response from the huddled figure and the constable, straightening his back, turned the light of his lantern more fully on it.

"Foxing," he reflected ponderously, "or so blind to the world that it'll be a case for the ambulance."

Then, as he stared at her, a doubt began to assail him. Women's fashions were beyond his ken, but there was something about the shape and texture of the neat black hat, tilted awry though it was on the bowed head, that did not fit well with his conception of a drunken drab. There was fur, too, on the collar of the dark coat, and expensive fur at that. Some old lady, perhaps, overcome with the fog on her way home. It behooved him to go carefully.

He leaned over once more, keeping the light of his lantern focussed.

"Anything wrong, mum?" he demanded, giving the shoulder he held a gentle shake.

The cloth of the coat slid from under his hand as the figure toppled woodenly towards him. The shoulders hit the steps with a soft thud, then slithered down them almost onto his feet. As the woman fell her hands dropped apart, dragging inertly from step to step.

He saw the hands first, red and glistening with blood, before his eyes fell on the gash in the upturned throat.

At midnight the fog lifted and, some twenty minutes later, a body of silent men filed through the gate into Eccleston Square and, for the next three quarters of an hour, spear points of light darted and probed among the bushes behind the railings. At the sound of a low call the dark figures foregathered, there was a whispered consultation and they slipped out as quietly as they had come in. They had found what they were searching for.

At nine thirty next morning Superintendent Thurston, his stocky figure jammed into a chair that looked at least a size too small for it, leaned forward and touched a button on his desk. He waited, impatiently fingering his grizzled moustache, until the door opened to admit Arkwright.

"Morning," snapped Thurston. His speech was invariably limited to the smallest possible quantity of words, released grudgingly from his mouth as though each one was a very small mouse escaping from a capacious trap. "Interested in this?"

He jerked his head towards an object on his desk. At the sight of it Arkwright's eyes snapped.

"That's not the Miller knife, sir!" he exclaimed.

"How d'you know that?"

Thurston had a grim, subterraneous humour of his own which he gratified occasionally by baiting his subordinates.

"There's a nick out of the blade of the other, but this one's the very spit of it. Where did it come from, sir?"

"Found early this morning in Eccleston Square."

"Eccleston Square?" said Arkwright slowly. "That's a far cry from Illbeck Street, but it's possible that our chap had got a pair of them and didn't dare keep the second one."

The Super snorted.

"Kept it all right *and* used it. Woman found stabbed on doorstep."

Arkwright fell headlong into the trap.

"Not with this knife, sir!"

Thurston's chair creaked as he jerked himself forward and glared at Arkwright with truculent grey eyes.

"Found at two o'clock. Expert's seen it, been dusted for prints, blood test taken, photographed and washed! That's why it's clean. Can you say as much for the Miller exhibit?"

Arkwright flushed.

"That's the trouble, sir," he said. "It *is* an exhibit, and I treated it as such. We shall need it at the trial."

Thurston froze him with a glance.

"If there is a trial," he barked contemptuously. "Slipshod methods! Blade coated with congealed blood, I suppose. If I hadn't been down with flu this wouldn't have happened."

Arkwright controlled his feelings and preserved a respectful silence. He had had flu not so long ago himself and recognised the inevitable after effects.

Thurston made a long arm and turned the knife over so that the other side of the blade lay uppermost. Then he jammed himself back in his chair and turned a sardonic, parrot-like eye on Arkwright.

Arkwright bent over the table and caught his breath. High upon the blade, close to the shaft, was a series of marks, roughly resembling letters, and, underneath them, unmistakably, a number: 620.

In answer to a nod from Thurston he picked the knife up and carried it to the window. The scratches showed clearly enough now.

"Amateur work," he said slowly. "The chap did that himself and didn't take much trouble over it. Looks more like English than Chinese. What does Grierson say, sir?"

"It's got Grierson beat, so you can take it it's not Chinese."

"The numeral's English, right enough," went on Arkwright, "and the first, second and fifth letters might stand roughly for M. A. and H. The fourth might be another attempt at H., but the third might mean anything."

The Super grunted.

"Try t'other way up," he growled.

Arkwright reversed the blade until the handle was towards him. The third letter now showed plainly enough as U.

"M.A.U.H.H.," he said. "With the U. upside down. That's not very helpful."

Thurston, who had been filling a peculiarly foul pipe, proceeded to light it.

"Neither are you," he mumbled, between puffs. "Get the Miller knife exhibit cleaned up and let me see it."

The Miller exhibit provided another bitter pill for Arkwright's palate, though he knew that, in leaving the weapon untouched, he had only followed the usual routine in such cases. In view of Thurston's jaundiced state of mind it was unfortunate that, when washed, the blade should be discovered to have been scratched in exactly the same way as that of the knife found in Eccleston Square. The lettering was, if anything, clearer, the only difference being in the numeral, which showed up distinctly as 300.

Taking the inscriptions into account it was impossible to ignore the probable connection between the two crimes, and Arkwright spent the greater part of the morning gathering what data there was from the inspector in charge of the case.

"Haven't been able to identify the woman yet, sir," was his discouraging report, "and it's not going to be easy. A foreigner, I should put her down as, and you know what those little lodging houses are Vauxhall Bridge Road way. Swarming with Frenchies and Italians, a lot of them without any friends or relations on this side of the Channel, and, if one goes missing once in a way, the landlady knows better than to report to us. Just hangs onto the luggage for six months or so and then bones it. The woman hadn't a pocket in her coat and her hand bag's missing. No papers, no money, nothing! There's the name of a Paris bootmaker, Dufour, in her shoes and there's a chemise that comes from The Louvre. That's all we've got to go on."

"How long had she been dead?"

"Over an hour, the surgeon says. She wasn't there at seven thirty, because the owner of the house went up the steps and let himself in then."

"Whom does the house belong to?"

The inspector grinned.

"Mr. Justice Farrer. I reckon we can rule him out. I've passed the tape over the household, but everything seems straightforward. The only person that saw her is a telegraph boy. He had a wire for a house two doors away and he noticed her sitting there as he passed, but, having no occasion to climb the steps, he didn't bother about her. He puts the time at round about eight o'clock."

"Which places the murder as having taken place between seven thirty and eight. That narrows it down a lot. Did the surgeon say anything about the wound?"

"He said as like as not it was done from behind. Whoever did it knew his job. Nearly took her head off. If the neck hadn't been muffled round with a shawl, that boy would have spotted the blood all right. As it was, there wasn't anything to show till the constable moved her."

"Sure there's nothing more in that shrubbery? The murderer may have chucked away her bag when he got rid of the knife."

The inspector shook his head.

"We've been over every inch of the whole Square. Tried the drains, too, round about, but there's nothing. I hear you're taking over, Sir?"

Arkwright sighed.

"I've got to. If there isn't some connection between this and the Miller business I'll eat my hat, but I can't see where the link lies. I'll go over to the mortuary now and see you later. Had many visitors there?"

"A good few. Mostly foreigners whose relations have gone missing, but no one that's ever seen her before. From the look of her I should say she's a bit better class than most of the people that have called, but it's difficult to tell nowadays."

Arkwright, in all the years of his service, had never been able to accustom himself to the mortuary. Today, the pitiful figure of the murdered woman, lying unknown and friendless on the marble slab, seemed to make the dreary sordidness of the place even more apparent.

As he took stock of the waxen face upturned to his he endorsed most of the inspector's comments. A white cloth had been folded and laid under the woman's chin, so that the cause of death was not apparent, and her face wore that enigmatic smile that is usually associated with a peaceful end. Her features had been handsome once, but trouble or illness had sharpened them and drawn deep lines about the mouth and round the eyes. Arkwright put her age at about forty-five, but realised that, had life proved hard, she might easily be younger. He examined the hands, smooth skinned and well cared for, with long, highly polished nails, and agreed with the inspector that she did not belong to the working classes. On one point, however, he differed from his subordinate. In spite of the marks on her clothing and the nails, cut into the sharp point so beloved of the foreign manicure, he had a strong suspicion that she was English, or, at any rate, Nordic, by birth. Her good looks had been of the milkmaid type, rarely if ever seen in any of the Latin countries, and her hair, though faded to a dull yellow and streaked with grey, was abundant and gave signs of having once been beautiful. Arkwright, who had crossed the Channel many times in the course of his service, knew that only one French woman in a thousand is so dowered.

He wrote "Dane or Swede, possibly an Englishwoman," in his note book and turned to her clothes, which lay neatly folded by her side. These confirmed his conviction that she was no working woman. Though not expensive, each item was well cut and of good material and showed a taste that even Arkwright's male eye could appreciate. The only labels on them were those of The Louvre and the bootmaker, Dufour, the shoes being, incidentally, exceptionally smart and expensive. "The shawl" which the Inspector had alluded to and which had been wrapped round her throat and upper part of her body to stem the flow of blood, turned out to be a plaid travelling rug and Arkwright's first step, on returning to the Yard, was to send a man to Victoria, on the chance that a porter might be able to identify her as one of the arrivals on the boat train. His next action was to ring up Miller's house.

Mr. Miller was at lunch, but, on hearing Arkwright's name, he came to the telephone.

"You have some news about the emerald?" he demanded.

"I'm afraid not," was Arkwright's answer, "but there has been an unexpected development. If you could give us a few minutes of your time here we should be grateful."

"You wish me to come to you?"

"At New Scotland Yard. Yes. If you will name your own time, I shall be waiting for you."

There was a pause, then:

"It is not convenient, but, if you think it necessary, I will come at once. As soon as I have finished my lunch. In three quarters of an hour I will be with you."

He was better than his word and was ten minutes before his time when he was shown into Arkwright's room.

As Arkwright rose to greet him, he found himself wondering whether he had not been doing him an injustice after all. Judging by his looks he was feeling his wife's death more deeply than had seemed possible the day before. His face was grey now, rather than sallow, and his shoulders sagged as though the mere action of walking was an effort. The man had aged ten years in a single night.

"This is very good of you, Mr. Miller," he said, drawing a chair out on the opposite side of the big office table.

Miller threw his hands out.

"Anything I can do to help," he intoned, in that surprisingly sonorous voice.

Arkwright sat down opposite to him, opened a drawer and took out the two knives. His eyes on the other man's face, he placed them on the table in front of him.

Miller's mouth twitched. He tried to speak, failed and swallowed convulsively. Then he mastered himself.

"Two knives?" he ejaculated. "But there was only one..."

"I'll tell you about the other in a minute, Mr. Miller" said Arkwright. "What I want you to look at is the inscription on them."

Miller peered at the blades, removed his glasses, slowly took a case from his pocket, extracted a second pair of horn-rimmed spectacles and adjusted them on his nose. Arkwright, watching him closely, noticed that his hands were not quite steady and wondered whether he were not playing for time.

"May one pick them up?" asked Miller.

"Certainly."

Miller pored over the inscriptions, compared them with each other, then laid the knives down on the table with a little shake of his head.

"The numbers are quite clear," he said, "but these signs, what are they? They do not look like Chinese."

"You don't recognise them as Chinese symbols?" enquired Arkwright blandly.

Miller shrugged his shoulders.

"I should not recognise them if they were," he pointed out. "As I told you, I know nothing of Chinese writing."

Arkwright sighed.

"I was in hopes you might be able to help us," he said. "You don't recognise them as belonging to any language you do know?"

Miller shook his head.

"I have never seen anything like them," he asserted. "It is curious about the numbers, though, of course, almost every nation in the world uses those numerals."

He hesitated, then:

"I remember you showed me the knife that was found beside my poor wife. Is it one of these?"

His voice broke on the words and he seemed genuinely affected.

Arkwright picked up one of the knives.

"This one," he said. "I'm sorry if this has been painful, Mr. Miller, but the inscriptions escaped our notice in the first instance and I had to make sure that they conveyed nothing to you. I suppose nothing has occurred to you in the interval that might have some bearing on the crime?"

Miller, who was replacing his glasses in the case, raised his head and met Arkwright's gaze with the utmost candour.

"Nothing, I regret to say," he asserted positively. "It is all a mystery to me. Is there anything else?"

"I'm sorry, but there's just one more thing I must ask you to do, rather an unpleasant one. I have not told you yet where we got the second of these knives."

Briefly he described the finding of the woman's body and the discovery of the weapon. Miller's expression, when he had finished, was one of pure amazement.

"But the whole thing is meaningless!" he exclaimed. "First my poor wife, then this woman, who can have no connection whatever with us. And yet, judging by the weapons, there must be some link between the two crimes. In my wife's case, I feel convinced that the motive was one of robbery, but this other was not a rich woman, you say?"

"In so far as one can judge, she was not, but it is difficult to say what she may have had on her. Everything was taken by the murderer."

Miller hesitated.

"You wish me to look at this woman?" he suggested unwillingly.

"I'm afraid so. Owing to the possible connection between the two crimes we must make sure that she was not known to you. Simply a matter of form, you understand."

Miller nodded.

"It is very unpleasant to me," he said, "but I see that it is necessary. Can we go now? I have a busy afternoon before me."

"By the way," remarked Arkwright, as he rose to accompany him, "you told me you were meeting a friend by the boat train last night. Was it very crowded?"

Miller glanced at him in surprise.

"There were a good many people. It was troublesome, as my friend did not come and I had to see them all off the platform before I was sure I had not missed her."

Arkwright turned sharply.

"You were expecting a lady?"

"An old friend of my wife's," Miller explained. "It was all a little awkward for me. You see, my wife had invited this lady to stay with us while she was in London and, in my trouble yesterday morning, I forgot all about her. When I did remember, it seemed best to meet her and explain the circumstances to her. It was a relief to me when she did not turn up."

"Had she mentioned that train specifically?"

"Certainly. She said she was coming by it. I have her letter at home. But it would not surprise me if she had changed her plans. She is an actress and was a friend of my wife's when she was on the stage, and, like all artistes, she is probably temperamental."

An idea struck him.

"You think this poor woman who was murdered may have come by that train," he exclaimed. "If she did and if, by some chance, I did miss my friend, it is possible she left the station alone. You are right. I must make sure that I do not know her."

"She was killed over an hour before that train got into the station," said Arkwright. "But, of course, there is a possibility that your friend changed her plans and crossed earlier."

He led the way down the stairs. On the road to the mortuary Miller's excitement grew as he discussed the possibility of his guest's having altered her arrangements, and by the time they got there he was already convinced that yet another appalling tragedy had come into his life.

"Why should these things happen to me?" he almost wailed. "Neither my wife nor myself have ever wished anyone any harm. It is as if a curse had come upon us."

Arkwright stared at him in surprise. This was a very different person to the pompous, rather rapacious individual he had interviewed the night before. At the door of the mortuary Miller paused.

"What a horrible place," he muttered, and again Arkwright had a feeling that he was trying to gain time. Then, suddenly, as though he had decided to get the thing over, he straightened his shoulders and walked ahead of his companion into the room.

"I have never seen her before," he announced, as soon as his eyes fell on the woman. "My God, what a relief!"

He pulled out a voluminous handkerchief and passed it over his forehead. Arkwright noticed with a certain grim amusement that the linen was none too clean.

"No doubt you'll hear from your friend tomorrow," he said reassuringly. "These convey nothing to you, I suppose?"

He indicated the neatly folded pile of clothing. Miller regarded the blood-stained rug with aversion.

"Thank goodness, no," he asserted with conviction, as he turned and made hurriedly for the door.

Arkwright saw him to his car and was on his way back to his room at the Yard when he was stopped by a constable with the news that a Mrs. Snipe had been enquiring for him.

His surprise was not unmixed with satisfaction. From the first he had hoped he might cull something useful from the garrulous dresser.

"Is she here now?" he asked.

"Waiting, sir."

At the sight of him she leaped to her feet, a dark flush looming through the crude make-up on her face.

"I've just seen the account in the papers," she panted. "Is it true that Sir Richard Pomfrey was in that house when my poor lamb was murdered?"

"He was in the waiting room," said Arkwright. "Why do you ask?"

"Because he was the only one there that knew Miss Lottie in the old days. You ask him if he didn't!"

Arkwright figured his chin thoughtfully.

"But it doesn't follow that he meant her any harm," he objected, hoping that opposition would only incite her to further revelations.

"No one could have wished her any harm," sniffed Snipey dolefully. "The poor lamb! But he was the only one there that knew her. You ask him!"

"He has made no secret of the fact. But I understand from him that, though he knew her, he was not an intimate friend of hers."

Snipey, her whole body quivering with indignation, thrust a flushed face into his.

"Wasn't he?" she snorted. "Then why did he give her that diamond brooch? The very brooch she was wearing when she was struck down!"

CHAPTER FIVE

CONSTANTINE WAS lunching at the Club. His companion, the expression on whose plump, good-natured face bore tribute to the excellence of his digestion, was senior partner in a well-known firm of chartered accountants and a noted chess player. The two men often fed together and, if Constantine seemed a shade more silent than usual today, Gibbs, who was as garrulous as he was amusing, did not notice it. He could be depended on to keep the ball rolling while his companion pursued his own line of thought uninterrupted.

Constantine had food for reflection. Arkwright had rung him up just before lunch telling him of the second murder and the finding of the weapon, and the letters M.A.U.H.H. were playing hide and seek in his mind as he automatically supplied the fuel necessary to keep his companion's tongue wagging. It was not until the meal was over and the two men had adjourned to the smoking room for their coffee that he resolutely dismissed the subject of this second outrage from his thoughts and deftly brought the conversation round to the Millers. It was a forlorn hope, but what Gibbs did not know about the financial status of almost any London firm was not worth knowing and there was just a chance that he might be able to contribute something useful. His response was immediate.

"I see you were there," he exclaimed, his fresh-coloured face alight with curiosity. "Must have been a ghastly business."

"I was," answered Constantine, humouring him. "I've never seen a more appalling sight."

Gibbs waited, in the hope of a more detailed description, then, as none came:

"What do you make of it? Robbery? The papers didn't give that impression."

"As a matter of fact, I understand that some jewellery is missing," answered Constantine, with the air of one imparting a state secret.

So far, the news of the missing pendant had not leaked out, but, knowing that Miller would make no secret of his loss, Constantine saw no urgent need for discretion. Gibbs' eyes gleamed. This was inside information, such as the layman loves.

"Then the police think that robbery was the motive?" he pursued eagerly.

"It seems the most obvious explanation," admitted Constantine. "The poor woman has been literally asking for trouble for a long time. The wonder is that no one has had a try at those jewels before. Miller's a rich man, I imagine, but, judging from what she was wearing when I saw her, he must have found her an expensive proposition."

"Oh, he's sound enough financially," said Gibbs. "He's not a client of ours, but I was talking yesterday to a fellow who went through his books a month or so ago. It's a very flourishing business, but, from all accounts, he didn't fork out easily. To his wife, least of all!"

"You don't think he was responsible for the bulk of the gewgaws she was wearing?" queried Constantine sharply.

Gibbs laughed.

"I wouldn't go so far as that," he said, "though I fancy some of them may be relics of the past. She was a bit of a gold digger in the old days, you know. But, apart from all that, she had a mania for buying jewels and what you saw must be only a small part of what she possessed. The trouble was, she didn't always pay for them. As I said, Miller didn't part with his money easily."

"Are you speaking from personal knowledge?" asked Constantine, "or just hearsay?"

"I know this," answered Gibbs drily. "She was on the black list of several of the big London people. I've seen their books. She used to say openly that her husband hardly ever gave her anything. Owing to his business connections and the fact that she was, in her way, a good customer, she got longer rope than most people and they generally managed to collect from Miller himself in the end, but she owed money everywhere and was always complaining that he kept her short of cash."

"In fact, instead of being the rich woman one thought she might have been actually hard up," suggested Constantine thoughtfully.

"She was being dunned right and left and, I should imagine, was afraid to appeal to her husband," asserted Gibbs.

After Gibbs had left him Constantine lingered in his chair by the fire, his eyes closed, engaged in the not too pleasing contemplation of the Miller menage. When he at last shook himself out of his abstraction and left the club it was to pick up a taxi and direct the driver to an address in Hatton Garden.

He found the man he was seeking in his office, a Greek, who had set up as a jeweller in London many years ago and who owed much of his success to the patronage of the Constantines. He greeted his patron's son as an old friend.

"You've come at the right moment," he exclaimed. "I've got an intaglio here that will make your mouth water. The museum people are after it already."

With the deliberation of the very old he unlocked his safe and produced a ring. If Constantine chafed under the delay he did not show it and the old man had no fault to find with his appreciation of the gem. It was not until it was safely stowed away again that he broached the real object of his visit.

"I suppose this Miller case has made something of a stir in this part of the world," he said.

The old Greek cast a shrewd glance at him as he unlocked a drawer in his table and produced the cigars that he kept only for his most favoured clients.

"So it was not only for my *beaux yeux* that you came to see me," was his dry comment. "If you would find out all about Miller, go to Hatton Garden, *hein?* When I saw your name in the papers I began to expect you."

He leaned forward to hold a match to Constantine's cigar, took one himself and, when it was well alight, leaned back in his chair and stretched his short legs out under the table.

"You shall have all I can tell you," he said. "There has been talk, yes, but they were not popular, the Millers, in this quarter. In business he was respected. There was nothing against him here, you understand. But his wife did not mix well, she had social aspirations and showed her opinion of her husband's associates too plainly. And, at best, Miller himself was not a pleasant fellow."

"You said there was nothing against him here," said Constantine. "Was there anything known to his disadvantage elsewhere?"

"There were rumours," admitted the old man cautiously. "I can only give them to you for what they are worth. The diamond people from the Cape declare that he was mixed up in a scandal there and was actually arrested and they are of the opinion that he made a cat's paw of his assistant, who was convicted and served his sentence. One of the De Beers men who was here not long ago declared that he had met the man shortly after his release from prison and that he had sworn to get even with Miller. He also said, by the way, that this man had left the Cape for Europe shortly before he did. I know nothing, myself, of Miller's past, but I must say that the story is generally accepted as true."

"Do you know the name of this man?" asked Constantine.

The Greek shook his head.

"I have never heard it, but it would be easy to trace."

"He would have had time to get over here?"

"Oh, yes. It is a month, at least, since I spoke to the De Beers agent and he had been to Berlin and Paris on his way to England. There has been plenty of time, but, my friend, it was Mrs. Miller who was killed! If it had been Miller, now!"

"Too oblique a form of revenge, you think?"

The old man's eyes narrowed.

"If it had been a peasant vendetta in our own country, no. It would have been as good a way as any other. But, in England, and in the case of a man whose relations with his wife were notoriously unfriendly?"

"The murderer may not have known that," put in Constantine quickly.

The jeweller shrugged his shoulders.

"It was common talk. If you ask me, I do not think he would try to hit him in that way. But the fact remains, this man had a grudge against him and he may be in England."

Constantine assented absently.

"Miller has assured the police, who, by the way, are aware of the arrest in Cape Town, that he knows of no one who could possibly wish him ill," he said.

"If you were in Miller's place would you voluntarily allude to that little episode in your past?"

Constantine's eyes twinkled.

"I suppose not," he admitted. "What is his standing here?"

The jeweller smiled.

"His reputation is unblemished. But he has been caught, once, remember, and he is very careful now. He is a clever man, Miller, and I think he has discovered that, in this country, honesty is the best policy. Certainly he has made it pay. He has built up a good business."

Constantine stayed to drink a cup of Turkish coffee with the old man, then took his leave. This time his thirst for information carried him to a very different quarter.

Old Lady Farnborough had never, even in her prime, been either beautiful or accomplished and now, in her extreme old age, enthroned beside a blazing fire in her stuffy, over-furnished drawing room, she would probably have had to depend on her two aged and obese fox terriers for companionship had it not been for two qualities that had survived the years and made her one of the most sought-after and detested old women in London. She was possessed of a retentive memory and a curiosity as vivid as Constantine's own. In the course of her long life she had known everybody worth knowing and never, so it was said, had she either failed to hear, or forgotten, the slightest whisper to the detriment of any one of them. Daughter of a famous politician and wife of one of the Stewards of the Jockey Club, she had two richly manured fields from which to cull her harvest and, as a result, her drawing room had become the haunt of those who love gossip for its own sake and the reference library of such writers of spicy memoirs who depend on "good stories" for the sale of their books. Of the Miller crowd she would, of course, know nothing. They belonged to a class of which she barely acknowledged the existence, but Constantine realised that, for the present, he had got as far as he was likely to get along that line. His object now was to forestall any information that might reach Arkwright's ears later.

Lady Farnborough was at home, which was hardly surprising, in view of the fact that she never went out if she could possibly help it. She received Constantine graciously. In her eyes he was still a "foreigner" and a nobody, whose charm, good looks and money had won him the entree into a magic circle that she would never realise had practically ceased to exist. But she liked him and would store up some of her choicest bits of scandal for his delectation.

"It is a long time since I've seen you," she panted gustily. "Betty Culmer tells me you've got yourself mixed up in this unsavoury business in Illbeck Street. Sit down and tell me all about it."

"I'm afraid I can't tell you any more than you've seen in the papers," answered Constantine, bending down to scratch the elder of the terriers cunningly behind the ear.

"Nonsense. Never look at the papers nowadays. My maid reads me as much as she thinks I can stand. It isn't good for me to get in a temper at my age. According to Betty, your dentist murdered some woman one's never heard of. How you were mixed up in it I couldn't make out. What's it all about? Dentists didn't murder people in my day."

Constantine chuckled.

"They don't now. Poor Davenport had nothing to do with it, but I was there when he discovered the poor woman. She was a Mrs. Miller, the wife of a rich jeweller."

"Extraordinary the people one meets at one's dentist's," murmured his hostess. Then, briskly: "Well, who did do it, if the dentist didn't?"

"That's what everybody would like to know. I fancy, however, you *have* heard of Mrs. Miller. She was Lottie Belmer before she married."

The old lady frowned.

"Wait a minute. It isn't like me to forget names. Of course, Lottie Belmer was that fat chorus gell Billy Anker tried to get into the Enclosure at Ascot. The old duke had to buy her off in the end. Cost him a pretty penny. And then, on the top of it, Billy married an appalling woman from Chicago, whose father kept a sausage shop. Rich as Croesus until just after the wedding. Then there was a corner in something and he lost every penny!"

"I remember now," said Constantine. "But there was somebody else, wasn't there?"

"Dozens, one would imagine," agreed Lady Farnborough airily. "She was Vallon's mistress for a time, I believe."

Constantine's hand paused in its progress down the dog's back.

"Is that a fact, do you think?" he asked.

"Can't say. Everybody seemed to know it. I never saw the woman myself. So someone's killed her? Well, that's the way most of those women end, isn't it? Hush, pets, it's only Cooper," as the two dogs burst into an asthmatic duet on the entrance of the butler with the tea.

Constantine waited till he had been provided with a cup and very buttery muffins before reverting to the subject of Lottie Belmer.

"Richard Pomfrey never got into her clutches, did he?" he asked.

"Whose? The Belmer gell's? Not he. He was otherwise engaged," she answered drily. "He used to be seen about with her though. Those gells all hang together."

"He went the pace while it lasted," said Constantine reminiscently. "Curious how he steadied down when he came into the property."

"Pity he didn't give up racing as well as the other things," retorted the old lady. "I hear he dropped a lot last year. Algie tells me he's giving up his stables."

This was news to Constantine.

"Selling, do you mean?"

She nodded.

"Getting rid of them, lock, stock and barrel. I knew he was hit pretty heavily. Poor Richard. If anyone had told me he would ever give up racing I should have refused to believe them, but I gather there's a counter attraction now! Curious that he can't keep his nose on this side of the footlights!"

"Mrs. Vallon, you mean?"

"Who else? He's been dangling round her for the last three years. Since her husband died it's only been a question of time before she led him by the nose to the nearest Registry Office. You'd have thought that other affair would have taught him a lesson!"

"Mrs. Vallon's a very charming woman," objected Constantine. "You can hardly class her with the Pagoda girls."

"Who was she?" came the swift retort, and Constantine had perforce to admit that he did not know.

When that night Arkwright dropped in on him, he did not tell him of his visit to Lady Farnborough nor repeat what she had said, but salved his conscience by making a detailed report of his interview with the old Greek jeweller. Arkwright was interested to hear of the release of Miller's former manager, but sceptical as to his possible connection with the murder.

"Unless Cattistock ..."

He hesitated.

"Unless Cattistock is the name he adopted on his arrival in England," finished Constantine. "Well, it's up to you to find out. Have you got on the track of that illusive gentleman yet?"

"Not a trace of him. It's an uncommon name, too. We've followed up two Cattistocks and drawn a blank. One is an auctioneer's assistant, who was in Liverpool at the time of the murder, the other's a bed-ridden old gentleman of ninety-two, a retired lawyer's clerk, who hasn't walked a step for the last five years. They've neither of them got any male relatives. We've had one piece of good luck, however. They've heard nothing at the hotel, but these arrived there for him by post today."

He untied the string of a flat package he was carrying and revealed a photographer's folder containing three unmounted prints, obviously proofs.

"Is this the man you ran into on the steps of Davenport's house?" he asked.

Constantine examined the three photographs. Each was taken from a different aspect and could hardly have been bettered from the point of view of identification. The trouble was that Constantine's glimpse of the man had been so fleeting. He said as much.

"If this isn't the man I met it is extraordinarily like him, but he was wearing a hat and only took his handkerchief away from his mouth for a moment as he passed me. I believe this to be the same man, but that's as much as I dare say. What about the photographers?"

"They know no more of him than we do. He simply went in, had his portrait taken and told them to send the proofs to his hotel. That was on the afternoon of the thirteenth, the day before the murder. Another blind alley."

He cast a side-glance at Constantine's face and went on more soberly.

"I got a curious bit of information from Mrs. Miller's maid. That diamond thing she was wearing when she was killed was given to her by Sir Richard Pomfrey."

But Constantine did not rise to the bait.

"That does not surprise me," was all he said. "There was money to throw away in those days before the war and Richard did his share of the throwing. It's probably Rue de La Paix stuff and a relic of some supper party or other at which all the girls got extravagant presents. I've given parties of that sort myself in my day. By the way, I suppose you've checked Miller's movements on the night of the murder?"

Arkwright flashed a surprised glance at him.

"Yes," he said. "He went straight home in the afternoon after leaving Illbeck Street and did not go out again until I called on him at ten o'clock at night. He left the house about ten thirty to meet a friend at Victoria. The servants and his secretary corroborate this. Why this interest in Miller?"

Constantine shrugged his shoulders.

"I don't like him, that's all. And, sorry as I am for Mrs. Miller, there must have been a certain temptation to get rid of her!"

Arkwright frowned and stretched his long legs out to the fire.

"About that woman," he said. "I got Miller to come down and have a look at her. He couldn't help us. Didn't know her. But he got me guessing. The man's all to pieces."

"He's been through a good deal in the last twenty-four hours."

"There's something he hasn't told us and, unless I'm imagining things, it isn't shock or grief he's suffering from now," insisted Arkwright stubbornly. "There's something on his mind, I'll swear, and, if I know anything of the symptoms, he's badly frightened."

CHAPTER SIX

"How DID YOU get onto him? Where? Guildford? Right. A widower, living alone. Sounds as if he might fit the billet. No, I'll see to it myself."

Arkwright slammed the receiver onto its hook, stretched out a long arm for the time-table and flicked over the pages till he came to the one dealing with the Guildford line.

Half an hour later his train was bumping over the points outside Waterloo and he was well on his way in pursuit of his third and most hopeful Cattistock suspect.

On his arrival at Guildford he went first to the police station. There he presented his credentials and arranged for help should he find it necessary to detain his man. This Cattistock, it appeared, was known to the police, though not in the derogatory sense the phrase usually conveys. Their account was that he had turned up in Guildford two years before and had leased a small house not far from the police station, establishing himself there with an elderly housekeeper, a local woman of undoubted respectability. He was known as the Rev. Charles Cattistock and was generally understood to be a missionary who had been obliged to retire on account of his health. He had twice spoken on Eastern Missions at a neighbouring Parish Hall and one of the constables had attended a lecture and was of the opinion that "the gentleman knew what he was talking about." Both the constable and the station sergeant recognized the photographs Arkwright showed them and he began to feel certain that he was on the right track at last.

"Anything been seen of him lately?" he asked.

Come to think of it, nothing had, according to his informants, and Arkwright's suspicion that his luck had been too good to last looked as though it was being verified. There seemed nothing for it but to interview the housekeeper and try to get some clue as to the man's whereabouts. Arkwright accordingly made his way to the neat little villa situated in one of the new streets that were already beginning to spread their tentacles round the old town.

The housekeeper, a pleasant looking elderly woman, opened the door and regarded him with just that shade of suspicion that a good servant who knows the house is empty feels towards the stranger.

"Mr. Cattistock is away, sir," she said, in answer to his enquiry.

"Can you tell me when he will be back?"

"I'm afraid I can't, sir. I've been expecting to hear from him." Her voice was frank and untroubled.

"Can you give me his address?"

By this time the woman seemed to have convinced herself of his respectability. Leaving the door open, she turned her back and took a postcard from the hall table.

"It's here, sir," she said, as she handed it to him.

Even before his hand closed on it Arkwright recognised the familiar paper heading of the Pergolese Hotel. Apart from the fact that the station sergeant had given her an excellent character, the woman's manner had been so natural and her response so ready that Arkwright found it difficult to suspect her of complicity and he decided to beat about the bush no longer. He stepped briskly across the threshold.

"I'm from the police," he said, "and there are one or two questions I must ask you. Is there anywhere where we can talk?"

The woman changed colour.

"Has the master had an accident?" she gasped, her hand going involuntarily to her throat. Arkwright let his eyes rest on her face for a moment before replying, but he read genuine concern, rather than fear in it, and he answered her frankly.

"We've reason to believe that he is quite safe," he said, "but he has left his hotel and we cannot trace him. We need him as a witness and I've come in the hope that you may have some idea where he's gone."

Through an open door he could see into a neatly furnished sitting room. Followed by the housekeeper he stepped into it, casting a keen glance round him as he turned and faced her.

"Are there any relatives or friends he would be likely to go to unexpectedly?" he asked.

She stared at him in utter bewilderment.

"I can't understand it, sir," she said. "His not being at the hotel, I mean. His instructions were to forward any letters there and he was to send me a card when he was to be expected back. The card I showed you came the morning after he left. There's nowhere else I can think of that he'd go to."

"No relatives or friends?" he repeated.

She shook her head.

"He hadn't got a soul belonging to him in this country. He belonged to an Australian family, so he told me, and there's only himself and a brother left. That was why he decided to settle in England when he came back from the East. His brother's out there still, so he said."

"Has he no friends over here?"

"Not that I've heard of, except the ones he's made since he came here. He's very well thought of in the town, let me tell you!"

Arkwright liked her all the better for the note of defiance on which she ended.

He crossed to the writing table and picked up a framed photograph that stood there. It portrayed a group of earnest, rather depressed looking gentlemen in clerical garb and he noticed, with a certain feeling of elation, that there were three Chinamen in native dress among them.

"Is your master among these?" he demanded. "Can you point him out?"

The woman laid her finger on a spare, middle-aged man in glasses in the centre of the group. Arkwright opened his packet of proofs and compared them with the photograph. The housekeeper peered over his shoulder.

"That's Mr. Cattistock," she exclaimed. "Where did you get it, sir?"

"You're prepared to identify that as your master?"

"Of course, sir," she agreed, in surprise. "It's the living spit of him. When did he get it done?"

"In London, the day before he disappeared. Where was this group taken, do you know?"

"In China, I believe. He was a missionary there for years till he retired."

"And this brother, where is he?"

"He's out there now, sir. Mr. Cattistock gets letters from him regular."

"Is he a missionary too?"

"No, he's a merchant."

"What kind of merchant?"

She hesitated.

"I don't rightly know, sir. He doesn't seem to have a shop, as it were. The master's told me about his house and the lovely things he's got. He's always buying silks and china and jewels. He sells them in England and America, so far as I can make out, more than in China."

Arkwright nodded.

"An Export House. Has your master ever had any connection with the jewellery trade, d'you know?"

"Oh no, sir. He's been in the Church all his life, Mr. Cattistock has. But he knows a lot about jewels and china and things through his brother. He told me that the most beautiful jewellery in the world was in China."

Arkwright slipped the photograph out of its frame and placed it in the folder.

"I'll take this for the present," he said. "It may be useful if we run across him. Has he ever gone off like this before?"

Again she shook her head.

"He always gives me his address and lets me know when to expect him back. He said this time he wouldn't be gone more than a week. I don't understand it at all, sir."

"Does he often go up to London?"

"Hardly ever, unless there's a Missionary Meeting or something of that sort. He went up once to meet a missionary gentleman he'd known in China, but he lives very quiet down here, as a rule. You don't think any harm could have come to him, sir?"

There was a quiver of anxiety in her voice and Arkwright smiled down at her reassuringly. Whatever Cattistock's faults might be he was evidently a good master.

"I don't think you need worry yourself," he said. "Though there is a possibility he may be suffering from loss of memory. Does he suffer from his nerves at all?"

She denied this emphatically.

"He's a very quiet, peaceful sort of gentleman, but no one would call him nervous. Very liable to colds, he is, but he says that's from living so long in the East."

Her work-roughened fingers were beginning to pluck restlessly at the strings of her apron. Not too quick at the uptake she was only just beginning to realise that there must be something seriously wrong if the police were concerning themselves with the matter. Arkwright extended a huge hand and covered both hers.

"Don't you worry," he said, giving them a reassuring little shake. "We've got the matter in hand and in a day or so we shall be able to tell you where he is, if you haven't heard from him by then. He may have paid a visit to someone and gone down with a touch of flu there."

There was something capable and protective about his very largeness and she felt vaguely comforted as he went on:

"There's one thing you can do for us. If you do get word of him, just go around to the police station here and let the sergeant know. He'll pass it on to us. Meanwhile, if we hear anything, we'll advise you."

He did not tell her that a watch would be kept on the house and that, should her master return unexpectedly, he would not leave again without the knowledge of the police.

He dropped into the police station to make certain arrangements and then caught the next train back to London. On his arrival there he went straight to Illbeck Street and showed Davenport the photographs. He identified them unhesitatingly.

Arkwright then returned to the Yard, only to find that there had been no startling developments there. The murdered woman was still unidentified and the man he had sent to Victoria had so far drawn a blank. He gave him one of the Cattistock proofs and told him to circulate it among the station officials on the chance that he had been seen there on the night of the murder.

Late that evening a cable containing a more detailed report on Miller arrived from the Cape Town police. After studying it he rang up Constantine and arranged to call on him on his way home. He knew the old man too well not to realise the concern Sir Richard Pomfrey's predicament was causing him, and if there were any comfort to be gained from the results of his day's work, he did not grudge it to him.

On his father's death Constantine had sold the huge, unwieldy mansion in Bayswater, divided the bulk of the treasures it contained among various museums, and established himself in a roomy and comfortable flat in Westminster.

Arkwright, as he stood waiting outside the familiar green door, pondered gratefully on the chance that had thrown him and the old Greek together in an old inn one snowy Christmas. Arkwright, a bachelor, whose heart and soul was in his job, had been rapidly falling into a dreary rut when Constantine had rescued him and introduced him to that curious and cosmopolitan fraternity that gathers round the chess board.

The man who opened the door was by now an old friend of his.

"Dr. Constantine all right, Manners?" he asked.

Manners permitted himself to smile.

"Dr. Constantine is opening a new box of Halva, sir," he said, as though that were more than sufficient answer to the question.

Arkwright, who shared his host's predilection for that sticky Eastern sweetmeat, took the stairs two at a time and peered round the door just as Constantine had finished extracting a last generous slice from the tin. He held the plate out in silence, with the result that the opening paragraphs of his guest's report were delivered with a diction reminiscent of a small boy at a school treat.

There was a glint of triumph in the old man's eyes when he had finished.

"So?" he said. "We seem to be getting somewhere. China, and a brother with unlimited opportunities for disposing of a stolen pendant. It fits in almost too well, Arkwright! There's a flaw somewhere!"

"The flaw's there, right enough," answered the detective. "For one thing, we haven't got Cattistock and he's had time to get through to Marseilles by now. We're having the seaports watched, but we didn't get onto the job till after the two o'clock boat train had gone. We can use wireless, of course."

"You can get to work at the other end."

"And meanwhile the whole thing will hang fire for months. You've been notified as to the inquest tomorrow, I suppose? We shall get it adjourned of course. There's the other unfortunate woman, too. We're neither of us involved in that, thank goodness. In any case, they are waiting for identification."

"Nothing further cropped up, I suppose?"

"This. We've got the name of that manager of Miller's."

Arkwright took an envelope from his pocket and produced a cablegram which he handed to Constantine.

The old man ran through it.

"Greeve," he quoted, "discharged July nineteen fifteen. Believed to have left Cape Town in the course of the last year, but no record of anyone of that name having sailed. Probably travelling under an assumed name."

Constantine glanced at the detective.

"He'd need a passport," he suggested.

"That wouldn't worry him," said Arkwright. "If he's served a sentence he'll have come across a dozen people who could have put him in the way of getting one. There's only one thing we can bank on. He's not Cattistock!"

"Unless he's done Cattistock in and taken his name," suggested Constantine, with a smile. "And that seems rather too far-fetched to be true!"

Arkwright straightened himself, a piece of Halva halfway to his mouth.

"There's something in that, all the same!" he exclaimed. "If Cattistock's a wrong 'un, they may have been in it together, Cattistock didn't come in or leave by the lavatory window, remember. I said there were flaws and this is the worst of them."

"Not to mention that Cattistock's a respectable member of the Church of England. You got onto him through the Clergy List, didn't you?"

"Time enough for him to convince us of that when we catch him," was Arkwright's sceptical rejoinder. "The Cattistock in the Clergy List may have died in China for all we know and this man may have been impersonating him at Guildford. That's an old game and far easier to pull off than you might think. The crux, from the beginning, has been that business of the next door house. Someone came in or left that way!"

"I wouldn't be too sure of that," said Constantine slowly. "What have we really got to go on? The fact that the key of the consulting room door was found on the leads outside, the traces outside the lavatory window and the open window in the house next door. But, remember, the only traces of blood were inside Davenport's house. Taking into account the fact that the house next door has been uninhabited for months, is there any reason why the entry into Davenport's house should not have been made any time within the past week and for some reason quite unconnected with the murder? I admit that it would be a coincidence, but stranger things than that have happened. There has been no rain for a week and nothing to disturb the traces. An open window in an empty house might not be discovered for a long time."

"The thing's not impossible," Arkwright agreed reluctantly. "We can find out from Davenport whether he's got reason to think his house has been entered at any time, but he's hardly likely to have had anything in the shape of a burglary without mentioning it. If he has, that will wash out the idea of an accomplice. All the same, we'll have a try at locating Greeve."

Constantine returned to the cablegram.

"I see that Miller came to Cape Town in nineteen eleven," he observed, "and left immediately after his acquittal in nineteen fourteen. He seems to have returned again in nineteen twenty-six and to have left the same year for England. Where was he in the interval?"

"I've got my own theory as to that," said Arkwright darkly. "We'll have his passport verified, but I'm willing to bet that he's down as a naturalised South African. That doesn't prevent his being a foreigner."

"And nineteen fourteen is a significant date!"

Arkwright nodded.

"Miller may have had his own reasons for leaving Cape Town just then," he said, "and, if he did offer his services, say, to the Germans, his nationality would make him doubly useful, from their point of view. His own account is that he was in Switzerland, but I'd give something to know what he was doing there, if only in the hope of establishing a motive."

"Aren't you rather ignoring the theft of the pendant?"

"If Cattistock, or anyone else, for the matter of that, murdered Mrs. Miller for the sake of her jewels," said Arkwright slowly, "why did he confine himself to the pendant? He could have got away with a bigger haul than that and, given this Chinese connection, he would have had no difficulty in disposing of it."

CHAPTER SEVEN

THOUGH Constantine attended the inquest on Mrs. Miller he did not have to give evidence. Knowing that the police were applying for an adjournment, the Coroner saw to it that only essentials were dealt with, in spite of which it was past lunch time before Arkwright managed to escape and snatch some food on his way back to the Yard.

He found the detective he had sent to Victoria waiting for him. He reported that he had struck oil at last.

"Got a man here, sir, a railway porter," he said, "who identifies the body as that of a woman who arrived on the seven fifteen boat train. He's been off duty since the murder or we should have got onto him before. He's positive that it's the same woman."

"Shown him the Cattistock photograph?" demanded Arkwright.

"Yes, sir. He declared he's never set eyes on the man. The photograph doesn't bear any resemblance to the person that met her."

Arkwright grabbed the report the detective had placed on his table. This looked like business at last.

"Send him along," he commanded briskly, as he read it.

His satisfaction deepened when, a few minutes later, the man was ushered into the room. Gnarled, grizzled and thick-set, his shoulders bowed by a life spent in the lifting of heavy weights, it was easy to place him as a porter of the old school, who had probably been for years in the Company's service. Arkwright knew the type, slow of brain and almost childishly observant of detail, a born gatherer of unimportant facts. He gave his name as Joseph Osborne.

"You were on duty at Victoria Station on the evening of Monday last?" said Arkwright.

Osborne considered the question.

"That's right," he admitted huskily. "I come on at seven and went off at eleven, an hour early on account of me cough. 'Orrid bad, it was. I didn't get back Tuesday nor yet Wednesday, owin' to bein' laid up. Reported this mornin' I did, that's 'ow I come to 'ear about that there enquiry."

Having said his say he passed the back of a horny hand across his mouth and waited. Arkwright, who had had experience of this kind of witness, shot another leading question at him and left him to tell his story in his own way.

"I understand that you recognised this woman when you were taken to the mortuary today. Know anything about her beyond the fact that you saw her at the station?"

The man shook his head.

"I carried 'er luggage, but I never see no name on the labels. Shouldn't 'a noticed it, likely, if I 'ad. It's 'er, all right, though. She come in on the seven fifteen. Three minutes late she were."

"You didn't hear the address she gave the taxi?"

"I didn't," was the deliberate answer, "because she didn't take no taxi. A gent met 'er and took 'er off in 'is car."

Arkwright leaned forward.

"What was this gentleman like?" he asked. "Is there any thing special you can remember about him?"

"There wasn't nothin' special, so far as I can remember," was the answer. "Of course, I didn't take special stock of 'im, if you understand me. 'Adn't got no reason to. Not too short, nor yet too tall, dressed in one of them Burberrys, or else a mackintosh, I'm not sure which. Think 'e must 'ave 'ad a soft 'at on. If it'd been a bowler or a cap I'd likely 'ave noticed, bein' as 'ow you don't often see 'em nowadays. Anyway, I'd say 'e was dressed quite ordinary. I didn't see much of 'is face, 'im bein' occupied with the lady, like, but I see 'is little grey beard. That I do remember, but it's the best I can do for you."

"A grey beard. You're sure of that?"

"Why shouldn't I be, seein' as I saw it?"

"What sort of beard?"

Osborne gave the matter his full attention.

"Smallish," he said at last. "Cut to a point, like. Very neat and tidy. Neat lookin' sort of gentleman 'e was altogether, now I come to think of it."

Arkwright visualised a certain, not uncommon type of Frenchman.

"Was he a foreigner, do you think?" he asked.

Osborne scratched his head.

"They was askin' me that at the station," he said, "but I told 'em as I couldn't say, one way or the other. 'E was talkin' English, that I do know. So was the lady. She looked foreign, all right, but she didn't talk foreign. I'd put 'er down as English, if you ask me."

"Did you hear what they said?"

"Not a word. I was follerin' up with the luggage, if you understand me, and, anyways, what with the noise in the station, you wouldn't 'ear nothin'. The gentleman's English seemed all right when 'e spoke to me."

"When was that?" Arkwright caught himself up and amended his question. "Wait a second. Better tell the story from the beginning in your own way."

"From where I first set eyes on the lady?"

"From the moment she engaged you. You actually saw her get out of the train, I suppose?"

"Couldn't 'elp it, seein' as I got out 'er luggage for 'er. A suit-case and one of them week-end cases. She was in a second class coach. I got 'em down from the rack and asked 'er if she'd got anythin' in the van. She said she 'adn't and would I get a taxi for 'er. I was just goin' after a keb when she 'ollered after me and I see this gentleman talkin' to 'er. So I waited and then follered them along to 'is car."

"Open or closed?"

"Closed, it was. 'E put 'er in and shut the door, then 'e told me to take the luggage to the cloak-room and bring back the ticket to 'im. So I off with it to the cloak-room. 'E'd got the door of the car open and was talkin' to 'er when I got back and when 'e see me 'e come to meet me and took the ticket."

"You've no idea where they went?"

"Didn't even see 'em drive off. 'E give me 'alf a crown for me trouble and that's the last I see of 'em."

Arkwright picked up the telephone on his desk and took off the receiver.

"Hullo, Atkins, is Gordon there? That you, Gordon? About this luggage in the cloak-room at Victoria. Is it still there? Right. Send someone down for it and have it brought to my room."

Arkwright consulted the detective's report once more.

"It's a pity you can't describe the car she went away in," he said. "Nothing special you can remember about it, I suppose?"

"Don't know nothin' about cars," was Osborne's emphatic rejoinder. "Don't want to. Nasty things. I 'ardly looked at it. Dark, I think it was and I know it 'ad one of them tops on because 'e 'ad to 'old the door open to talk to 'er."

"Had he got a driver?"

"'E was drivin' it 'imself. That was the last I see before I turned away, 'im sittin' down in the driver's seat behind the wheel."

"Do you know what time they left Victoria?"

"If they drove off at once it would be round about seven thirty-five, seein' as I went straight off from there to meet the seven thirty-seven, and she was on time."

Arkwright looked up from his notes with a friendly smile.

"Sure that's the best you can do for us? Nothing else you can remember?"

A gleam of humour appeared in Osborne's faded blue eyes.

"Not unless I pitches you a tale, and I take it that wouldn't be much good to you. I 'andles too many people's luggage for me to remember much about 'em. Sorry I couldn't do no better for you."

"You've given us a shove in the right direction," said Arkwright, as he dismissed him. "Someone else may have noticed them. If you pick up any information, you let us have it."

Osborne nodded, rose stiffly to his feet and began winding an enormous and apparently interminable muffler round his neck. He was drawing the end through the knot when Arkwright's last words, which had been slowly germinating in his mind, bore fruit.

"I reckon as the railway constable might 'ave somethin' to tell you if you asked 'im," he volunteered.

Arkwright looked up quickly.

"Where does he come into it?"

"It was when the lady first got into the car. I was waitin' with the luggage and the constable spoke to the gentleman. There was a taxi wanted to draw up and there wasn't no room for it. 'E 'ad to 'op in and back the car nearer to the one behind. That's when I first see 'e was drivin' it 'imself."

"Did he speak to the constable?"

"There couldn't ave been more than a couple of words passed between them. Then 'e got down and signalled me to come over to 'im."

Arkwright frowned thoughtfully. He had an eye for detail that had stood him in good stead before now.

"Why did he do that if he wanted the stuff taken to the cloak-room?" he asked abruptly.

The porter shifted his cap to his other hand and scratched his head.

"Now you come to mention it, I don't know," he said slowly. "I was nearer the cloak-room where I was and that's a fact."

"What were his movements exactly?"

Osborne's eyes closed in an effort at concentration.

"Well, first 'e 'opped up, like I told you, and backed the car. Then 'e 'opped down and went round behind, and I thought 'e was lettin' down the luggage rack, so I started to move. I 'adn't 'ardly started when 'e looks round the back of the car and beckons to me, but when I gets round to the back 'e tells me to take the lot to the cloak-room. I thought to myself as 'e'd changed 'is mind, like."

"And when you brought back the cloak-room ticket he came to meet you and took it from you. Is that right?"

"That's right."

After he had gone Arkwright added his notes to the detective's report. On the arrival of Gordon with the murdered woman's luggage he sent him back to Victoria to fetch the station constable while he«embarked on a careful inspection of the contents of the two cases. They were both locked, but the locks were of the kind that are invariably supplied with inexpensive luggage and presented little difficulty. As it turned out, Arkwright might just as well have spared himself even that slight exertion, for there was literally nothing in either of the cases that provided even the smallest clue to the woman's identity. The larger contained clothing, including a couple of evening dresses, of the same style and quality as the dress she had been wearing when she was killed. The smaller case held only toilet articles and the things necessary for one night. There was not a letter, document, photograph, or even a newspaper cutting in either of them.

Arkwright sat back on his heels and regarded the two cases on the floor before him, his face dark with perplexity and exasperation. If the murdered woman carried one of those voluminous hand-bags that are so much in use nowadays there was every reason to suppose that she had her passport and any private letters with her when she was killed, but such a complete dearth of the usual epistolary moss gathered even by the most confirmed rolling stone was, to put it mildly, unnatural. And she had told the porter that she had no big luggage! The only remaining possibility was that she had followed the custom in vogue with wealthy Americans and had forwarded her trunks through an agent, in which case they would materialise in a day or so, but Arkwright did not feel hopeful. He was gradually being forced to the conclusion that she had only come over for a couple of nights and that the bulk of her possessions was still on the other side of the Channel. If, as he was beginning to think, she had no friends in England and her papers remained ungetatable, things were at a hopeless deadlock. The only chance, in that case, was to concentrate on the car and its owner and, unless the constable on duty at Victoria possessed an unusually retentive memory, it did not look as if that line was going to lead far. Arkwright settled to wait for his arrival in a mood that was not lightened by the receipt of a report from the Guildford police to the effect that nothing had been heard of Cattistock. His housekeeper had called at the police station to ask what she was to do with his correspondence and was beginning to betray acute anxiety as to his welfare. She had been directed to deliver all letters to the station. The three she had brought with her accompanied the report.

Arkwright opened them, only to fling them on the table with a snort of exasperation. Two small bills from local tradesmen and a form from the secretary of a well-known charity committee to say that Cattistock's annual subscription of five shillings was overdue. Arkwright reflected dourly that if the sums had been larger the correspondence might have furnished proof that the man was pressed for money, but the three claims together did not amount to fifteen shillings and there was no reason to believe that they would not have been met promptly if he had been at home. According to the report he was, as the housekeeper had said, well thought of in the neighbourhood and had the reputation of settling his accounts regularly.

To Arkwright, in his present frame of mind, the statement of the constable was as the first bright gleam of sun on a dull day. He proved to be young and earnest, with the tan of his native Dorset still on his cheeks. He had been only two months in London and was inclined to take both himself and his job with a seriousness that would have been amusing under other conditions. As it was Arkwright blessed the gods that had placed this particular man on such a spot at such a time, for he not only remembered the car, but could describe it and even had ideas about the number.

"I wouldn't like to say for sure, sir," he said, with a caution that betrayed his peasant stock. "There were five cars I took count of that evening and I may have got them a bit mixed."

"Can you remember the others?"

The constable reeled off five sets of numbers with commendable precision.

"How did you come to have them so pat?" asked Arkwright, with a gleam of amusement.

The constable flushed.

"I started doing it for practice, sir," he explained. "Then I got into the way of it. Being in the station yard there, I often have to say a word to the drivers and, when I do, I make a note of the number of the car in my mind, as it were, and go over them in the evening, just to see how many I can remember. It's just a sort of habit."

"An uncommonly good one," said Arkwright. "It's a thing I've recommended to any number of recruits, but I've never caught one at it till now! I gather that you're not too sure of these?"

"The numbers themselves are all right, sir," was the reply. "I can pretty well vouch for that. I've got a sort of system of my own for remembering them. What I'm not sure about is whether I gave you the right one. I'm a bit hazy about the order in which that car came."

"Then if we follow up the lot we can be pretty sure of hitting on the car? They're all London numbers, I see."

"That's right, sir. Morris Oxford, dark green or dark blue, I'm not sure which."

"Notice anything special about the driver?"

"I'm afraid not, sir. He wasn't looking my way when I spoke to him and he didn't turn round. Just muttered something and climbed into the car and backed her. I could see he had a beard, but that was all. Once he'd cleared the way I didn't take no further notice of him."

Arkwright dismissed him, making a mental note to keep an eye on him if he went on shaping well, and stepped across to the Traffic Branch. There he had little difficulty in tracing the owners of the five cars in question.

Having more faith in the constable's memory than the youngster had himself, he decided to begin with the number he had first mentioned. The owner of this car, it appeared, ran a public garage near Buckingham Palace Road. He accordingly went there.

At the sight of his card the proprietor left his office and came to meet him, revealing himself as a short, stocky little • man, badly hampered by an artificial leg which he managed with difficulty. He had ex-officer written all over him and Arkwright, at the sight of him, blessed his luck for sending him yet another witness capable of making a coherent statement. The man's greeting was characteristic.

"What are you trying to fasten on me, Inspector?" he demanded, with a grin. "Whatever it is, I didn't do it!"

"We're letting you off lightly this time," Arkwright assured him, "though I'm not sure that one of your cars hasn't been up to mischief."

The man stared at him for a moment, then his eyes narrowed.

"Bet I can tell you which it is," he exclaimed. "Have a look at this."

He limped ahead of Arkwright down a long alley of cars into the back of the garage and stopped opposite a dark green Morris Oxford.

"How's that?" he asked.

Arkwright glanced at the number plate.

"That's the offender," he admitted.

The little man cocked a shrewd eye at him.

"Want to know where she was last Monday evening, the fourteenth, by any chance?" he asked.

Arkwright smiled.

"We should be glad of any information you can give us," he agreed noncommittally.

"Properly speaking, it ought to be the other way round," grumbled the proprietor. "However, I'll do what I can for you. As a matter of fact, I've got it all pat. At about seven o'clock on Monday night a man came in and said he wanted a car for the evening. I gathered that it was the usual restaurant and theatre business. As he hadn't dealt with us before and wasn't taking a driver I had to ask him to pay in advance, which he did."

"He paid in notes, I suppose?" put in Arkwright.

"Yes, and there was nothing fishy about them. I tried one on my bank manager next day."

"Can you describe the man?"

"Medium sized, middle-aged, with a small, pointed grey beard. Dressed in a good quality rain-coat and a felt hat. That's all I can remember."

Arkwright nodded.

"That's near enough. It's our man all right," he said. "Did he give his name?"

"No. To tell you the truth I didn't bother much about him. One gets pretty good at sizing people up in this business and I put him down as all right. Looked well to do and respectable and all that."

Arkwright stared at the car thoughtfully.

"Don't happen to have kept any of those notes, I suppose?" he asked.

The other nodded.

"Owing to what happened afterwards I felt a bit suspicious about them, so I stuck them in an envelope, and when I went to the bank I got the manager to vet them for me. He passed them all right and changed one of them for me into silver. I've been carrying the other two about with me ever since, meaning to shove them in the till."

He took a wallet from his pocket and extracted an envelope which he handed to Arkwright. Arkwright inspected the two pound notes it contained and held one of them up to the light.

"Was this green stain on it when you got it?" he asked.

"Yes. Nobody's handled it but myself and the bank manager."

Arkwright took two pounds from his pocket and gave them to him, keeping the others in exchange.

"I'll take charge of these if you don't mind," he said. "And now I'll ask you how you knew that this was the car I was after?"

The proprietor glared at him.

"I like that!" he exclaimed indignantly. "Considering you had a full description of this car first thing Tuesday morning!"

"There are about two hundred police stations in London," suggested Arkwright mildly. "Which of them did you patronize?"

The glare subsided, to be replaced by a broad smile.

"One up to you," admitted the little man. "Honestly, I thought that was what you had come about."

"On the contrary, I came for information."

"Then you shall have it," was the sardonic answer. "Though you may not know it, you were looking for that car, at least, in my ignorance, I thought you were, through the greater part of Tuesday morning. That chap who took it out forgot to bring it back."

"Seeing that it is back, may I ask where we found it?"

"In a mews near Grosvenor Place," answered the owner. "I can't help feeling you ought to have known that!"

CHAPTER EIGHT

"So that's what you thought I came for," said Arkwright solemnly, giving quite an able imitation of the imbecile stage policeman. But the little ex-officer at his elbow did not miss the dry humour that lurked in his grey eyes and was not surprised when he continued, with a complete change of tone: "Now it's my turn. This is a case of murder and there seems every reason to believe that your little tin Lizzie, there, is an accessory!"

But the manager had played poker, too, in his day. His face remained imperturbable.

"You don't say so," he drawled. "I must admit I'm surprised at her. She's been a quiet, well-behaved little body up till now. Are you going to arrest her? I've got my living to make, you know."

"Depends on what I find in her. Has she been overhauled since she came in that night?"

"She has been looked over cursorily, just to make sure that no damage had been done to her, but it was the engine we were interested in, mostly. She hasn't been cleaned yet."

"Been out since then?"

"No. As a matter of fact, she's a bit of a maid of all work. I use her sometimes myself, but, as a rule, I only let her out to customers like that chap the other night, people I've had no dealings with before and who aren't taking a driver. There's been no demand for her since Monday. Except for the engine, she's just as she was when your people brought her in on Tuesday."

Arkwright opened the door, climbed onto the running board and ran his eye over the cushions and wood-work. The proprietor watched him for a moment, then turned and limped off in the direction of his office, to return almost at once carrying an electric torch.

He handed it silently to Arkwright, who grunted his acknowledgments. His head was under the steering wheel and he was examining the wood-work of the door next the driver's seat. He turned the light of the torch on it and watched the beam as it travelled slowly upwards until it reached the seat itself. The cushions revealed themselves as rubbed and dusty, but otherwise uninjured. Slowly the little disk of light swung round and rested finally on the upholstery to the left of the seat.

"Got it, by Jove!"

The exclamation came from the garage proprietor, who had climbed onto the running board beside Arkwright and was peering over his shoulder.

Beginning about eight inches above the edge of the cushion of the seat and running down to it, was a long, dark brown smear.

The proprietor heaved himself to the ground, hobbled round to the other side of the car and hoisted himself once more onto the running board. His round face sharpened with curiosity and excitement, he resembled a fox terrier at the mouth of a rat hole.

"Let me get that cushion out!" he exclaimed. "If that's blood, somebody's hand's been down there."

Arkwright straightened his back and stood waiting.

"Careful you don't shift anything," he enjoined, keeping the torch focussed on the cushion as the proprietor lifted it carefully out.

Underneath, jammed into a corner, was a pair of motor gauntlets. Arkwright bent over and picked them up gingerly. They were literally stiff with dried blood.

The proprietor gaped at him, his face considerably less florid than it had been but a moment before.

"So that's that," he said. Then, with an attempt at his former manner. "Poor old Lizzie! What a damned shame!"

He helped Arkwright to make a careful search of the whole of the interior of the car, but there was nothing further of any interest to be found.

"Chap must have been killed outside the car," he said, when they had finished, "and those gauntlets just shoved down there afterwards."

Arkwright picked up a bit of newspaper from the floor and wrapped the gloves in it.

"The murder was committed inside the car, I suspect," he asserted, "and a shawl muffled round the neck of the victim in time to catch the spurt of blood."

"Spurt?"

Arkwright nodded.

"Jugular. The shawl was saturated."

The little man looked as if he had suddenly come across a very nasty smell.

"Good Lord!" he ejaculated. "It seems to have been a pretty skillful job! Sort of professional touch about it, what?"

"There was," assented Arkwright grimly. "And about the other, too!"

The proprietor's jaw dropped.

"What other? Isn't one of this sort enough for you?"

Arkwright, the parcel containing his gruesome find under his arm, turned to go.

"It's a comfort to feel that we've got something under our hats at the Yard that you don't know," he said complacently. "We must ask you to leave that car as it is and keep it in the garage for the present."

"Do you think I'm likely to send it out in that state? This is a garage, not the Chamber of Horrors!" exclaimed the proprietor disgustedly, as he accompanied him to the door. He did not speak again till they reached the street, then:

"You didn't tell me that poor old Lizzie's victim was a lady. Very discreet of you. But I do read my paper in the morning and when two women get their throats cut on the same day one can't help wondering! How does the official hat feel now, Inspector?"

Arkwright took his off and examined it critically.

"Smaller than the civilian head," he retorted with a grin, as he departed.

Back in his office at the Yard he examined his find more carefully. The gauntlets bore no mark except their size number, stamped inside the cuff. They were of inexpensive make and had seen a good deal of service before they had been ruined so irretrievably. Arkwright pushed them aside and turned his attention to the notes he had taken from the garage proprietor. These were both new and, which was more interesting, bore consecutive numbers. Across the corner of one of them was a green stain. While he was considering them the telephone bell rang. Arkwright took off the receiver to find Constantine at the other end.

"I've had a stroke of luck," he said, "and, as a result, I've got a suggestion to make to you. Did Miller tell you anything about that woman he was by way of meeting at Victoria on Monday night?"

"Nothing, beyond the fact that she had not arrived. As I told you, he got the wind up before his visit to the mortuary. Thought the murdered woman might out to be his friend, but he failed to identify her."

"He did definitely fail to identify her?"

"Said he'd never seen her before. It was evidently a great relief to him."

"Does Miller strike you as being the sort of person to feel acute concern as to the fate of a vague friend of his wife's? He didn't give the impression that she was an intimate friend of his own, did he?"

"No, I rather gathered that he didn't know her well and was annoyed at her coming. What *is* the bright idea, sir?" Constantine countered with another question.

"Have you had tea? Or does Scotland Yard not run to such effeminacies?"

"As one old lady to another, I have not," retorted Arkwright, "but, as a means of changing the subject. ..."

"Then I'll be with you very shortly and join you in a cup," went on Constantine imperturbably. "Then, if there's nothing in my idea we shall neither of us have wasted our time."

"Delighted," assented the mystified Arkwright, his finger already on the bell. He sent the messenger who answered it out to buy cakes, cleared a space on his table for the tray and waited. If Constantine said "shortly," he meant it and he knew him well enough to be certain that any idea of his would be worthy of consideration.

The old chess player's eyebrows went up at the sight of the tray.

"So this is where our money goes, is it?" he remarked plaintively. "Well, I don't grudge it to you. Between mouthfuls I'll try to prove to you that I'm not so senile as I may have sounded on the telephone. I had a chat with Miller today."

Arkwright paused in the act of pouring out tea.

"Did he go to see you?" he asked in surprise.

"Hardly. Fate threw us together. I decided to indulge my old bones in a Turkish Bath this morning. Simmering on the next slab to myself was Miller. We could have hardly devised a more informal meeting and I may mention that he looks singularly unprepossessing in a Turkish Bath."

"So I should imagine," answered Arkwright appreciatively. "I gather you exercised your well known powers of conversation on him?"

Constantine smiled reminiscently.

"I did my best. He was more than ready to talk about the murder, in fact I had difficulty in keeping him off the subject. He wasn't nearly so anxious to discuss his wife's old friend."

He paused.

"Has it struck you that he took her non-arrival rather casually?" he demanded.

"He didn't seem worried, certainly," admitted Arkwright, "but considering what had happened that day he would have had every excuse if he had forgotten all about her."

"That wouldn't have surprised me in the least. What does strike me as curious is that, having remembered her, he wasn't at more pains to discover why she never turned up."

"There had been all this business connected with his wife's death."

"Oh, he's every excuse, I admit. In spite of which his attitude towards her does not ring true. Anyway, it roused my curiosity, and when I found that he showed distinct reluctance to discuss the matter I'm afraid I used all the guile I had at my command to extract information. He couldn't very well refuse to tell me who she was and he admitted that he had made no effort to find out whether she had arrived in London. There was one thing that, with all my efforts, I could not persuade him to do. That was to describe her."

Arkwright frowned.

"Do you mean to say that he refused to tell you what she looked like?" he demanded.

"I mean that he evaded giving any description of her so persistently and so cleverly that a suspicion slowly began to form in my mind."

Arkwright stared at him.

"You're not suggesting that he did recognize the woman in the mortuary?" he said.

"No. I'm suggesting that he didn't, because he couldn't. Did he ever tell you in so many words that he had ever met this friend of his wife's?"

Arkwright hesitated.

"He certainly implied it," he said at last. "What object could he have in concealing the fact that he didn't know her?"

"None, unless he wanted to delay the identification as long as possible. Supposing, when he told you his wife's friend had never turned up, he had also told you that he did not know what she looked like, what would you have done?"

"I should have worked on the assumption that she might have come on an earlier train and endeavoured to find out whether she was missing, I suppose, merely on the chance that she might prove to be the murdered woman."

"Helped by the fact that Miller, though he had never seen her, could supply you with all particulars as to her identity. By implying that he knew her and did not recognise her, he managed to evade this. Why?"

"But he hasn't admitted to you that he has never seen her, sir," objected Arkwright.

"In all but actual words, he has admitted it," asserted Constantine impatiently. "I can't prove it, but I tell you I know he was unable to describe her and that he didn't dare take the risk of giving a false description."

"I can't see why he should have hesitated there. If the woman lives in Paris, as he said, her friends would not be here to refute him."

"Her friends are not in Paris. She brought them with her when she came to England. I literally forced that out of him. Miller, if he had never seen this friend of his wife's and had omitted to tell you so, found himself in a cleft stick this morning. When I tried to get her description out of him he had already told me her name and that she was a member of a troupe of Russian singers and dancers that is appearing at the Parthenon Playhouse next week. That being the case, he did not dare describe her. It would not take half an hour to get in touch with the manager of the troupe and find out if the description were correct."

"And less than an hour, probably, to get one of them down to the mortuary. That's what you're driving at, isn't it, sir?"

"It's what I hoped you might do," agreed Constantine placidly. "I admit that I've given you very little to go on, but, if this friend of Miller's turns out not to be missing, or even if she has not arrived, but is proved to have no connection with the murdered woman, you will be no worse off than you were before. I think it's an idea worthy of your consideration. I suppose Miller's alibis are air-tight?"

Arkwright grinned.

"I think you would find it difficult to pick a hole in them. He was at his office from ten till twelve thirty. We have his staff's word for that. Mrs. Miller was murdered between eleven forty-eight and twelve five, as you know."

"What about his movements in the evening?"

"Scheduled to the minute! The footman, who made up the fire in the library at seven twenty-five states that he was there then; the butler spoke to him in the library at seven forty-five and saw him cross the hall from the secretary's room at a few minutes to eight. We know that the murder in Eccleston Square took place somewhere between seven thirty and eight. The secretary, who was working in his room all the evening, states that he took letters into the library for Miller's signature several times during the evening. No, however fishy his behaviour may have been since, he was not concerned in the murder."

Constantine deliberated for a moment.

"It looks as if he were lying low about something that happened in the past," he said, at last. "Something fairly significant, I should think. I have a strong suspicion that he knows, or at least suspects, who killed his wife."

"The man's frightened," insisted Arkwright. "I can tell you that. Shouldn't wonder if he thinks he'll be the next to go."

"If that's the case his obvious course should be to ask for police protection," was Constantine's dry comment. "I'd give a great deal to know why he doesn't. Some queer things happened in Switzerland during the war. Have you worked on that line at all?"

"I've tried the Special Branch. There's nothing doing there. They've no record of anyone of that name, but then, of course, he may have called himself anything. He was certainly in funds when he got back to Cape Town in nineteen twenty-six. It was understood that he had been dealing in jewels in Switzerland for some time."

"With Russian refugees pouring in from all sides there was a good field for business there. He may have made his money honestly. All the same I think our friend Miller is worth watching."

Constantine leaned forward and picked up The Times from Arkwright's desk.

"The Russian show opens on Monday next at the Parthenon Playhouse," he said. "They are running a kind of variety performance between the two big films. It would be interesting to know whether any member of the cast is missing."

Arkwright gathered himself to his feet.

"The resources of the Yard are at your disposal, sir," he announced, with a grin. "But, honestly, I think you are drawing a bow at a venture."

"Well, if we do hit anything the credit will go to you," retorted Constantine, "and the Yard has plenty of arrows at its disposal."

Arkwright applied himself to the telephone and had no difficulty in getting the address of the manager of the Russian Company from the box office at the Parthenon. After a short conversation he hung up the receiver with a sigh.

"He's at a small hotel off the Strand," he said. "I'd better see the man myself. Interviewing temperamental foreigners on the phone is a poor business at best. What will you do, sir? I shall come straight back here, I expect."

Constantine smiled shrewdly.

"If only for the pleasure of saying 'I told you so,' to a fussy old gentleman," he replied. "On the whole, I should prefer to be present at the scene of my humiliation. Unless you feel that I shall mar the official atmosphere?"

Arkwright executed a neat continental bow as he picked up the receiver once more and gave the number of the manager's hotel.

"I shall welcome your assistance, my dear colleague," he asserted floridly.

The manager was at home and, ten minutes later, Constantine having insisted on a taxi on the score of his advancing years, they entered the hotel.

Monsieur Karamiev, a short, immensely fat individual, whose clean-shaven, very sallow face seemed permanently afflicted with that look of vague discomfort and apprehension so often to be observed on the Channel, hurried down from his room at the sight of Arkwright's official card and professed himself entirely at his service. He protested volubly and in excellent English that his papers and those of his artistes were all in order.

Arkwright, who, on the way from the Yard, had suggested that Constantine should take charge of this, his own, investigation, reassured Monsieur Karamiev on this point and introduced his companion.

"This gentleman has one or two questions to ask concerning a member of your troupe," he said, and then, with a mischievous side glance at Constantine, retired into the background.

Constantine opened negotiations with a bow as elaborate, if slightly less florid, than the Russian's.

"I must apologise for troubling you, Monsieur," he said, "but I have been given to understand that Madame Abramoff is a member of your company."

Monsieur Karamiev's look of nausea became more pronounced.

"Ah, Monsieur," he exclaimed tragically. "I knew it! You have come to tell me that Madame Abramoff is unable to play on Monday! You are a doctor, yes?"

Constantine smiled.

"Not a doctor of medicine, Monsieur," he assured him. "I have no message from Madame Abramoff. On the contrary, I was depending on you for information concerning her. Could you oblige me with her address?"

The manager threw out his fat little arms in a gesture expressive of tragic despair.

"But I have it not! Imagine, Monsieur, we arrive on Monday, last at the station here in London. My artistes go to the lodgings I have engaged for them, all of them except Vera Abramoff. She leaves the station with a friend with whom she is to stay during our engagement here. Before she goes she tells me that she will telephone to me concerning the times of our rehearsals and other important arrangements we have to make between us. From that time until now I hear nothing of her."

The amusement faded from Arkwright's eyes and he took a step forward, only to subside at a warning gesture from Constantine.

"You arrived, I think, at seven fifteen at Victoria, Monsieur," suggested the old man.

Karamiev bowed.

"That is so, Monsieur."

"And this friend of Madame's? You saw him?"

"Assuredly, Monsieur. A very correct gentleman, the husband, I understand, of the friend with whom Madame was to stay."

"He was dark and clean-shaven, this gentleman?"

"But, no, Monsieur. He wore a little grey beard, cut as one sees them in France and also in my country. I said to myself, that Madame does not stay, as I thought, with her compatriots."

"Madame Abramoff is English, then?"

The apprehension on the Russian's face deepened.

"I assure you that Madame's papers are correct, Monsieur," he vociferated. "All through France and Germany they have never been questioned. Madame is a Russian subject by marriage, but she is of English parentage. Until her husband's death during the Revolution she was a rich woman, well known in society in Riga. There can be nothing against her."

Constantine's smile was a miracle of polite deprecation.

"Believe me, Monsieur," he said, "we are not questioning Madame's credentials. My interest in her is purely friendly. But we have lost sight of her for many years and anything you can tell us of her life in Russia would be of the greatest assistance to us. Shall we sit down while you are kind enough to satisfy our curiosity?"

Herding the little man towards a chair he took out his cigarette case and offered it to him,

"You need be under no apprehension," he assured him. "The police here haven't the smallest intention of interfering with your performance. This is a purely private matter, in which my friend here, Chief Inspector Arkwright, has kindly consented to help me. These friends, now, of Madame Abramoff's, can you tell me anything about them? Are they friends of long standing?"

Monsieur Karamiev shrugged his fat shoulders.

"I can only tell you what she has said to the other members of my company, Monsieur," he answered. "Myself I know nothing. The lady, I understand, was an old stage acquaintance of Madame's in the days before her marriage. Madame met Abramoff in England, married him and went to Russia, where she has lived ever since. Her husband was killed in the early days of the Revolution and Madame was left penniless. Before I met Madame she had been acting as dresser to a dancer, a woman of the new regime who treated her worse than a dog. She was brought to me by a member of my Company and, finding that I could use her in my performance, I engaged her and she has been travelling with us ever since. She can only play certain parts, you understand. Hardship has altered her voice and her looks, but for what you call the character parts she is useful and I am glad to employ her."

"Can you think of anyone, Monsieur, who might wish her ill? Is there any enemy she might have made during those years in Russia?"

Monsieur Karamiev looked sceptical.

"It is difficult to believe, Monsieur," he answered. "Vera Abramoff is so gentle and kindly. But during those years, you understand, many strange things happened. She may have made enemies, yes, in spite of herself. That she was ill-treated, I know, but I have never heard that she harmed anyone."

"She has never spoken of anyone whom she might have reason to fear?"

For a second tragedy looked out of the eyes of the Russian.

"There was a period, Monsieur," he said, "when we feared everybody in Russia. Even those nearest to us. But Vera Abramoff, once she had crossed the frontier, showed no special fear. I think she is happy with us."

"She showed no reluctance to come to England."

"None, Monsieur. She seemed to be looking forward to renewing her old friendships. She certainly spoke with pleasure of this visit she was about to pay."

Constantine rose.

"Then I think I need trouble you no further, Monsieur," he said. "You have heard nothing from her, you say, since she left you at the station?"

"Nothing. It is that which was making me anxious. To-morrow we rehearse and she left me no address with which to reach her. I feared she was ill."

Constantine turned to the window and stood there, looking out into the narrow street, while Arkwright explained matters to Monsieur Karamiev. He accompanied the two men to the mortuary and waited outside for them, but he had little doubt now as to what the result of their visit would be.

One glance at the Russian's face when he emerged was enough. The identity of the victim of the Eccleston Square murder was established at last.

CHAPTER NINE

Monsieur Karamiev had gone back, considerably shaken, to his hotel.

"So much sorrow in her life and at the end, this," he had muttered, wiping the tears unashamedly from his eyes.

Constantine watched the obese figure and queer, rolling gait of the Russian as he hurried on his way, blowing his nose sonorously on a gaudy check handkerchief.

"That is a good little man," was his comment.

Arkwright, his hands deep in his overcoat pockets, was staring at the pavement at his feet.

"It takes a lot to stir my imagination nowadays," he said slowly, "but that woman in there has got me thinking. It's a queer story, isn't it? God knows what her father was, but the chances are that she was brought up in a respectable, middle-class home. Semi-detached villa in the suburbs; chapel-going parents; Monday's washing hanging out in the back garden, and all that sort of thing. Could anything be duller and safer? Probably went on the stage in search of a bit of excitement, met this Russian chap, married him and found herself playing the great lady among the richest and gayest people in the world. I don't suppose she'd ever even imagined anything like it. And then the crash. Karamiev said she was at breaking point when he met her. And then, just at the moment when she must have felt safest, this vile business! I'd like to get my hands on the beast that did it!"

Constantine's eyes hardened.

"Do you know," he said, "this is about the first time I have found myself envying you your job. I wish I could see a light anywhere in this puzzle!"

Arkwright kicked a piece of orange peel savagely into the gutter.

"It's all too damned geographical for my taste," he growled. "This Chinese knife business, then Cattistock, with his Chinese connection; Miller, with a past that covers South Africa, Switzerland and, for all we know, Germany. And now this woman and her Russian antecedents, as if things weren't complicated enough already! We've got enough to choose from!"

"And Miller's the link," insisted Constantine doggedly. "Don't forget that. His wife was the first victim and this woman was on her way to stay with him when she was killed."

Arkwright grunted.

"I'm beginning to think kindly of the American third degree," he said morosely. "I'd give a good deal to make him talk. He's got to produce a satisfactory reason why he kept back the fact that he had never met this Abramoff woman and I'm off to get it!"

He found Miller out. Bloomfield, the secretary, received him. His manner was courteous, but he gave the impression of having detached himself with difficulty from his work to deal with the detective and, on the arrival of his employer, ten minutes later, vanished with unflattering celerity. Bloomfield had been discretion itself when Arkwright turned the conversation to Madame Abramoff. Mrs. Miller had mentioned her once or twice and he understood that she had invited her to stay in the house during the run of the performance at the Parthenon, with a view to saving her expense, as she had lost all her money in the Russian revolution. Asked whether Mr. Miller had ever met her, he said he could not say, but that, unless she had been in England lately, it was unlikely, as, with the exception of an occasional business visit to Amsterdam and Paris, he had not left this country since his marriage in nineteen twenty-seven.

Miller, when he came in, was palpably ill at ease though he tried to hide his discomfiture with an assumption of annoyance that crumbled slowly before Arkwright's curt officialdom.

"I can give you ten minutes, Inspector," he snapped, with a glance at his watch. "Unfortunately, my time is not my own."

Arkwright sat down uninvited, his feet planted firmly, his huge hands on his knees, policeman written all over him.

"We have identified the murdered woman, Mr. Miller," he announced briskly.

Miller ceased drumming impatiently with his fingers on the table and stared at him.

"Ah, the unfortunate creature in the mortuary," he said vaguely. "I had forgotten for the moment. My poor wife..."

"Your wife's friend was a Madame Abramoff, I think," continued Arkwright inexorably.

Miller bowed.

"That is so," he admitted.

Arkwright leaned forward.

"Mr. Miller," he said. There was a new ring in his voice now. "Why didn't you tell me when we were at the mortuary that you had never met Madame Abramoff?"

Miller's face exhibited blank amazement.

"But surely you knew that. I thought I had given you to understand that I had never seen my wife's friend. I merely told you at the mortuary I could not identify the murdered woman."

"You gave me to understand that you had never seen her, but I've reason to think that you deliberately withheld the fact that Madame Abramoff was unknown to you. Had you any reason to suspect that this woman might be Madame Abramoff?"

A mottled flush crept under Miller's thick skin.

"Aren't you taking a good deal for granted, Inspector?" he retorted acidly. "A woman is found murdered in the streets of London and, by pure chance, I happen to be expecting a lady from Paris on the same evening. Can you suggest any reason why I should have jumped to the conclusion that these two people were identical? If I omitted to tell you that I had never actually met Madame Abramoff, I can assure you that it was only because the fact did not strike me as relevant."

"You had no reason to fear that any ill might have befallen this lady?"

"What possible reason could I have for suspecting such a thing? Does it not strike you as possible, Inspector, that my mind may have been too full of other things to give this friend of my wife's much thought? I went to meet her at the station as a courtesy which I felt was due to her, but, when she did not arrive, I must confess that I was, if anything, rather relieved. It was not unreasonable to suppose that she had changed her plans."

"You said, I think, that she had written a letter to you saying that she intended to travel by the ten fifty-two train?" pursued Arkwright steadily.

"She had written to my wife," corrected Miller. "I have the letter here, if you wish to see it."

He pressed a button, picked up a speaking tube from his desk and spoke down it.

"Bloomfield, get me the package of letters on Mrs. Miller's writing table. The one in her sitting room."

With the efficiency that, Arkwright suspected, characterised all his movements, Bloomfield materialised, almost immediately, placed the package at his employer's elbow and vanished. Miller slipped the top letter from under the elastic band and, as Arkwright watched him, he reflected that it looked uncommonly as though it had been placed there in readiness for his visit.

He took it from Miller, but, before reading it, he examined the envelope. It bore the Paris post-mark and was dated two days before Mrs. Miller's death. The letter was short and to the point. It was written on flimsy foreign paper in the characterless, rather ornate hand-writing one would have expected from such a correspondent. In it Vera Abramoff said that she was coming to England with the rest of the Company on November the fourteenth and would arrive at Victoria at ten fifty-two. She expressed her delight at renewing her acquaintance with her old friend and the hope that she might find work that would keep her in "dear old England." On the face of it there seemed no reason to doubt that Miller actually had been expecting her by that train.

Arkwright handed the letter back in silence. Miller eyed him truculently, but Arkwright, seeing his tongue pass swiftly over his thick lips and watching his fingers fumbling nervously with his watch chain, knew the man was nervous.

"Well?" demanded Miller, as the silence grew oppressive. "Are you satisfied? I do not know what you are driving at, Inspector, but if you are trying to suggest that I had any knowledge ..."

He pulled himself up sharply, but Arkwright could have sworn that he had been about to say "Vera Abramoff's death." As it was, he wriggled clumsily enough out of the trap into which he had fallen.

"Are you trying to connect me with this unfortunate person's murder, Inspector?" he demanded.

"I have made no such suggestion," answered Arkwright. "My object is to find out why you deliberately misled the police. You have heard nothing further from this Madame Abramoff?"

Miller shrugged his shoulders.

"Nothing, though I have been expecting a telegram every day. It is possible that, if she decided to remain another day or so in Paris she may have seen the news of my poor wife's death in the papers. In which case she would hardly expect to come here."

Arkwright looked him squarely in the eyes.

"Madame Abramoff is dead," he said bluntly.

Miller stumbled to his feet and stood leaning heavily on the table.

"Dead!" he repeated. "When did she die? And where? If she is in Paris ..."

"She died in England, Mr. Miller. You saw her yourself when you failed to identify her on Tuesday."

Miller's grip on the edge of the table tightened. He stared at Arkwright as though he could not believe his ears.

"That woman? But this is appalling, Inspector! Are you sure there is no mistake?"

"None. The body has been identified by the manager of the Company in which she was playing."

Miller groped for his chair and sank into it. His truculence had collapsed like a pricked bladder. He looked utterly shaken.

"But this is awful," he muttered. "First my wife and then this poor woman. And for no reason! What is the meaning of it? My wife had not seen this woman for years. There could not be any connection between them. No one's life is safe now ..."

He was almost incoherent with sheer terror and would have babbled on interminably if Arkwright had not cut him short.

"What reason have you to think that there is any connection between the two crimes? After all, it's by mere chance that Madame Abramoff happened to be putting up at this house rather than at a hotel."

Miller wrung his hands together.

"I wish I could think there is none, but Lottie was my wife and Madame Abramoff her friend. Isn't that enough? And, according to the papers, Vera Abramoff died in the same way as my poor Lottie!"

He paused, staring at Arkwright with dilated eyes.

"That second knife you showed me ..."

Arkwright nodded.

"I told you at the time where we had found it," he said.

"I knew then that some influence was at work against me," groaned Miller. "Are the police doing nothing? Do you propose to allow these crimes to continue?"

"If you wish to lay hands on the murderer, Mr. Miller," answered Arkwright bluntly, "it is up to you to tell us anything that may have any bearing on the case. It is to your own advantage to be frank with us. Is there nothing, no matter how trivial, that you can think of that might establish a connection between these two cases?"

"There is nothing, nothing, I tell you! I have already given you all the information I possess. You cannot expect me to do your work for you. If the police are incompetent, I am not to blame, but I demand to know what you are doing. Have you made any progress whatever, Inspector? After all, my wife has been brutally murdered and I have a right to ask."

"I am afraid I cannot discuss the case, even with you," said Arkwright, as he rose to go. "But I suggest that you think it over, Mr. Miller. If there is anything you have to tell me, you know where to find me."

He left the house more firmly convinced than ever that Miller was concealing something that he was either afraid or unwilling to tell the police. That the information he had brought him was no news to him he was certain and yet he could have sworn that Miller, when he saw the body at the mortuary, had been under the impression that it was not that of Vera Abramoff and that he was speaking the truth when he insisted that he had expected her by a later train. Had he merely put two and two together after reading the newspaper reports of the second murder or had something happened in the interval to convince him that the victim was Madame Abramoff? Then there was the question of the letter, which he had been more than ready to produce. That it was genuine seemed indisputable, and yet Karamiev had assured him that there had never been any suggestion that the troupe should travel by a later train. Owing to the fact that they were burdened with scenery and various theatrical properties their arrangements had been made well in advance and there had never been any intention of altering the time-table. Madame Abramoff had never expressed a desire to travel alone, and, he was sure, had not intended to do so. And yet she had written from Paris announcing her intention of coming by the later train.

Arkwright called at Karamiev's hotel on his way back to the Yard and interviewed him once more. The Russian was able to produce several specimens of Madame Abramoff's signature and had often seen her handwriting. After inspecting the letter to Mrs. Miller he gave his opinion that it was genuine, but again expressed his conviction that she had never intended to travel by the later train. He was able, however, to clear up the mystery of her luggage. A large theatrical dress basket had gone through the Customs with the rest of the baggage of the troupe and was at present in one of the dressing rooms at the Parthenon. At Arkwright's request he accompanied him to the picture theatre and pointed out the dress basket to him. Presumably Madame Abramoff's keys had been in the missing hand bag, but Arkwright had little difficulty in forcing the lock and getting the basket open.

He examined the contents and, at the bottom of the trunk, found a large accumulation of old letters, programmes, photographs, etc. These he took back to the Yard with him.

He went through them carefully, only to find that there was little to be gleaned from them. Mrs. Miller's letters to her she had evidently destroyed and there was no mention of her or of any of Mrs. Abramoff's English connections among her papers. It looked as if she had lost sight of her people during the years she had lived abroad and, without the help of her passport, it would be difficult to get in touch with them, even if anything were to be gained in that direction. Arkwright compared her handwriting with that of the Miller letter and was forced to the conclusion that the latter was genuine.

Constantine, meanwhile, had gone straight back to his flat on leaving the mortuary. He was met by Manners with the news that a lady had called during the afternoon. She had left no name, but had expressed herself as very anxious to see him and announced her intention of coming again later in the day.

"Very worried she seemed, sir, at finding you out," volunteered Manners. "She wouldn't leave a name, but said she'd take her chance of finding you."

"What kind of lady, Manners?" demanded Constantine, knowing from experience that Manners' judgment was to be relied on.

"Very nice, sir. Very nice indeed. Not at all the kind of lady to be collecting subscriptions. You'll be having your bath now, sir?"

Constantine intimated that he would and undressed slowly to the sound of running water. He had barely got into the bath, however, before Manners knocked at the door with the information that the lady had returned. Constantine, more mystified than annoyed, sacrificed his usual quiet hour with a book and dressed hurriedly.

He was astonished to find Mrs. Vallon waiting for him.

"But this is delightful," he exclaimed, with perfect truth. "You will let Manners mix you a cocktail?"

"I'm full of apologies," she declared. "I have just realised that I must have interrupted the one quiet moment of your day. I ought to have telephoned."

"And spoiled a most pleasant surprise! I'm glad you didn't!"

Her smile was very charming.

"You're making it too easy for me," she said, "but, all the same, you are wondering why I have come. The truth is, I had an impulse this afternoon and then, when I found you out, I felt I must see you. Now I'm here, I feel a little foolish."

"My feeling, on the contrary, is entirely one of gratitude," Constantine assured her. "At this hour of the day I know myself to be an old man. If it were not for you, I should be dropping off to sleep over a book, a delightful sensation when one is young, but humiliating and ominous at my age."

He was interrupted by Manners with the cocktails. When he had gone Constantine cast a whimsical glance at his unexpected guest.

"That was a more subtle compliment than you realise," he said. "I was just about to order these. When Manners brings them of his own accord it means that he thoroughly approves of my visitors. And Manners is a potent factor in this household, let me tell you. He said, by the way, that you were not at all the kind of lady to be collecting subscriptions! He has all the well trained servant's snobbish dislike for charitable enterprise!"

Mrs. Vallon laughed, but her eyes were distrait. Constantine knew that she was aching to broach the reason for her visit and was finding it difficult.

"It is curious that we do not know each other better," he went on, more to give her time than for the sake of conversation. "We must have nearly met so often in the past."

She leaned forward impulsively.

"You are a good friend of Richard's, aren't you, Dr. Constantine?" she demanded.

"And of yours, I hope," he added quietly.

She flashed a grateful glance at him.

"Thank you," she said. "I mean that, you know. I have an idea that soon Richard and I may need all the support our friends can give us. Dr. Constantine, they say that you have some influence at Scotland Yard. Is that true?"

"I'm afraid it is a gross exaggeration. I know the Assistant Commissioner rather well and I have several good friends among the police, but that is all."

"But you hear things, don't you? Is it true that Richard is under suspicion?"

Constantine did not try to evade the question.

"In connection with the Miller murder, you mean?" he said. "I think perhaps that is putting it too strongly. I suppose I ought not to give away official secrets, but, as a matter of fact, the police have another, very definite suspect in view. I will say this, though. I could wish that Richard had not chosen just that particular moment to leave Davenport's waiting room."

"But you don't believe he could possibly have done such a vile thing?"

"I don't," answered Constantine, with conviction.

"You know they've been bothering him? He's been questioned and his servants have been got at. Richard's not a patient person and I'm so afraid he'll put himself in the wrong with the police. And yet it's so obvious to anyone that knows him that he couldn't be anything but innocent. Can nothing be done about it, Dr. Constantine?"

"If you mean as regards the police, any attempt to interfere with their activities would be the gravest mistake, from our point of view. Arkwright has got the case in hand and he's scrupulously fair in his methods. He's a good friend of mine and he knows that Richard's arrest would hit me heavily. He won't move unless he has good reason to. If you're afraid that the police will make Richard a scapegoat simply with a view to saving their face, you can dismiss that idea from your mind completely. My only anxiety is as to how far he actually is implicated."

Mrs. Vallon turned on him, her eyes flaming.

"Then, in your heart of hearts, you do suspect him!" she exclaimed. "And I came to you because I thought you were his friend!"

"I am a good enough friend to face any possibility," answered Constantine gravely. "Can you say the same?"

If she hesitated, it was only for a moment.

"Yes," she said softly. "Even if I knew he was guilty, I should stick to him. I couldn't help it. But he didn't do it, you know."

Constantine smiled.

"I wanted to hear you say that," he told her, "because, though I share your conviction that he isn't guilty I have had an uneasy feeling in my bones from the very beginning. I can't define it, but I never see Arkwright without dreading some fresh piece of evidence he may have picked up against him. I've nothing to go on beyond an impression I got from Richard himself on the day of the murder."

He waited, his wise old eyes on the glowing coals in the grate, but he could feel the impulse to speak flame and then die within her and knew that, as he had suspected, she had come to him driven by more than just a vague fear for Richard's safety.

"Dr. Constantine," she said at last, "there is something Richard ought to tell you, though, seeing that you are in touch with the police, I don't know whether it will help or hamper you. You are the only person who can judge of that and, without Richard's permission, I would rather you did not hear it from me. May I ask him to come to you?"

"I can assure you of one thing," answered Constantine. "I do not consider myself by any means bound to pass on everything I hear to our friends at New Scotland Yard. And I should feel a great deal happier if I could get a square look at the bogey that has been lurking in the dark corners of my soul for the last few days!"

She rose and began to draw on her gloves.

"You have laid some of my bogies, I think," she said, with a little laugh that broke suddenly in the middle. "I shall sleep better now that I know you are on his side. Richard is such a dear fool and when his back is up he's capable of any idiocy. If I can persuade him, he will come to you and, if I can't make him do that, I shall make him understand that I intend to tell you myself. The worst of it is, he's so unreasonable, bless him. He's furious at what he calls the interference of the police and yet I can't make him see that there is any real danger."

"Send him to me," agreed Constantine, with more cheerfulness than he felt. "It won't be the first time I've spoken my mind to Richard, you know! And, for both your sakes, may I say how glad I am that you decided to come and see me?"

She had not been gone ten minutes before the telephone bell rang. Arkwright was at the other end.

"Davenport has just rung up," he said. "He's heard from Cattistock! Got a polite note from him by this evening's post making an appointment for tomorrow! He's in a nursing home! What price our fugitive, fleeing from justice, now?"

CHAPTER TEN

THE REVOLVING DOORS of the Hotel Pergolese led straight into the lounge. Arkwright had hardly passed through them before he recognised the original of the photograph he had been carrying about with him so assiduously seated in a wicker chair reading the identical copy of "Esmond" that had been found beside his bed by the police on their first visit.

At the sight of the little, white-faced, sandy-haired man, who looked as if the torrid Eastern sun had sapped what little vitality his meagre frame had ever possessed, Arkwright recalled Mrs. Miller, vast and domineering and still retaining, in spite of years of soft living, the muscular vigour of her type. Cattistock would have been helpless as a rabbit in her hands and, as his eyes fell on him, Arkwright saw his case against him crumbling ominously.

At the sound of his own name the little man raised a pair of gentle blue eyes from his book.

"I am Mr. Cattistock," he said courteously, "but I don't think I have the pleasure of your acquaintance."

Since his painful interview with the dentist he had mastered at least some of the difficulties of enunciation, but the effort entailed made his words sound curiously prim and pedantic.

Arkwright introduced himself and the little man's pinched features relaxed into a smile that, owing to his complete lack of front teeth gave him somewhat the air of a very sophisticated baby.

"The manager told me that you had been enquiring for me," he said. "He gave me the impression that the matter was one of some importance and I was intending to call at Scotland Yard first thing tomorrow morning to inform you that I had returned to the hotel. If it were not for the fact that I have been unwell and am still in the doctor's hands I should have done so this evening."

Arkwright did not tell him that, not only had the manager rung up the Yard within five minutes of his return, but that one of his own men had reported his presence in the hotel and had been keeping him under observation ever since his arrival.

"I understand that you have been laid up ever since your visit to the dentist on Monday last," he said.

Cattistock once more inflicted his toothless smile on him and Arkwright's lips twitched in spite of himself. So long as his mouth was closed the little man bore himself with a certain prim dignity, once it opened he had the aspect of some fantastic, fairy-tale changeling.

"I have had a very distressing experience," he said. "The dentist was not in any way at fault and I am afraid I have only my own unfortunate constitution to thank for what happened. I had had several teeth extracted and was on my way back to this hotel when my gums began to bleed so badly that I became alarmed and called on a doctor who had treated me for malaria when I first returned to England. He did his best to stop the haemorrhage, but it persisted, in spite of his efforts, until early on the following morning. I was so weak from loss of blood that I was only too glad to comply with his suggestion that I should go into a nursing home that night and, on his advice, I remained there until all danger of a return of the trouble was over. Owing to severe attacks of fever in the past my heart is not all it should be and it was only today that I was able to leave the home and come back here."

"I take it, then, that you have not seen the newspapers for the last few days?"

Mr. Cattistock gave what in other circumstances would have been a wan smile.

"I must confess I had little inclination to read. I was feeling so ill that I even omitted to inform this hotel of my whereabouts, thereby causing you some inconvenience, I'm afraid I shall have to ask you to give me the names and reason you can have for wishing to see me."

"We are endeavouring to ascertain the movements of everyone who was at forty-two Illbeck Street on the morning of Monday last and you are naturally on our list. I'm afraid I shall have to ask you to give me the names and addresses of the doctor and the matron of the nursing home you mentioned, after that, should our enquiries prove satisfactory, I think I can promise you that you will not be troubled again."

Mr. Cattistock blinked at him in mild amazement.

"I hope this man, Davenport, has been doing nothing irregular," he said apprehensively. "He was very strongly recommended to me by the manager here, and I must say the place seemed to be run on excellent lines. I observed nothing unusual myself, though, I confess, I was hardly in a condition to be very critical."

"If you had stayed a few minutes longer you would have found yourself involved in something that, I am happy to say, is still very irregular in this country. A patient whose appointment came shortly after yours was very brutally murdered in the dentist's consulting room."

Mr. Cattistock recoiled.

"By the dentist who extracted my teeth?" he gasped. "He certainly struck me as somewhat callous, but ..."

Arkwright laughed.

"The dentist had nothing to do with it," he said. "You needn't worry yourself about him, his reputation is good enough to stand even this nasty business. It was done while he was out of the room and our job is to find out who did it. That's why we have been concerning ourselves with your whereabouts. Could you give me a rough idea of the time you left Davenport's house and the hour at which you arrived at the doctor's?"

Mr. Cattistock hesitated.

"I'm usually a fairly reliable person," he declared conscientiously, "but you must remember that I was more than a little dazed that morning, indeed, as time went on, I became too faint to realise anything very clearly, but, so far as I can recollect, I must have left the dentist's house somewhere about twelve o'clock. My appointment was for eleven and, after he had finished with me, I sat for a time in the waiting room. Then, as the bleeding grew worse, I went to the lavatory to try to make myself look a little more presentable. It grew so much worse there that I went straight to the doctor's and I can remember noticing that the clock in his consulting room said twelve twenty. I am estimating the time I left the dentist's on that."

"I wish everybody was as conscientious as you are, Mr. Cattistock," said Arkwright, with a smile. "Now can you go one further and tell me what other patients you saw in Davenport's house?"

Cattistock described Sir Richard Pomfrey, Mrs. Miller and Mrs. Vallon with an earnest eye for detail.

"I sincerely trust that that good-looking man was not the victim of this shocking affair," he concluded.

"Sir Richard? No, the victim was a woman, the large, overdressed lady whom, from your description, I gather you did not much like, Mr. Cattistock."

The little man's reaction was immediate.

"Dear, dear! The poor creature!" he lisped, in a voice full of contrition. "It was heartless in the extreme of me to have given that impression!"

He hesitated for a moment, then his natural honesty triumphed.

"The truth is, I did not like her," he admitted. "But, as I have said, I was feeling ill and perhaps a little morbid. I certainly wished her no ill, poor woman."

"You saw no one else? Either coming in or going out?"

"I passed someone, an elderly man, on my way out, but I could not describe him."

"You saw no one else? In the hall or coming out of the lavatory?" insisted Arkwright. "We believe the murder to have taken place between eleven forty-eight and twelve five."

Cattistock looked mildly agitated.

"Then I may actually have been on the premises when it was committed!" he exclaimed.

Arkwright nodded.

"That is why I hoped you might help us," he said. "You saw nobody but the people you have mentioned?"

"No one. Except the dentist's assistant, who crossed the hall as I was on my way to the lavatory."

It was Arkwright's turn to look startled.

"Was he wearing a white coat?" he demanded.

"Yes. A long white coat, like the one the dentist had on."

"Where did he come from?"

"From the lavatory. He crossed the hall and went into the consulting room."

"Could you describe him, Mr. Cattistock?"

But Cattistock shook his head.

"I'm afraid not. If you had not been so persistent in your questions I should not even have remembered him. He simply passed across my vision, as it were. Even if I'd wished I couldn't have observed him closely."

Arkwright sighed.

"Well, you enjoy the unique distinction of having seen the murderer, Mr. Cattistock," he said. "I only wish you could have got a better look at him!"

Then Cattistock said a surprising thing.

"I have seen, aye, and spoken to, many murderers in China," he announced calmly, "but, curiously enough, I have never been affected as I am now. I find this rather horrible, Inspector."

Before he left Arkwright questioned him more closely as to his own movements.

"We found traces of blood in the lavatory," he concluded, "Until now we were under the impression that they had been left by the murderer."

Cattistock blushed.

"I'm afraid I was responsible," he confessed. "I know I was driven to use a towel owing to the deplorable state of my handkerchief and I no doubt left the basin in somewhat of a mess. If I had not been feeling so ill, I should, I hope, have been less inconsiderate."

Arkwright's main feeling was one of regret that Constantine had not been present at this interview. The old man would have appreciated every moment of it. As a matter of routine he went straight from the hotel to the nursing home Cattistock had just left. Here the matron corroborated his story. It was too late to get in touch with the doctor that night, but Arkwright was under no delusions as to what the result would be when he did succeed in interviewing him. As a potential murderer, Cattistock was a complete failure.

He said as much to Constantine when he dropped in to the Club to snatch a hasty meal before returning to the Yard.

"He's an absolute wash-out. A queer little chap, but he wouldn't, and couldn't, hurt a fly. He saw the murderer, all right, though."

Constantine listened while he described the interview.

"And that leaves us, where?" was his comment at the end.

"Pretty much where we were at the beginning," admitted Arkwright, with a wry smile.

"With Richard as your only hope?"

"I'm sorry," said Arkwright, and Constantine knew that he was speaking the truth. "He had the opportunity, he's an old acquaintance of Mrs. Miller's and I fancy the motive won't be too difficult to find."

"In fact, he's got everything but the mental and moral equipment necessary for the murder," concluded Constantine drily.

"You might say that, superficially, of a dozen murderers. It doesn't alter the fact that they did do the job."

"My knowledge of Richard's character is not superficial. He's hot-tempered, even violent, in anger, but utterly incapable of cold-blooded brutality. Apart from which, what motive can you possibly assign to him? To begin with, his association with Lottie Belmer was never of an intimate nature. She can have had no possible hold over him."

"You admit that if she had, she might have used it to her own advantage?"

"From what I have heard of her, I think she might," agreed Constantine.

"Miller kept her short of money and she was hopelessly extravagant. If it was a question of hard cash, I don't fancy she would be too scrupulous. And, if what one hears about Mrs.

Vallon is true, this is the last moment that Sir Richard would wish for any kind of scandal."

"Mrs. Vallon isn't a young, romantic girl," objected Constantine. "She's a sophisticated woman of the world and she must have heard a good deal of what was common gossip at one time. It would be unlikely that Mrs. Miller could tell her much that she doesn't know already."

Arkwright pushed his plate aside and planted his elbows on the table.

"Look here, sir," he said. "Laying all prejudice aside, what is the situation? Mrs. Vallon and yourself are beyond suspicion. Davenport could have committed the murder, but, so far, we have been unable to trace any possible motive for the crime. I think we can take it that, by tomorrow, Cattistock will be safely out of the picture. If the murderer came from outside he may have entered through the house next door, but you yourself have pointed out that the traces we found there could have been made any time during the past week. On the other hand, there is nothing to prevent Sir Richard from having concealed the overall and gloves in the lavatory and gone there to put them on. Having killed Mrs. Miller the murderer left his disguise in the consulting room and departed, either by the front door or across the leads into the next door house. Now, just before twelve, Cattistock saw him cross the hall on his way to the consulting room. We can take this for granted, as Davenport, when he left Mrs. Miller, went straight downstairs and did not go near the lavatory. His assistant was in the basement, with another mechanic, who can vouch for it that he did not go upstairs until he was sent for to force the lock. If the man Cattistock saw was the murderer, that clears Davenport. All this narrows down the time of the murder to between twelve and twelve five, though it is possible that it actually took place while Davenport was trying to get the door open. By twelve fifteen the room had been entered, so that we can now place it pretty definitely as between twelve and twelve fifteen. Therefore, unless the murderer made his get-away across the leads, he must have been someone who had a definite right to be in the house, owing to the fact that Betts was standing on the doorstep until twelve five, and from then onwards, he and Davenport and the assistant were outside the consulting room door. There was only one person who did go down the hall while they were there, and that was Sir Richard."

"Perfectly logical, if you exclude the house next door," agreed Constantine. "When I pointed out that the traces we found need not have been made on the day of the murder I did not for a moment suggest ruling them out altogether."

"Well then, assuming that it was an outside job, we have to find someone who not only knew Mrs. Miller and had a motive for getting rid of her, but who was aware, first that she had an appointment with Davenport for that particular day and time, and, second, that the work he was doing for her would necessitate his leaving her alone in the room at some period during the consultation. We have ruled out her husband, who might very well have known these things. Can you suggest anyone else?"

"I cannot, but that doesn't mean that Miller couldn't, if you are right in your assumption that he is holding something back. As I see it, your job is to concentrate on Miller s past and leave me to get on with mine."

"Yours being?"

"To clear Richard, seeing that you're too pig-headed to accept my point of view," snapped the old man.

After Arkwright had left him Constantine rang up his friend, the Greek jeweller, at his private address and asked him if he could ascertain for him which of the West End firms had been specially favoured by Sir Richard Pomfrey in his more palmy days. Half an hour later the old jeweller telephoned to him to say that he had rung up various friends of his in the trade and had found his man almost immediately. He gave Constantine the name of a firm in Bond Street with which Sir Richard had at one time dealt almost exclusively. If Constantine cared to call there the proprietor would see him himself and give him any information he required.

By ten o'clock next morning Constantine was in a private room behind the shop in Bond Street. The proprietor, a man almost as old as himself, had known Sir Richard for years, though of late he had not dealt with him. He remembered the great days of the Pagoda and sent his clerks for the ledgers that covered the period of Sir Richard's connection with the theatre.

"Did he ever bring Lottie Belmer here?" asked Constantine.

"It's curious you should ask that," answered the jeweller, with a reminiscent smile. "I was talking to my head clerk here only yesterday about her. We were discussing her death and found ourselves raking up old memories. She was the daughter of a piano tuner out Wandsworth way, did you know that? The old man's still alive and appeared at the inquest, I believe. So far as I can remember, Sir Richard only brought her here once. I happened to be in the shop myself that day and it's an occasion I'm not likely to forget."

Selecting one of the ledgers, he flecked over the pages.

"I can place it fairly accurately," he murmured. "It must have been just about a week before Derby Day."

He ran his finger down a page and gave a little exclamation of triumph.

"That's what I'm looking for," he exclaimed. "Here it is. Diamond star brooch, twelve points, to be delivered to Miss Lottie Belmer, Pagoda Theatre, tonight without fail. Sir Richard Pomfrey's account. That's the only time he ever got anything from us for her. There was a strong counter-attraction at the time, you know, and I don't mind admitting to you, sir, that we did well out of that!"

"I quite see that her tragic death must have brought Lottie Belmer back to your mind, but you will forgive me for asking whether this remarkable performance is the result of an incredibly efficient system of book-keeping or is merely an astounding feat of memory on your part," enquired Constantine, with pardonable curiosity.

The jeweller laughed.

"I hoped you would appreciate it," he said. "The truth is, I'm hardly likely to forget that visit of Sir Richard's! He gave me a tip for the Derby that day that brought me in fifteen hundred pounds. I'm not a betting man as a rule and when I do back a horse I invariably lose my money. That Derby Day will remain in my memory till the end of my life!"

"The brooch wasn't paste, I suppose?"

"Paste? Not for Lottie, sir! There was very little she didn't know about diamonds, even in those days. That brooch cost Sir Richard a cool five hundred!"

Constantine walked back through the Green Park to his flat. After Manners had relieved him of his hat and coat he stood for so long staring into space that that faithful guardian of his comfort began to grow anxious.

"Is there anything I can do for you, sir?" he asked.

Constantine glared at him.

"You can't tell me, I suppose, why a man should suddenly give a woman in whom he has never shown the slightest interest a brooch worth five hundred pounds?"

"No, sir, I'm afraid not, sir," answered Manners imperturbably.

Arkwright rang up in the course of the morning.

"That diamond thing that Sir Richard gave Mrs. Miller wasn't Palais Royal," he said. "Very much the reverse. I've had a look at Miller's insurance policy and it's listed as being worth six hundred and fifty pounds."

It is to Constantine's credit that he answered Arkwright in his silkiest voice and then replaced the receiver quite gently on its hook. He had seldom spent a more aggravating morning.

CHAPTER ELEVEN

CONSTANTINE, still suffering from a severe attack of what he described as spiritual indigestion, betook himself to his Club. But before leaving his flat he rang up Mrs. Vallon.

"No sign of Richard yet," he said. "How are you getting on at your end?"

A sigh was wafted gently over the wires.

"He's being difficult," she answered. "His attitude is that the police can go to Hell for all he cares."

"You might point out to him that they certainly won't go anywhere at his bidding and that he, just as certainly, will go to prison at theirs if he refuses to see reason."

"I did that for a solid hour last night and, when I'd finished, he told me that I was overwrought and nervy and that what I needed was a good, long day in bed or a whiff of sea air! If I'd hit him, as I felt inclined to do, he'd merely have said I was hysterical. I'm not sure that I wasn't!"

"If hysteria will do the trick, use it!" Constantine admonished her shamelessly. "Seriously, I am relying on you to send him to me as soon as possible."

He deliberately chose the Club's prize bore to lunch with and did his best to keep the conversation on Vallon and the Pagoda girls. But, beyond fully justifying his reputation, the man, a garrulous egotist, looked like giving little in return for Constantine's patient endurance. Being a snob of the first water, he took no interest in the Miller murder, and Lottie Belmer, who at best, had been an unimportant member of the Pagoda galaxy, he had never considered worthy of his notice. Sir Richard he could gossip about and did, but, after the manner of his kind, he had only managed to amass those facts that were already common property. Owing to an unhappy blend of inaccuracy and discursiveness even these lost all zest in the telling. Constantine was already regretting this lost venture in Sir Richard's cause when, at the end of a long and depressing list of the casualties that had befallen the bulk of the young sparks of his day, his companion casually let fall one sterling piece of information.

"Phipps tells me that he saw Richard Pomfrey with one of the old Pagoda girls the other day. Lottie Belmer, it was. Never knew her myself, but he appears to have recognised her. Says she had grown fat and coarse. They all do, curiously enough. I remember seeing ..."

He prattled on unheeding. Constantine shook him off as soon as possible and went in search of Phipps. He found him in the library, his broad, florid face flushed with the unwonted exertion of putting pen to paper.

"What's that? Hubbard told you? Well, he was right for once. It was this way. My wife arranged to meet me at the Futurist Galleries, of all ghastly holes, and of course she was late, so I toddled round and had a look at their funny pictures. Of all the rubbish! However, that's neither here nor there. Anyway, who should I see, jammed up next to a fat woman on one of those sofa things, but Richard! Looking pretty sick he was, too, I can tell you. Thought he'd been lugged there by one of his rich aunts or something of the sort and I was having a quiet chuckle to myself over it when I caught sight of the woman's face. Blessed if it wasn't old Lottie Belmer! She'd put on a bit of flesh since the Pagoda days, but she was unmistakable. She and Richard had got their heads together, going it hammer and tongs, so I sheered off. Shouldn't have thought of it again if it hadn't been for what happened two days later. Seemed to bring it home to one, somehow, seeing her like that and then hearing that she'd been done in. At a dentist's too, of all places. Seems to make it worse, what?"

Constantine agreed that it did and drifted gently but firmly away. The news he had just heard, disquieting though it was, merely confirmed his suspicion that Mrs. Miller had got some hold over Richard Pomfrey and had decided to put the screw on shortly before her death. That she had applied it at least once, long ago, he shrewdly suspected, unless the diamond brooch had been the result of a wager, the only other convincing explanation he could think of.

Constantine was well known to most of the London picture dealers and, when he strolled into the Futurist Galleries, the secretary hurried to meet him with a hopeful gleam in his eye. This Constantine, in his most urbane manner, proceeded to extinguish.

"I'm not buying today," he said. "The truth is, I find myself a little old for this sort of thing, interesting as it undoubtedly is. You will see me next month, however, if the advance notice you sent me is correct. At the moment I'm in search of a little information."

The secretary cast a deprecating glance at a nude which the artist had innocuously camouflaged as a cooked beetroot, expressed himself as entirely at Dr. Constantine's disposal, and supplied him with a specimen of the New School of furniture, the object of which seemed to be to discommode the sitter as much as possible. Constantine fitted himself cautiously into it.

"Did you or any of your bright young men know Mrs. Miller by sight?" he asked.

The secretary's eyes lit up with interest.

"The poor woman who was murdered?" he exclaimed. "I'm afraid I can't help you. One of our assistants is at lunch, but I can send for the other if you like, though I doubt if he has ever seen her. Was she interested in this sort of thing?"

Constantine's eye lingered for a moment on the walls of the gallery.

"Not greatly, I should say," he said, with a solemnity that would have delighted Arkwright. "We won't bother your assistant for the moment. Can you carry your mind back to the afternoon of the twelfth of this month?"

"Our opening day? Certainly."

Choosing his words carefully, Constantine described Sir Richard and Mrs. Miller. He was, he felt, pursuing a forlorn hope, but the gallery was a small one and the secretary, trained to observe and canvass possible buyers, could hardly have failed to notice anyone so patently opulent as Mrs. Miller.

"These two people were here for some time, I believe," he concluded. "They probably met by appointment and certainly sat talking for some time on one of these abominably uncomfortable seats. I should doubt whether they looked at the pictures at all."

"They sat on this seat," answered the secretary surprisingly. "I remember the lady well. She looked just the sort of client we hope to attract and I admit I was disappointed when I realised that she had not come with any intention of looking at the pictures. She and the man with her were deep in conversation for a long time and they left the building together."

"Did the conversation strike you as being friendly or the reverse?" asked Constantine.

The secretary hesitated.

"They were not quarrelling, though the lady struck me as being annoyed. I had an impression that she was getting the worst of it. Until they actually left the building I didn't give up hope of doing a deal with her and there was no one else in the gallery at the time who looked in the least promising, so I gave a good deal of attention to her. Was she really Mrs. Miller, Dr. Constantine?"

"It seems more than likely that she was. You inspected her pretty closely, I gather, so you ought to know," said Constantine, with a smile.

"The only portraits published by the Press were old ones, taken in her chorus girl days," pointed out the secretary. "They conveyed nothing to me when I saw them but, now that you've put the idea into my head I can quite imagine that she might have grown into the woman I saw. A Press photograph isn't exactly helpful as a means of identification."

Constantine cast a mischievous glance at the beetroot nude.

"You find this sort of thing more inspiring perhaps," he enquired politely.

The secretary laughed.

"Strictly between ourselves, I am less to be blamed than pitied," he answered. "I do my best to sell these, but I don't buy them. May I give you my frank impression of Mrs. Miller's interview with the man who was with her?"

"That's precisely what I've come to hear."

"Frankly then, I concluded that the man had tired of her and that she was doing her best to get him to take her back. In the end I believe she went so far as to threaten him."

"What makes you think that?"

"From the only sentence that I overheard. I was crossing the room and passed close to them. I caught the words 'Scotland Yard' and involuntarily pricked up my ears. It was followed by 'rather than submit to anything of the sort' or words to that effect. They left almost immediately afterwards. Mrs. Miller, if it was Mrs. Miller, looked pretty poisonous and I remember wondering whether there wasn't going to be a first-class row on the pavement outside."

Constantine rose stiffly.

"If they sat for long on one of these instruments of torture," he said drily, "their conversation must have been an engrossing one. I am very grateful to you and should be still more so if you would keep what you have told me to yourself for the present. If it got about it might involve a person who is innocent of any complicity in the murder and who, incidentally, is a very good friend of mine."

"I've mentioned it to no one," the secretary assured him, "and you can trust to my discretion now. If you could let me have a photograph of Mrs. Miller's companion I should no doubt recognise it."

Constantine thanked him and hurried out to his waiting taxi. He had made up his mind. Sir Richard would have to be dealt with at once and drastically. Arkwright used the Club a good deal in his spare time and, at any moment, might stumble on Phipps' information. Richard must be made to understand that the time for playing the fool was over.

He drove first to Sir Richard's rooms. He was out. At his club, his servant believed. Constantine climbed back into his cab and took up the chase once more, only to find that his quarry had left the Club five minutes before his arrival. Undefeated, he returned to Sir Richard's flat and announced his intention of waiting there until he came back.

He had been nursing his impatience for a good half-hour when he heard the latch-key turn in the lock of the front door and the sound of voices in the hall. He opened the door and was just in time to see Sir Richard making for the street, his coat over his arm.

"That you, Richard?" he remarked urbanely. "Glad to have caught you."

Sir Richard was a poor dissembler and his plight was accentuated by the knowledge that he was no match for his father's astute old friend. He threw his coat and hat on the table and followed Constantine into the room, looking so like a sheepish schoolboy who has been caught red-handed that it was all the old man could do to keep the amusement out of his voice as he turned on him and launched his attack.

"Did Mrs. Vallon give you a message from me?" he asked abruptly.

Sir Richard looked acutely uncomfortable.

"She suggested that I should see you," he answered, with an attempt at bravado. "But as the matter did not seem urgent ..."

He caught a withering glance from Constantine's dark eyes and the sentence tailed off into silence. The years seemed unaccountably to have rolled away and, to his disgust, he found himself slipping back into the attitude of futile defiance which, in years gone by, had failed to carry him through many a painful interview with his elders and betters.

"Won't you sit down, sir?" he said awkwardly, as the silence grew oppressive. Constantine ignored the invitation.

"Are you going to treat me as a friend or an enemy, Richard?" he demanded, with more ferocity than he felt. There was something absurdly disarming about this well-groomed, florid giant who, for all his years, still retained so much of the clumsiness and naivete of a boy. "I've put myself out considerably to see you today and it rests with you whether I have wasted my time or not."

Sir Richard shifted his feet uneasily.

"I'm sorry you had all this bother, sir ..."

Constantine cut him short.

"You've got yourself into a devil of a mess," he snapped. "What do you propose to do about it?"

Sir Richard flushed a deep red. For a moment it seemed as though the interview was going to terminate swiftly and violently. Then he controlled himself.

"I think you can trust me to manage my own affairs, sir," he said with ominous quietness.

"You are no longer in a position to control them," Constantine assured him. "In a few hours' time the police will have charge of both you and your affairs and the only person at liberty to do anything will be your solicitor. I don't envy him."

"If the police are such damned fools as to lay their hands on me ..." began Sir Richard.

"The police are not damned fools. That's where your danger lies. They've got a sound case against you, so sound that, if I did not know you, I should be convinced of your guilt myself. It's because I do know you that I've come here today. It so happens that I am in a better position to help you than any other of your friends. I, at least, know exactly how you stand in the eyes of the police and, if you decide to pocket your pride and behave like an ordinary human being we still have time to map out some sort of defence before they act. Are you prepared to meet my offer reasonably or do I leave you now and wash my hands of the whole business?"

Constantine's words fell slowly; cold, biting and contemptuous, but behind them burned an anger so sudden and so un-English that Sir Richard's hot-headed bluster collapsed before the shock of the encounter. He had never met the old man in this mood before and was unaware that he had deliberately unleashed the pent up exasperation of the last twelve hours in his determination to achieve his aim. He waited now, passive and inexorable, for the other's answer.

Sir Richard took a quick step forward.

"I never dreamed you'd take it like that, sir," he exclaimed. "The whole damned business is so confoundedly silly."

"Get that out of your head, once and for all," cut in Constantine. "The situation is serious, far more serious than you seem able to realise."

Sir Richard stared at him, hesitated, then capitulated completely.

"What do you want me to do about it?" he asked.

"Tell the truth. You made a fatal mistake when you led the police to believe that you had had no communication with Mrs. Miller for years. How long did you suppose it would take them to unearth the fact of your meeting with her at the Futurist Galleries on the day before her death?"

Sir Richard looked genuinely startled. He opened his mouth to speak, but Constantine continued, ruthlessly pursuing his advantage.

"How long had that woman been blackmailing you?"

His victim made a final attempt to assert his independence.

"Look here, I'm dashed if I'll parade my private affairs for the benefit of the police! If they think I'm guilty of Mrs. Miller's murder, let them say so. They'll find it uncommonly difficult to prove a case against me and, if they don't prove it, I'll have the coat off the back of the fellow who is in charge of this!"

Constantine's voice, following on his outburst, was cold and smooth as ice.

"If they fail to prove it, you will be discharged. No satisfaction will be given you and, in the meanwhile, your private affairs, as you call them, will have been dragged, wholesale, into the open, torn to pieces, examined and commented on. You will have to sit helpless while every sort of construction is placed on them and, by the time the trial is over, there will not be a shred of your private life that is not common property. Is this your conception of dignified reticence? That is all you will gain by these heroics. Suppose you drop them and give me a clear account of your dealings with Mrs. Miller. Have some pity, Richard, and grant me the privileges of a friend instead of making me feel like the front row of the stalls at a cheap melodrama!" This sudden and whimsical twist at the end of a furious tirade produced just the effect he had counted on. A slow, deprecatory smile broke over Sir Richard's face.

"I'm sorry, sir," he said. "I suppose I have been making a bit of an ass of myself, but it's no fun to have one's old follies raked up and served on a salver for a lot of fools to gape at. I always did jump first and look afterwards and now it seems I've got to pay for it. What, exactly, do you want to know?"

"Where and when this business started and to what extent it involves you in the Illbeck Street affair."

"I fail to see why it should involve me in any way," objected Sir Richard stubbornly, "but, if you say so, I'm ready to take your word for it that the situation is serious. The whole thing started, roughly speaking, about a month ago. I hadn't seen Lottie Belmer for years when she came up to me one night at the Savoy and asked me if I didn't remember her. As a matter of fact, I didn't at first. We had a chat, a half sentimental, good old days, sort of business. She told me about her marriage and asked me to call and I tried to get out of it as politely as possible. I'd never liked her and time certainly hadn't improved her. As a matter of fact, I never did go to her house, but, after that, though I did my best to dodge her, she seemed to be continually cropping up. I know there was one big charity show at which she fastened onto me and I literally couldn't get rid of, her. It never occurred to me that she had anything up her sleeve. Frankly, knowing she'd married money, I thought she had social aspirations and was looking to me to further them. Then I got a letter from her, saying that she was in a devil of a mess and wouldn't I advise her what to do. There was a good deal about old lang syne and the happy old days and that sort of thing in it and she finished up by asking me to meet her at this Futurist place and talk things over. I shouldn't have smelt a rat even then if she hadn't alluded to something that happened years ago and which I'd every reason to believe was over and done with. The last thing I wanted was ever to see her again, but I went. She was out of money, of course, but I'll do her the justice to admit that she tried hard to get a loan out of me before showing her hand. She'd got a letter I'd written years ago to Nancy Conyers and was keeping it up her sleeve as a last resource. When I told her the truth, which was that I wasn't in a position to lend my best friend a farthing, she offered it to me for a consideration."

He paused, his florid face growing several shades pinker.

"It was a damn silly letter," he burst out at last. "Everyone knows I made an ass of myself over Nancy and I suppose I was luckier than I deserved when she gave me the push and married Selkirk, but I only hope no one gave me credit for the sort of drivel I managed to put on paper in the course of that affair! It was the sort of stuff that comes out in breach of promise cases, utterly nauseating when you meet it later in cold blood. We'd got idiotic nicknames for each other and all that sort of thing. It makes me hot to think of that letter now. When she found she couldn't get the money in any other way she threatened to send the letter to Mrs. Vallon unless I could see my way to lending her a cool thousand. Lend was the word she used all through the interview. It was a pretty maddening situation. There was nothing much to the letter except that I was head over ears in love with Nancy when I wrote it and, as I said, it was such confounded drivel! At best I should have felt a consummate fool if it got into Mrs. Vallon's hands and, naturally, she was the last person I wanted to read it. Half a dozen years ago, if the situation had been the same, I might have paid up and have done with it, but, as things are, I should be hard put to it to lay hands on the money. As a matter of fact, I'm cutting down expenses and getting things straightened up, before settling down for good. Mrs. Vallon's agreed to take me on, you know," he finished, with an embarrassment that made him look more absurdly like an over-grown schoolboy than ever.

"Delighted to hear it. You've got my heartiest congratulations," Constantine assured him, concealing his feelings admirably. To be side-tracked with so stale a piece of news at this juncture was annoying, to say the least of it. Sir Richard continued, showing, in the process, how little he still realised the seriousness of his position.

"We're hoping to get married next month and, if anything should happen to me I want to leave her something better than a pile of debts to carry on with. You can imagine how I felt when, just as I was trying to set my house in order, Lottie Belmer came along and tried to upset the apple cart. I'd every reason to feel sick with her, too. She'd let me down pretty badly, considering that she'd had her little whack years ago and the whole matter was dead and buried, as I thought."

Constantine looked up sharply, the light of comprehension in his eyes.

"At the price of a diamond brooch?" he suggested.

Sir Richard stared at him.

"Now how the devil did you hear about that?" he demanded.

"My dear Richard, the whole of Scotland Yard knows about it," snapped Constantine, goaded beyond endurance. "For pity's sake, stop behaving like the proverbial ostrich and, if it's in you, give me a clear account of your transactions with Lottie Belmer from the beginning. How did she get hold of this correspondence?"

"Through her dresser, who was a friend of Nancy's maid. The fact is, they used me pretty ruthlessly between them. I was a young fool and they knew it! As it turned out, there were three letters, not two, as I thought. Lottie got them from her dresser and held them over Nancy's head. They always hated each other like poison and she knew, what I didn't, that Nancy was all but engaged to Selkirk and would have died rather than let them fall into his hands. Nancy came to me about it and, seeing that I'd written the letters and that she was worrying herself stiff over them, I undertook to settle the matter. Mind you, I'd no idea that Selkirk was in the running then. Well, I got the two letters at the price of a brooch which Lottie was to choose herself. I'm sure Nancy was under the impression that those were the only two that were missing, but, as it turned out, Lottie must have been keeping the third back in case it came in useful. To do her justice, she must have been in a pretty tight place before she decided to use it. As far as the brooch was concerned, she was always as greedy as they make 'em, but I believe she was actuated by spite more than anything else then. This last time it was different. She was out for hard cash and hoped to get it."

"I gather she did not get it?"

"She didn't. For one thing I hadn't got it, for another I wasn't at all sure that she was speaking the truth when she said that that was the only letter she had. I'd been stung once, you see. If I paid her what she asked now there was nothing to prevent her from turning up again with another later. I told her to do her worst and even threatened to go to the police, in the hope that she'd think twice about using the letter. We parted outside the Gallery and that's the last I ever saw of her, except for that glimpse we had of each other in Davenport's waiting room. I was terrified then that she'd recognise Mrs. Vallon and would say something. Fortunately Mrs. Vallon had no idea who she was, but it was a nasty moment for me and I admit I felt pretty sick about it, but not sufficiently so to follow her into the consulting room and stick a knife into her."

For a moment Constantine was silent, aghast at the completeness of Sir Richard's case against himself, then:

"So that, if anyone was out to gain anything by Mrs. Miller's death it was yourself," he said slowly. "You realise the construction that will be put on that?"

Sir Richard smiled cheerfully down at him from his great height.

"Not a bit of it," he retorted. "I always was an unlucky beggar! When she was killed, Mrs. Vallon had already read the letter! I'd nothing to gain by Lottie's death—she'd sent the letter to her directly after our meeting the day before!"

CHAPTER TWELVE

"The letter had already reached Mrs. Vallon," repeated Constantine slowly. "Did you know it had been sent to her?"

"Of course I did. I was dining with her and was there when it arrived."

"Did she read it?"

Sir Richard nodded.

"She was amazing! Lord knows what I've done to deserve such luck! She didn't say anything. Just read it through to the end. Of course I'd no idea what she'd got hold of, but I looked up and saw her staring at me exactly as if she'd never set eyes on me before. Couldn't think what was up. Then I saw the letter and recognised it! It was a pretty awful moment! I didn't know what to say."

"What *did* you do?" asked Constantine. He had a conviction that, whatever it was, it would be wrong and wondered whether Mrs. Vallon's intuition had outweighed Richard's notorious lack of tact. But he had done Sir Richard an injustice.

"I just stood there, looking as big an ass as I felt, I suppose," he continued. "She didn't say anything, simply walked over to the fireplace and read the thing right through again. Then she did the most extraordinary thing."

"Well?" prompted Constantine impatiently.

"She laughed," Sir Richard informed him, in awe-struck tones. "Not a nasty laugh. As if she was really amused. She said: 'How old were you, Richard, when you wrote this?' And I knew it was all right."

"I confess I should like to have seen that letter," murmured Constantine reflectively.

"You can't. We burned it. Of course, we talked things over a bit and I told her about my meeting with Lottie Belmer. That's why I got the wind up when they ran into each other at Davenport's. As soon as Lottie saw us together she must have known she'd made a mess of things. She looked furious and I was terrified for a moment that she was going to let herself go, not about this business, but about Vallon. She could have, you know, if all I've heard was true and I'm not sure she wouldn't have, just to get her own back, if Davenport's man hadn't come for her just in time."

When Constantine left Sir Richard he drove straight to Scotland Yard, where he was fortunate enough to find Arkwright. He told him what he had just learned.

"You must admit that that pretty well disposes of any motive for the murder," he concluded. "Mrs. Miller had already shot her bolt and failed."

"It weakens our case against Sir Richard," assented Arkwright, "but there still remains the fact that he possessed both the knowledge, which we agreed was necessary, and the opportunity."

"I refuse to admit the knowledge," objected Constantine. "He was not on intimate terms with Mrs. Miller and certainly did not expect to see her at Davenport's."

"We have only his word for that. He could have known of the time of her appointment either from Davenport or his man and he was undoubtedly familiar with the disposal of the rooms on that floor of the dentist's house."

"And the fact that the nature of Davenport's work on her denture would necessitate his leaving her alone in the consulting room? Do you suggest that he was aware of that?"

"He may have simply awaited his opportunity. I'm not saying that, so far as I myself am concerned, I am not coming round to your point of view or that, at present, we have sufficient evidence to act, but we cannot afford to disregard Sir Richard altogether yet. It would have been better for everybody if he had been frank with us in the beginning."

"It would be better for Richard if his first impulse was not always that of an impetuous fool," agreed Constantine tartly. "All the same, you must admit that I've gone at least part of the way towards establishing his innocence."

Arkwright grinned.

"You've succeeded in tying my hands a bit tighter," he retorted, but there was no malice in his voice. "But, while you're about it, I wish you'd go a little further, sir, and find the murderer for us. If you could make anything of the inscriptions on those knives it would be a beginning."

He went to the safe and opened it. Constantine watched him.

"What about those notes you got from the garage proprietor?" he asked suddenly. "One of them was stained, I think you said."

Arkwright placed the two knives and the stained note on the table.

"There are the exhibits," he said. "If you can make anything of them I shall be grateful."

As he spoke the telephone bell rang and, for the next few minutes he was busy with the instrument. When he turned round again Constantine was snapping the elastic band round a small pocket book.

"Well, sir," asked Arkwright. "Got anything?"

"Two facts that you and your myrmidons seem to have missed," was the old man's exasperating answer, as he slipped the book into his pocket. "I wish I'd seen these things before."

He rose and held out his hand.

"But look here, sir," expostulated Arkwright, as he took it. "This isn't fair ..."

Constantine beamed on him. Arkwright was annoyingly aware that something had happened within the last few minutes to alter his mood for the better.

"You won't listen to my convictions," he retorted. "If you insist on proofs you must wait till I can supply them. I'll give you something, though, little as you deserve it. Your Chinese expert could make nothing of those inscriptions. You should have tried a Greek."

The latch clicked softly and Arkwright found himself staring at a closed door. Knowing better than to pursue the old man in his present mood, he continued to stare.

Constantine's first act when he got home, was to ring for Manners.

"I believe I'm right in assuming that you're not one of those misguided people who never touch intoxicating liquor?" he remarked in his most urbane tones.

Manners's expressionless eye became if anything more glassy. Though he never allowed himself more than an occasional glass, he was fully aware of the excellence of his master's port.

"I believe in moderation, sir," he admitted with dignity.

"I wonder if you would feel inclined to practice it on the other side of the Green Park? I'm not casting aspersions on your favourite house of call, merely suggesting that you should repeat your very able performance of last year, when, if you remember, you beat the police at their own job."

A ripple passed over Manners's countenance. For a second he looked almost animated.

"The matter of the window cleaner?" he suggested respectfully.

"Precisely. While the police were still engaged in taking notes you rounded him up and got my silver salver back for me. I haven't forgotten the neatness with which you pulled off that job, Manners."

Even Manners was not proof against so calculated and graceful a piece of flattery.

"We should have won our case if you'd cared to make a charge against him, sir," was all he said, but the note of gratification in his voice was unmistakable.

"It was on your recommendation that I didn't," Constantine reminded him, with a quizzical gleam in his eyes.

"The man had a good record, sir. If it hadn't been for that I shouldn't have taken the liberty."

"Considering that he had just spent three months in hospital and had a wife and family on his hands, I wonder, Manners?"

Manners looked positively uncomfortable. Behind his pontifical manner he concealed a heart so soft that even Constantine, in whose service he had been for years, was sometimes surprised by its manifestations and occasionally amused himself by baiting him mildly on what he knew was looked upon by Manners as a deplorable weakness in an otherwise inflexible character.

"What did you wish me to do, sir?" he asked, placing the conversation firmly on a more seemly footing.

"To work on the same lines as you did in the case of the window cleaner. How you found out which pub he was in the habit of frequenting, I don't know, but, roughly, what I want is any information you can gather concerning a certain Mr. Charles Miller or his late wife. I don't fancy you will find either his butler or his footman very congenial companions, but I should be very much obliged if you would sink your prejudices and join them in a friendly glass wherever they may be in the habit of foregathering. I leave you to find out where that is."

"Is that the husband of *the* Mrs. Miller, may I ask, sir?" enquired Manners, in a voice carefully devoid of all interest.

"If, by that, you mean the lady who was killed the other day, it is. I am anxious to disabuse the police of certain ideas they persist in holding regarding Sir Richard's presence in the house at the time, but I must warn you that I may be giving you a hopeless task. There is nothing against Mr. Miller save his very unpleasing personality, but I'm going on the principle of leaving no stone unturned."

"I will do my best, sir. Would it be possible to ascertain the names of the persons in question?"

Constantine telephoned to the Yard and had no difficulty in getting the required information.

"Remember I want all the gossip. The more, the better," were his parting directions, as he added Miller's address to the names of the two servants.

His next act was to ring up Davenport.

"I'm sorry to bother you at the end of a long day's work," he said, when the dentist had, with difficulty, been persuaded to come to the telephone himself. "But can you tell me who owns the empty house next door to you? I have my own reasons for asking. Your own landlord? No, it doesn't matter about his name. I can get that from the agents if you'll put me onto them. Thearle and Thearle. Yes. By the way, has that house been done up lately, do you know? A couple of months ago. Thank you. I'm very grateful. No, I'm very well satisfied where I am, but a friend is interested."

Next morning he called on Messrs. Thearle and Thearle. He had heard through Mr. Davenport of a house in Illbeck Street that he thought might suit him and he understood that it was in their hands. Messrs. Thearle's urbane young man said that it was. If it hadn't been for the fact that rents were high in that part of the world and times bad they would have disposed of it long ago. As it was, they could offer it at a comparatively low rental. Would Dr. Constantine like to look over it now? He had already risen when Constantine stretched out a detaining hand.

"I'm afraid I haven't made myself clear," he said briskly. "I'm not interested in the rental. I want to buy. From something Mr. Davenport said, I concluded that the house was for sale, or I shouldn't have approached you about it."

The agent's face fell, but he acknowledged defeat slowly, after the manner of his kind.

"I couldn't persuade you to go over it, I suppose?" he urged. "I think we might persuade our client to consider a slight reduction in rent if the house met with your approval. We can strongly recommend it and if, after you have seen it, you feel inclined to change your mind ..."

Constantine cut him short ruthlessly.

"Unless you can persuade your client to sell, I am not interested."

"We could approach our client," said the agent doubtfully, "but I doubt whether we should be successful. He purchased four houses in that block, including Mr. Davenport's about a year ago and it is unlikely that he would sell again. We have several admirable properties on our books, suitable for the medical profession, if you would care to consider them."

He was assuming that his visitor was a doctor of medicine and Constantine did not undeceive him.

"I've set my heart on Illbeck Street," he said, with convincing finality, "and I shall be leaving for the Continent in a day or two. I suppose, as time is short, you could not put me in touch with your client? I might be able to persuade him to sell. I need not say that all future negotiations would, of course, be conducted through you."

"'I'm afraid I cannot even give you his name," answered the agent. "All our negotiations have been through a firm of solicitors. We could put you onto them, of course."

Constantine shook his head.

"No good," he said. "I haven't time for that sort of thing. Unless I can get in direct touch with the owner I must give up the idea. It is a pity. If the house suited me I should be prepared to make a good offer."

The agent, seeing the chance of a profitable deal slipping through his fingers, made a final effort.

"We could approach the solicitors," he suggested. "In the event of their being willing to negotiate, how long could you give us?"

Constantine looked dubious.

"I've had too much experience of the dilatoriness of lawyers," he said. "If you can give me the name of the actual owner of the property this evening I will undertake to approach him myself. If I can persuade him to sell I will communicate with you."

Leaving his address with the agents he was about to depart when he paused as though a sudden idea had struck him.

"By the way," he said, "I understand that these houses were redecorated not long ago. If this deal goes through I may want to arrange about certain alterations in a hurry. Can you recommend the firm that did the work?"

The agent could and was only too ready to supply the name: Dicks and Hoskins, Quebec Street. Constantine thanked him and, placating his conscience with the thought of all he had suffered at the hands of house agents in days gone by, went back to his flat and rang up Arkwright. He was not at the Yard and it was late in the afternoon before Constantine could get onto him.

Arkwright was aggrieved.

"Look here, sir," he complained, "those inscriptions may be in Greek, but they're absolutely meaningless. If you've made anything of them ..."

"I haven't. When I do I'll let you know. Meanwhile, I've a job here that your people can do far more quickly and efficiently than I can. How goes the official conscience?"

Arkwright's disappointment was reflected in his voice.

"That hardly comes into it, sir," he said. "After all, we're both working for the same ends."

"We are not, if, by that, you mean your case against Sir Richard."

Arkwright chuckled.

"You can only upset my apple-cart by producing the murderer," he pointed out. "We're willing enough to help you there, sir."

"This may be a step on the way, it's true, though I don't guarantee any results."

"Good enough. What do you want us to do?"

"Get in touch with a firm of decorators named Dicks and Hoskins and run your rule over the men who were employed in redecorating that empty house in Illbeck Street. The keys must have been in their possession for a considerable period."

There was a pause, then, ruefully:

"You've got us there, sir. An ordinary routine job we ought to have seen to. I'll get onto it and let you know the result. Anything else?"

"Nothing at present."

Constantine replaced the receiver with a sigh. Arkwright, with a fixed object in view, was in a better case than himself. It had amused him to score over him, but he had been speaking only the truth when he admitted that the inscriptions on the knives conveyed as little to him as to the police. He had sent Manners on his quest on the vague chance that, if Miller were concealing something, his servants might let fall some clue as to its significance. As for the empty house, it was a forlorn hope at best. Even if the murderer had make his escape that way, there was no reason to believe that he had had any previous connection with it. A window left unlatched by a careless painter would have given him the means to enter and he could have left by the front door in the ordinary way.

The knowledge that he had thought it worth while to waste a large portion of his day on the empty house only served to increase Constantine's sense of his own futility, and the return of Manners with his report did not tend to raise his spirits, though, in the time, the man had performed wonders. He had spent the hours between tea and dinner in visiting the bars of various houses he described as "well spoken of" and had succeeded in locating the one patronised by Miller's butler. Though he had not seen the man himself he had established relations with the landlord and had found no difficulty in getting him to talk about the murder. The man, proud of being in possession of information straight from the horse's mouth, as it were, had passed on all that Miller's butler had told him. That Miller had been at his office at the time of his wife's death, there seemed no doubt. One of his clerks, who had called at the house since the murder, had told the butler that he was actually in the room with him at the time it had taken place. The whole of the domestic staff, including Mrs. Snipe, had been in the house all the morning. The secretary had been seen by the butler to enter the Square with the dog, and a small girl, whose nurse was an acquaintance of the butler's, had played with the dog while it was in the Square. In fact, the butler had been talking to the nurse when the secretary returned to the house. Evidently the crime had been discussed exhaustively, in all its aspects, in the bar of the public house, many times before Manners came on the scene.

"That was the best I could do, sir," he finished. "Would you wish me to see Mr. Miller's man personally? I have ascertained when he is to be found there and, as it appears that he is a keen billiard player, I should have no difficulty in approaching him, being fond of a game myself."

"How did the landlord's account strike you?" asked Constantine.

"Very reliable, I should say, sir. The police had been questioning Mr. Miller's man and he seems to have repeated his conversations with them to the landlord, with a bit extra, on his own, as it were."

"In fact, if anything, we now know a little more than the police," suggested Constantine.

"Exactly, sir. It is unfortunate that it all points the same way, seeing that it's extra knowledge," assented Manners ponderously and Constantine could only agree with him.

"All the same," he told him, "you might see the man for yourself. Get him to gossip, if you can."

At seven o'clock a note arrived from the house agents. The owner of the property in Illbeck Street was a Mrs. Marks. It was most unlikely that she could be persuaded to sell.

"Thank goodness for that small mercy," murmured Constantine, as he sat down to his dinner and the contemplation of a wasted day.

CHAPTER THIRTEEN

ARKWRIGHT SWUNG round the corner into Shepherd's Market and barely escaped a collision with two men who were walking in the opposite direction. He flashed a swift, appraising glance at them, stopped dead in sheer amazement, then, with a delighted chuckle, pursued his way. He had come within an ace of bowling the irreproachable Manners into the gutter and the companion with whom Manners was progressing sedately along the pavement was none other than Miller's rather raffish looking butler.

His amusement was enhanced by Manners's reaction to the meeting. For the first time in their acquaintance Arkwright saw his imperturbability badly shaken. At the sight of the detective his hand went involuntarily to his hat, then, realising that Arkwright must be well known to Miller's servants and that he would be severely hampered in his task if they suspected him of any connection with the police, he stiffened. The uncertain, almost appealing glance he threw at the detective as he passed on, cutting him deliberately, was a comedy in itself. Arkwright was quick to grasp the significance of the encounter. So Constantine was on the job! If there were to be any results, he would no doubt arrive at them, he reflected rather ruefully, realising that Manners was in a far better position to collect stray gossip than any of his own men.

He was on his way to Miller's house. Having failed to discover anything of interest among the murdered woman's possessions he had asked Miller to go through his wife's papers on the chance of there being old letters of Vera Abramoff's among them. The jeweller had promised to do so and now Arkwright, realising that two days had gone by with no word from him, had decided to see to the matter himself. He had telephoned to Miller's office to find that he was not expected there that day and actuated by that indefinite feeling of distrust with which the jeweller had begun to inspire him, had decided not to warn him of his coming but to take his chance of finding him at home.

As he approached the house a man who had been walking ahead of him turned up the steps and rang the bell. Arkwright instinctively slackened his pace, preferring to wait until the coast was clear. He saw the door open and Miller's secretary, Bloomfield, on the threshold. There was a short colloquy, then Bloomfield handed something to the man, went back into the house, and closed the door. His visitor ran down the steps and walked briskly along the Square ahead of Arkwright, carrying the object Bloomfield had given him, a large white envelope, in his hand. Arkwright quickened his steps once more, only to be brought again to a halt by the reopening of the front door. The secretary emerged, wearing a hat and a heavy overcoat, shut the door gently behind him and, with a rapid, curiously furtive glance at the windows of the house he was leaving, followed hurriedly in the wake of his late visitor. Ordinarily speaking there was nothing out of the usual in the whole transaction, and, had it not been for Bloomfield's manner, Arkwright would not have given it a second thought. As it was he was sufficiently interested to follow the secretary until he turned the corner and stand watching the two men as they made their way down the narrow side street.

Bloomfield did not attempt to diminish the distance between himself and the man he was following, neither did he make any endeavour to attract his attention, and Arkwright watched with increasing interest as they continued on their way until, halfway down the street the front man turned into a small post office. Bloomfield, in his wake, peered for a moment through the glass of the office door, then went in.

His back had hardly disappeared before Arkwright was off the mark and, a few minutes later, he, in his turn, had his nose pressed against the glass of the post office door. There were several other customers grouped in the constricted space in front of the counter, but he could see his men clearly enough. The first was bending over the narrow ledge that served as a desk for those unfortunates who might be driven to use it, and was engaged in tying up and sealing the envelope Bloomfield had given him, obviously unaware of the presence of that gentleman, who stood behind him, shamelessly peering over his shoulder. Arkwright took advantage of his absorption to slip through the door and into the solitary telephone booth that stood at Bloomfield's elbow. Leaving the door ajar and keeping his back turned he buried his nose in the Directory and waited. The moment he had hoped for soon arrived. Some movement of Bloomfield's must have warned the other man for he swung round with a swiftness that caught him utterly unprepared.

"Na yer don't!" he snarled. "Follerin' of me, was yer? Think yerself clever, I suppose. Well, yer can tike yerself orf, see? Yer can foller me to every post orfice in London, but yer won't see me address this parcel. I got plenty o' time on me 'ands. And now I've spotted yer I know what to do with it!"

Then, as Bloomfield did not answer:

"Well, what abart it?"

Bloomfield remained silent and Arkwright, realising that, at this juncture, he would hardly have eyes for anyone but his companion, turned until he could see him clearly through the glass door of the booth.

He watched the secretary unbutton his coat, take a bundle of notes from his pocket and count out five of them onto the ledge at the man's elbow. Keeping his hand on them he echoed the other's words.

"What about it?"

A slow grin spread over the man's face.

"What d'jer think?" he jibed. "I've got my whack comin' to me, all right, and don't you worry. I've only got one thing to say to you. You 'op it, mister. It's no manner o' use yer follerin me, no matter what yer got in yer pocket."

Bloomfield spoke again.

"I'll make it ten if you give me that address."

The other's only answer was to thrust the envelope into his pocket, keeping his hand on it.

"Orl right, smarty," he jeered, settling his back more comfortably against the shelf and crossing his legs. "'Ere we are and 'ere we stays."

For a moment Bloomfield glared at him with baleful eyes, then, seeing himself beaten, swung round, pushed his way through the little crowd round the counter and vanished. The other man watched him off the premises, gave him time to get away, then, with a wary eye on the door, busied himself once more with the envelope.

Arkwright waited till he had finished laboriously printing the address before he stepped out of the booth. The man, having nothing to fear from that quarter took no heed of him and when a huge hand descended on the envelope his consternation was such that he could do no more than make a feeble snatch at his property. Arkwright's other hand closed on his like a vice.

"Oy, what jer doin'?" squealed his victim.

Arkwright surveyed him and beheld a square-shouldered, pug-nosed youth of about twenty. His clothes were neat, shoddy, and altogether atrocious, but he bore none of the earmarks of the habitual criminal. Arkwright turned the hand he held palm up and looked at it. Bending forward he sniffed the air appreciatively.

"Potman, aren't you?" he demanded.

"What's that to you? 'And over that there parcel!'"

Arkwright caught the eye of the post office clerk goggling at him through the wire netting over the counter. He took a step nearer to her, dragging his captive with him.

"It's all right, Miss," he said in a low voice. "I'm a police officer."

At the words, the wrist he held gave a convulsive twitch and then lay passive and he knew that the bolt had gone home. Before the man had time to recover, he shot another at a venture.

"Blackmail's a criminal offence," he said. "How did you come to be mixed up in it?"

The pasty face grew a shade whiter. Then the words came, a spate of them, tumbling over each other.

"I ain't got nothin' to do with it, mister. You can't put it on me. Actin' for someone else, I am. Honest, I don't know nothin' about it. Chap asked me ter collect a letter and send it to 'im. There ain't nothin' you can bring up against me!"

The torrent of words abated and finally ceased as Arkwright, shifting his grip to the man's cuff, marched him to the door and out of the post office. A swift survey of the street satisfied him that there was no sign of Bloomfield. He led his captive to the cab rank at the corner and pushed him into a taxi, ignoring his renewed expostulations, which grew shriller and more incoherent as they neared Scotland Yard. By the time they got there he had reached a state bordering on hysteria.

Arkwright felt certain now that he was dealing with a first offender. He gave him no time to recover. Once he had him within four walls he put a quick end to his protestations.

"That will do," he commanded curtly. "I'll do the talking now. May as well go back to the beginning. You're a potman, aren't you?"

"Yes," was the sullen answer.

"Where?"

"Goat and 'Orns, Tallow Street, Battersea,"

"Name?"

"'Arry 'Oover. You got it wrong, mister. There ain't nothin' against me. Mr. Proctor, of The Goat and 'Orns'll speak for me."

Arkwright ignored the outburst. He held out the envelope.

"How did you come to be fetching this? I want the whole story."

"All through me offerin' to do a favour. That's what comes of bein' soft! It's the last time, I can tell yer!"

Arkwright glanced at the inscription on the envelope.

"This man, Edward Parker, who is he?"

"Chap as I met in the bar. Honest I don't know nothin' more about 'im than that."

"How did you come to take on this job, then?"

"'E come in three nights ago and asked me to meet 'im after closin' time. We went for a walk together and 'e said as how 'e wanted someone to do an errand for 'im. Said 'e'd make it worth anyone's while. So I offers to do it. That's all I got to do with it."

"What were your instructions?"

"I was to go to the 'ouse and see a cove as would give me a letter. Then I was to address the letter and register it, like you see me. I don't know no more than that."

"Why couldn't you take the letter to Parker yourself?"

"Dunno. I reckon 'e was afraid of me bein' follered. 'E told me 'e didn't want no one to know 'is address."

"What were you to get for this?"

"Arf a crown and me fare," answered Hoover glibly.

"Yet you refused a tenner because you'd got your whack coming to you! Not good enough, my lad. You'd better come clear. How much were you to get if the deal went through?"

Hoover's unsteady eyes sought the window, as though for inspiration. None came, and, with his weak mouth obstinately closed, he sat hunched, in silence. Arkwright leaned forward, his hands on his knees.

"Want me to tell you what happened?" he said. "Parker told you he'd got the goods on Bloomfield and was going to bleed him, but he didn't want to collect the money himself. He gave you a chance to stand in if you'd do the collecting. You were to send the money by registered post and keep away from him, for fear Bloomfield might follow you and find out where he hangs out. That right?"

Hoover shifted uneasily in his chair. He was beginning to waver, but his fear of Parker was still paramount.

"You can't make me say nothin'," he muttered sullenly. "I know me rights. You ain't even warned me."

"I haven't warned you because you're not under arrest, yet," answered Arkwright sternly. "I've got a right to hold you for twenty-four hours before I charge you. What you get when I do charge you depends largely on how you behave now. If you come clear I'll undertake to speak for you when the time comes. I'm giving you your chance. How much was Parker to get out of Bloomfield and what was your share?"

Hoover leaned forward suddenly.

"Looke 'ere, mister," he said earnestly. "You can't fix this on me. I ain't never 'eard of any Bloomfield. I don't know what's in that there letter, but it ain't from anyone of that name. You're on the wrong track, mister."

A sudden light of comprehension dawned in Arkwright's eyes.

"Was Charles Miller the man you were to see?" he demanded.

Hoover's face gave him away though he tried to bluster.

"I don't know what you mean ..."

Arkwright cut him short.

"Very well, then, if you prefer it."

He pressed a bell on his desk and waited in silence till a constable appeared in the doorway. Then, jerking his head in the direction of Hoover:

"You can take him," he said curtly. "I'm holding him till we pull in his friend."

Hoover's eyes were fixed glassily on the constable. The sight of him had shattered what little nerve he had left. He clutched at the table convulsively.

"I'll tell what I know," he babbled. "I ain't done no 'arm, mister."

At a gesture the constable vanished.

"Get on with it," said Arkwright. "What's in this envelope?"

"Eight 'undred pounds there should be. I ain't looked."

"How much were you to get?"

"Fifty."

"What for?"

"Leavin' the letters and fetchin' the answers. And puttin' of 'im off if 'e tried to foller me."

"Whom were these letters addressed to?"

"Charles Miller. I never 'eard of no one else."

"Never heard the name of Bloomfield?"

"No."

"What was in Parker's letters to Miller? I suppose Parker did write them?"

"That's right. 'E never told me what was in them and I knew better than to ask. 'E told me 'e was goin' to put the screw on 'im, that was all I knew."

"Who is Parker? How did he come to pitch on you?"

"Dunno. Said 'e didn't know no one in England. I reckon that's right. I know 'e was a stranger to London. 'E came into the bar and we got talkin'. 'E asked me the next night if I'd go a job for 'im. I said, 'yes, if it was safe.' And that's all I know about it."

"It's a large sum of money to trust to anyone he knew so little about," said Arkwright incredulously. "How did he know you'd send it on?"

"Dunno. I got a good name where I work. Besides 'e said 'e'd get me and 'alf kill me if I went back on 'im," answered Hoover simply.

Arkwright, his eyes on the weak mouth and indeterminate features, decided that Parker had chosen his tool well.

"Is this his right address?" he asked.

"So far as I know."

"How many letters did you take to Miller?"

"Only one. It was mostly the answers I 'ad to fetch."

"Did you never see Miller?"

Hoover shook his head.

"Never see no one else. Thought this chap was 'im."

"What does Parker look like?"

"Ugly lookin' chap about my size."

"Clean-shaven?"

"Yes."

"Hair?"

"Brown, turnin' grey."

"Complexion?"

"White. Pastiest lookin' chap I ever see."

"Any distinguishing marks?"

"Not as I know of."

"Right. We shall have to detain you. If Parker corroborates your story I'll do my best for you."

He pressed the bell again. Hoover rose from his chair.

"I say, mister, you'll see 'e don't get 'is 'ands on me. 'E'd 'alf kill me if 'e knew."

Arkwright reassured him.

"You'll be safe enough here and, when you get out, he's not likely to be in a position to annoy you."

Taking a plain clothes detective with him he went direct to Parker's address in Battersea. There would be time enough to tackle Miller when he had got his man. The job proved easier than he had expected. Parker was lying on his bed in his shirt and trousers and was taken completely unawares. If he possessed a weapon he had no opportunity to lay his hands on it, but there was a look on his colourless face as he silently hitched himself into his coat that made Hoover's attitude easily explainable. He never betrayed himself by look or gesture or opened his lips from the time of his removal from the frowzy room in which they found him till his arrival at the Yard, but Arkwright had an impression of seething emotion rigidly kept in check for so long that the repression had become part of the man's nature. His face was a mask in which only the eyes, hot and tormented, seemed alive. His voice, when Arkwright, in the seclusion of his room, tried to break through the barriers of his reserve, was toneless and hardly above a whisper. That he was a much better educated man than Hoover was apparent as soon as he opened his lips.

Arkwright confronted him with the letter.

"This is addressed to you," he said. "Have you anything to say about it?"

Parker's lips barely moved as he answered.

"Nothing."

"We have reason to believe that it contains money paid to you as the result of certain letters from you to a Mr. Miller. What was in those letters?"

"If Mr. Miller has complained to you he no doubt told you what was in them," was the answer.

"Am I to take it that you refuse to answer?"

"I've a right to keep my correspondence private if I choose. If Miller cares to bring the matter into court I can defend myself."

"Mr. Miller is on his way here. I'm giving you your chance before he comes."

Parker's thin lips did not smile, but his eyes were derisive.

"I've nothing to say."

Arkwright had him removed and rang up Miller's house. He was still out and was not expected back to lunch, but the secretary was in and announced his readiness to come to the Yard immediately. Arkwright was hanging up the receiver when the detective he had left behind in Parker's room returned. He reported that a careful search had revealed nothing incriminating. The man seemed to have very few possessions and, judging by the complete lack of correspondence found in his lodgings, no friends.

"This was underneath his mattress, though," he said, holding out a dirty envelope. "It's his passport. Parker's not his name."

Arkwright drew out the passport and, balancing it on his hand, stared at it thoughtfully.

"He's got no friends in London and he talks like an old lag," he said slowly, "and he's got his knife into Miller. Looks as if the name on this passport might be Greeve."

The detective smiled.

"You've got it, sir. And the passport's his all right, there's the photograph to prove it. He's the chap that was mentioned in the Cape Town report, isn't he? Looks as if he'd got Miller by the short hairs over that receiving job. There was an impression that Greeve had been used as a scapegoat, wasn't there?"

Arkwright nodded.

"Greeve served his time and if he's come over now to get his own back, I don't envy Miller. Blackmail's a filthy business, but, if that's all there is to it, I could find it in my heart to be sorry that I wasted my time over him. I was hoping for something better. We don't want to be sidetracked just now."

After the detective had gone he sat turning the envelope Bloomfield had given Hoover over and over in his hands. If he had been certain there was anything to be learned from it he would have opened it long ago and taken the consequences, but, certain as he was that it contained money, he was equally sure that it held nothing else. If Miller had decided to pay for Parker's silence he would be careful to give him no further hold over him. How much Bloomfield knew was an open question, but Arkwright had every intention of getting that knowledge out of him and was not sorry that circumstance had forced him to deal with him before seeing Miller himself.

Bloomfield, when he came, was very much himself. His manner was brisk and business-like and gave the impression that he had torn himself from more urgent affairs to clear up what might, or might not, prove to be an important point, but that, in any case, he was anxious to get back to his own work as soon as possible. It struck Arkwright for the first time that this pose of efficiency was a little overdone.

Bloomfield placed his hat on the table, pulled a chair brisk-ly into position and sat down.

"You gave me to understand that something important had transpired, so, as it may be some time before I can get in touch with Mr. Miller, I came at once," he announced in his rather guttural voice. His accent was more pronounced than that of his employer, but his English was, if anything, more fluent.

"Is Mr. Miller out of town?" asked Arkwright.

Bloomfield raised his eyebrows.

"Oh, no, but he is attending a luncheon party, a business affair, and, as he may very likely go home with one of the oth-er guests afterwards I should not know where to find him at a moment's notice. He will not be at the office today. Is there anything I can do for you in his absence?"

"The matter concerns both you and Mr. Miller. To begin with, this is your property, I think."

Arkwright held out the envelope.

Bloomfield stared at it, then thrust out a quick hand to take it, but Arkwright evaded him and replaced it on the table in front of him.

"I think not, Mr. Bloomfield," he said drily. "We will keep this for the present, if you don't mind. Am I right in assuming that it contains money?"

Bloomfield hesitated. Arkwright could see that he was thinking rapidly.

"Well?" he continued briskly. "When I tell you that we have two men in custody here in connection with this letter you will realise the necessity for being frank with us."

Bloomfield settled himself more comfortably in his chair.

"I fail to see what bearing my private correspondence can have on the matter," he said, at last, with a hint of insolence in his voice.

"This hardly comes under the head of private correspondence," said Arkwright. "From certain information I have received I understand that you were acting for Mr. Miller in the matter. As the result of certain letters which passed between him and one of the people we have detained he agreed to pay this man a sum of money. I am asking you whether this letter contains the sum in question."

Bloomfield nodded.

"It does," he said coolly. "What of it?"

Arkwright eyed him narrowly.

"Blackmail is a criminal offence in this country, Mr. Bloomfield," he said slowly. "If Mr. Miller is wise, he will refuse to submit to it. We shall ask him to charge these men and, once he has done so, he can rest assured that his name will be kept out of all subsequent proceedings. In the meantime, I am ready to listen to any statement you may care to make. Anything you say here will be treated as confidential."

Bloomfield's answer was to rise slowly to his feet. He picked up his hat and stood looking down at the Inspector.

"I am sorry, Inspector," he answered, with every appearance of regret, "but I really know nothing about the matter. My instructions were to place a certain sum of money in an envelope and hand it to a messenger who would call for it. With that my duties ended."

"Was it in pursuance of your instructions that you followed the messenger and endeavoured to bribe him into giving you the address of the man to whom the money was being paid?"

For a moment the man was startled out of his equanimity. Arkwright saw his hands clench and then relax as his quick brain raced in an effort to cope with this unexpected development. Then he evidently realised that frankness was his best policy.

"I hope you will not find it necessary to report this to Mr. Miller," he said earnestly. "It would cost me my job if it came to his ears. I was a fool to do such a thing, but practically all Mr. Miller's business deals go through my hands and this was the first time he had not taken me into his confidence. I am afraid I yielded to curiosity and tried, very stupidly, as it turned out, to find out what he had not told me for myself. I intended no disloyalty to Mr. Miller."

"And you were willing to pay for your curiosity to the tune of ten pounds?"

Arkwright's voice was frankly incredulous. Bloomfield reddened, opened his lips to answer and was silenced by the clamour of the telephone bell. Arkwright put the receiver to his ear.

"Send him up," he said. Then, turning to Bloomfield: "Mr. Miller has arrived. He found your message waiting for him and came straight on. Now perhaps we shall get to the bottom of this business."

Bloomfield's distress at the news was so acute that Arkwright felt almost sorry for him. He craned over the table, his prehensile nose within an inch of Arkwright's face.

"Inspector," he gasped, "this means a lot to me! Let me tell him later in my own way of the part I have played in this. If he hears from you that I followed this man, I am done for."

"If Mr. Miller charges these men," said Arkwright, "you will have to give a more convincing explanation of your part in the affair than you have given me. All I can undertake to do at present is to keep your name out of it until you have had an interview with him. I will do that much, if possible."

He rose as the door opened to admit Miller. The jeweller had evidently lunched well and was in one of his more affable moods.

"Ha, Bloomfield," he exclaimed at the sight of his secretary. "You here? What is all this about, Inspector?"

Arkwright told him briefly of the detention of the two men and of Hoover's admissions, finishing up with a repetition of the little homily to which he had already treated Bloomfield.

"We are doing our best to put a stop to this sort of thing, Mr. Miller," he finished, "but we can only hope to be successful if we have the co-operation of the public. Should you decide to prosecute, you will figure as Mr. X. in the subsequent proceedings and we will undertake that your name shall be kept out of the matter altogether."

Miller stared at him as though he could hardly believe his ears, then, for the first time, Arkwright saw him smile, and was irresistibly reminded of one of those ivory figures of the more amiable Chinese deities. The smile broadened, as though Miller was slowly digesting his own private joke.

"But this is funny," he said, at last. "It would give me pleasure to oblige you, Inspector, but I am afraid I cannot bring any charge against these men."

CHAPTER FOURTEEN

ARKWRIGHT MASTERED his annoyance with difficulty.

"Am I to understand that you refuse to charge these men?" he asked, his voice ominously quiet.

Miller beamed on him.

"But certainly, Inspector. I am sorry, very sorry, you should have been put to so much inconvenience, but you must admit that it would have been wiser if you had seen fit to consult me in the first instance. As it is, much as I should like to oblige you, I cannot ask you to arrest these men for a crime they have not committed. That would hardly be in accordance with your English ideas of justice, I think?"

Arkwright did not miss the covert sneer that underlay the last sentence. He had learned self-control in a hard school, but even he was hard put to it to keep a hold on his temper now. Hoover's confession had effectually removed any doubt he had had that the case was one of blackmail, and, knowing from experience the reluctance the victims of this basest form of extortion almost invariably showed to take any risk of publicity★ he had been prepared for trouble in persuading Miller to act. But that he should blandly deny having paid Parker for his silence was carrying things too far. A glance at Bloomfield did not serve to smooth his feelings. The secretary's dark face was impassive, but the derisive triumph in his eyes was unmistakable.

Miller, having shot his bolt, sat waiting, with something perilously like a smirk on his wizened face. Arkwright eyed him coldly.

"I'm afraid I must ask you to explain yourself, Mr. Miller," he said.

Miller threw out his hands, palm upwards.

"Of course. Though, frankly, it is an explanation I should have preferred to avoid. It is not surprising that you should have mistaken a purely business transaction for something much more irregular, but I think I can set your mind at rest. This man, Parker, came to me some time ago with a story about an Italian he had met here in London. At the time, he would not tell me the man's name, but he declared that he was the head of an old and very impoverished Italian family and was being forced by circumstances to sell certain of his family effects. As you may know, there are very stringent laws in Italy against the removal of such things from the country and, according to Parker, he had already helped this man to dispose of a picture which he had managed to smuggle over to England. He was anxious now to find a market for a piece of jewellery. Now pictures do not interest me, but jewels do and, according to his description, this one was a collector's piece. An Italian sixteenth century pendant, in enamelled gold, representing Apollo, and set with diamonds, emeralds, rubies and pearls. These transactions are more common than you might think and, though they might be called irregular, they are not illegal in this country. Parker undertook to arrange for the safe transport of the pendant, which was still in Italy, to London, provided I were prepared to pay the price the owner was asking. This would, of course, cover Parker's commission. As it happened I had a customer who I knew would be interested, and Parker's offer impressed me as being so genuine that I got in touch with a friend of mine, a jeweller, in Berne and asked him, next time his business took him to Italy, to call on the owner and inspect the pendant. He did so, verified Parker's story and reported that the piece was well worth the sum asked for it. I therefore approached Parker again and told him that I would deal, provided he could deliver the goods. How he proposed to get the pendant out of Italy I naturally did not ask."

Arkwright's eyes narrowed.

"How did you get in touch with Parker?" he asked sharply.

There was the fraction of a pause before Miller answered, but his explanation was glib enough when it came.

"I had told him at our last meeting to ring me up in a fortnight's time. He never gave me his address and I did not ask for it. I was naturally anxious not to be mixed up in the transaction before the actual sale took place and the less I knew about him the better."

Bloomfield's chair creaked gently as he recrossed his legs. Arkwright had a sensation of tension suddenly relaxed.

"What passed between you when you telephoned? Did he arrange to call on you?"

Miller shook his head.

"After the first interview I never saw him again. His letters to me were brought by hand and the messenger waited for an answer. If I was out he called again on the following day. I had no objection to the arrangement. From my point of view the less he came to the house the better."

"You could identify this messenger, I suppose, if necessary?"

Miller threw out his hands in a gesture of hopelessness.

"I never saw him. Mr. Bloomfield had instructions to receive the letters he brought and hand him mine in return. I should like to make it clear that Mr. Bloomfield was acting quite blindly in this matter. The whole business was, as I say, irregular and I felt that the fewer people who were involved in it the better."

Arkwright picked up the envelope.

"I take it that this contains the price of the pendant?"

"That is so."

"The thing is already in your possession?"

"Parker left it at my office yesterday. I suppose he did not care to trust the messenger with it. I am going by my head clerk's description of the man who brought it. I was not there myself at the time. As soon as I arrived I examined the pendant carefully, decided that it was up to the specification and handed the money to Mr. Bloomfield, telling him that it would be called for. So far as I was concerned the deal was over. I was absolutely astounded when you announced that Parker was in custody."

"Is it customary to carry through transactions of this sort through comparative strangers? Weren't you taking a good deal for granted in dealing with Parker?"

"It was not until after I had received my Swiss friend's report that I consented to deal with him," pointed out Miller. "Once I had satisfied myself that he could deliver the goods and that the article had been come by honestly I considered that I had taken all necessary precautions. In my profession one has to take certain risks. Owing to the circumstances, the deal was an exceptionally good one from my point of view and, if I had refused to negotiate, Parker would have taken his offer elsewhere."

"It seems a risky business to entrust to a stranger. Parker had never carried through any such transaction for you before, had he?" suggested Arkwright, deftly leading him on to the admission that was to be his undoing.

But, even as he spoke, he knew he was too late. He saw Miller's hand close with a convulsive grip on the arm of his chair and, following his eyes, caught them as they rested for a fraction of a second on the passport that lay beside Bloomfield's envelope on the table. He knew he had only his own carelessness to thank for what followed.

Miller hesitated, then, with an admirable assumption of confusion, told the truth.

"I am afraid I may have misled you as to my acquaintance with Parker," he admitted. "The man has been unfortunate and is trying his best to make a fresh start and I was afraid if I told you what I knew about him it would serve to prejudice you against him. But, as you have asked the question, I must answer it. Parker was not unknown to me, though I have never had any dealings with him in this country. He was, however, in my employ in Cape Town at one time and, until he was suddenly arrested for dealing in stolen property, I had every faith in him. The most painful part of the whole affair to me was the fact that he had used my business as a cloak to cover his transactions. He was convicted and has already paid in full for what he did. When he came to me I was glad to help him. Parker is not his real name, by the way."

He had wriggled out of an awkward corner with amazing swiftness and dexterity. Not only had he been quick to realise the probable significance of the passport, but, handicapped by his ignorance of whether Arkwright had heard of the Cape Town episode, he had neutralised it by cleverly backing his horse both ways. If Arkwright knew nothing he would naturally look upon Parker as the sole culprit; on the other hand, should he be in possession of the real facts, he could hardly blame Miller for telling only a half truth. He had hampered Arkwright effectively, if only temporarily, by a story which, he was bound to admit, might be true, but which he viewed with the utmost scepticism.

"May I have the address of this Swiss gentleman?" he said. "And I'm afraid I must ask you to let me see the letters that passed between you and Parker."

"My friend's name is Herr Oppenheimer, and his address, 7. Alpenstrasse, Berne. As regards the letters, I am afraid I destroyed them on receipt of the pendant. My business takes me occasionally to Italy and, should any details of the affair leak out later, the less trace of my part in it the better. Parker gave me his word that he would do the same with my letters to him. I can show you the pendant, of course."

"And the name of the original Italian owner?"

Miller drew himself up with a fine assumption of dignity.

"That, Inspector, I am within my rights in refusing to give you." he exclaimed, with some show of indignation. "I have submitted meekly to questions which I might very well have declined to answer and have succeeded in proving to you that I have not acted in any way against the laws of this country. But this Italian gentleman is in a very different position. He is liable to prosecution if the truth leaks out in his own country."

Arkwright nodded.

"I see," he said slowly. "I don't think I need trouble you further, Mr. Miller. You have no reason to believe that this man, Parker, or Greeve, bears any grudge against you, I suppose?"

Miller stared at him, wide-eyed.

"Considering that I have just put a fat commission in his pockets, certainly not. I should say he had every reason to be grateful."

There was nothing for it, after he had gone, but to hand the envelope to Parker, with as good a grace as possible and then release the two men. Parker was cautioned that any attempt to molest Hoover would meet with swift retribution.

"I've done with him," was his contemptuous rejoinder. "He's safe enough as far as I'm concerned."

Hoover plucked up sufficient courage to run after him as he left the building.

"What about me money?" he was heard to say as Parker shook him off.

Parker's reply was lost in the roar of the traffic.

Arkwright sent a cable to the police at Berne, asking them to look up Oppenheimer and get him to confirm Miller's story. Later in the afternoon Miller's clerk called at the Yard with a parcel in which was a leather case containing a very beautiful enamel and jewelled pendant. He also brought a letter from the jeweller, emphasising the value of the piece and demanding a receipt for it. Arkwright regarded the pendant with a distaste it certainly did not deserve and that night, when he dined at the Club, he carried it with him. His own knowledge of such things was nil, but Constantine, if he were lucky enough to find him, would be able to tell him if Miller's estimate of its worth were correct.

The old man came in just as Arkwright was beginning his soup and joined him. Arkwright handed him the case.

"What would you say that was?" he asked. "Date, value and that sort of thing. Is it what you would call a collector's piece?"

Constantine examined it carefully.

"I'm not an expert," he said at last, "but if this is genuine I should say it was a Renaissance jewel, probably sixteenth century Italian. If it *is* genuine, probably worth anything from five to eight hundred pounds."

"Are these things rare? Of this date and quality, I mean?"

"I saw one at Christie's, practically a replica of this, about six months ago. So far as I remember it fetched just under eight hundred."

Arkwright's eyes narrowed.

"You said practically a replica. Could it have been this one?"

Constantine bent over it once more.

"It might have been. As I said, I'm not a collector, so I didn't examine it carefully. I do remember the price, as the bidding was very hot and a friend of mine, who goes in for this sort of thing, only dropped out quite at the end. I don't know who bought it. The one I saw was an Apollo with Lute and it was jewelled in much the same way. More than that I dare not say."

"One could find out, I suppose?"

Constantine looked dubious.

"You might meet with success," he said, "but I'm afraid it's not so easy as you would think. Christie's have no doubt got the specifications and may know the present owner, but it's not unusual to find replicas of these pendants and there are some admirable forgeries in existence. This may very well be a copy. So far as the present owner is concerned, he may have bought it through an agent or it may have been sold again, not once but several times, since it came up at Christie's. It would be worth trying, however."

Arkwright repeated to him Miller's story of the pendant.

"How does it strike you?" he asked, when he had finished.

"It's clever," answered Constantine, with a mischievous gleam in his eyes, "so clever that I can quite appreciate your feelings! And it may be true. Such things do happen. The worst of it is that it's perfectly in keeping with what we already know of Miller. According to all accounts, he has kept carefully on the right side of the law since he came to England, no doubt as the result of the lesson he learned in Cape Town, but a deal of this kind is exactly what would appeal to him. He would safeguard himself in precisely the way he described. But there is one thing that, in my opinion, does not ring true."

Arkwright raised his eyebrows.

"There's a good deal, to my mind, but you know more of the tricks of the trade than I do. Where's the hitch?"

"He's the last man, I should imagine, to hold out a helping hand to Greeve, after what has happened. I should even doubt his employing him, however advantageous the deal might be to himself. His instinct would be to keep clear of the man at all costs."

"Unless Greeve has some hold over him."

"Exactly. But we must take into account that, if Miller is under the impression that no one in this country is aware of the Cape Town scandal, Greeve is in a position to make himself very troublesome. In view of Miller's business connections here he may have found it worth while to buy his silence."

"Meanwhile he's got us cold," assented Arkwright grimly. "Our only course is to get what information we can from this fellow, Oppenheimer, and he's probably hand and glove with Miller. I'll try my luck at Christie's and then send this thing back to Miller. Anyway, he's produced a pendant, which is more than I expected!"

Arkwright's visit to the auctioneers turned out much as Constantine had predicted. While admitting that the pendant might have passed through their hands, they could give no definite opinion. Neither could they say, at a glance, whether it was genuine or not. It was certainly a fine piece of work, but these pendants had been extensively copied and, supposing it to be genuine, there were probably several in existence. It might be identical with the one they had handled six months before, which had been knocked down to an agent who acted for several prominent firms in London. On asking his address Arkwright learned that he had died about four months ago. He reflected bitterly that, if Miller's story were a fabrication, the gods certainly seemed to be on his side.

He said as much to Constantine, who rang him up soon after eight thirty that evening.

"You sound exasperated," was the old man's unfeeling comment. "Would it be rubbing it in unduly if I rounded up a satisfactory day's work by calling on you for a little information?"

"Not at all," Arkwright assured him. "Why so abominably cheerful?"

"Possibly because I am not dependent for my information on Mr. Miller," chuckled Constantine maliciously. "Expect me in half an hour."

When the door opened to admit him Arkwright, who had barely recovered from the exasperations of the afternoon, eyed him fretfully.

"You look as jolly as a sand boy," he said disapprovingly. "I believe you really enjoy a good murder."

The animation died out of Constantine's eyes.

"A shrewd hit," he said, "but an unkind one. I love a puzzle of any kind, and, for my own peace of mind, I find it pleasanter to disregard what the newspapers call 'the human interest' and approach the thing as I would a chess problem. For the last few hours I've been trying to keep those two poor women out of my mind."

"For the last few hours?" queried Arkwright shrewdly.

There was no doubt about Constantine's gravity now.

"It is just beginning to dawn on me," he said, "that this is a more abominable business than either of us suspected."

Arkwright stared at him.

"Miller?" he queried. "But he's definitely out of it. His alibis are unassailable."

Constantine's lips curved, but his eyes did not lose their sternness.

"That's where my problem becomes interesting," he replied. "I went one step towards solving it this afternoon, but I must admit that I don't see my way ahead yet. I came for another look at those notes you got from the garage proprietor."

Arkwright produced them and watched the old man as he spread the soiled notes out in front of him and, with a piece of green billiard chalk, proceeded to copy the stain onto a clean pound note that he took from his case.

"Billiard chalk," he exclaimed. "It's an idea!"

"Say rather, a forlorn hope," amended Constantine. "A good many things might have caused that stain, and billiard chalk is one of them. I'm banking on the habit many players have of keeping the chalk in their waistcoat pockets."

"And the next step?" enquired Arkwright.

"I'll keep that to myself till I know whether it is a next step or not," retorted Constantine, as he slipped his note into his case and handed the original back to Arkwright. "I'm not trying to annoy, but I dislike making a fool of myself as much as you do."

"So, going on the principle that no man is a hero to his valet," murmured Arkwright.

It was the first time he had ever succeeded in putting the old man out of countenance and he duly chronicled it as the one bright spot in a gloomy day. Constantine recovered himself with remarkable quickness.

"So Manners has been making himself conspicuous," he said. "Now I wonder when you spotted his activities? But, if you think I have taken him into my confidence, you're mistaken. One of the many good points about Manners is that one merely has to give him instructions and he carries them out with remarkable efficiency."

"I wish I could say the same for some of my myrmidons," replied Arkwright. "It's only fair to say that I stumbled on him by accident. May one enquire, sir, if you have been defacing the currency of the realm for the benefit of Manners?"

"If I say, for the benefit of certain of Manners' acquaintances I shall be telling you more than you ought to know," smiled Constantine. "Fortunately, I'm in a generous mood."

"Won't you go further and tell me what you were doing this afternoon?" enquired Arkwright, with his most engaging grin.

"If, in return, you will do something further for me," answered the old man. "There are certain questions that Mrs. Miller's maid might be able to answer and you can approach her more easily than I can. If you'll give me a piece of paper, 111 jot them down."

He scribbled a few lines and handed them to Arkwright.

"The major part of my afternoon was spent at Somerset House," he said, "looking up the will of a certain Mr. Isidor Marks. As a document I commend it to your notice."

After he had gone Arkwright gave his attention to the sheet of paper he had left behind him. It consisted of three questions:

"How and when was Mrs. Miller's denture broken?

Was she in the habit of sleeping in it?

If not, where did she put it at night?"

He was still staring thoughtfully at the list when a messenger arrived with a cable from the Berne police, in answer to the one Arkwright had sent earlier in the day.

At the sight of the smudgy, typewritten message Arkwright's temper slipped its leash at last. It ran:

"Oppenheimer left Berne three days ago for England stop present destination unknown."

For ten lurid minutes Arkwright gave expression to sentiments that would possibly have caused Miller considerable gratification had he been there to hear them.

CHAPTER FIFTEEN

CONSTANTINE WAS still in bed when Arkwright rang him up next morning.

"Shall I take the message, sir?" enquired Manners, who was as fussy as a hen over his master and strongly disapproved of any form of exertion before breakfast.

Constantine, wide awake in an instant, raised himself on his elbow.

"No, put him through to me here," he ordered, the receiver already in his hand.

"I've got the information you asked for," Arkwright reported. "Mrs. Snipe is a Roman Catholic and goes to Mass every morning at seven. As luck would have it she mentioned the fact to my man, among about a thousand other bits of extraneous information, and he caught her on her way back this morning. She says Mrs. Miller never slept in her denture. It was kept in a tumbler in the bathroom adjoining her bedroom. Mrs. Snipe does not know precisely what went wrong with the denture, but her mistress was very much annoyed as the damage prevented her from wearing it and Davenport was unable to give her an appointment before eleven thirty. I gather that in consequence Mrs. Miller was in a pretty bad temper all the morning and Mrs. Snipe had to bear the brunt of it. Anyhow, plenty was said about the teeth. Mrs. Snipe thinks Mrs. Miller must have damaged them herself when she cleaned them the night before, though she refused to admit this and accused Mrs. Snipe of having dropped them when she was preparing her bath in the morning. There seems to have been something of a scene over it."

"The damage was actually discovered, then, on the morning of the murder?"

"When Mrs. Miller tried to wear the teeth, to be exact."

"Did anybody use the bathroom besides Mrs. Miller?"

"She and Miller shared it, but it has a second door opening into the passage. When the door into Mrs. Miller's bedroom was shut, any member of the household could have entered the bathroom unperceived. Miller, apparently, was not by way of using it in the morning. He always shaved in his dressing-room. That's as much as she could tell us. I see what you're driving at, but Miller's alibi still holds, remember. And we've no evidence that he ever touched the denture."

"We've no evidence against Miller at all, come to that," agreed Constantine, "but, if there is a crack in that alibi we ought to find it. And why all these lies?"

"The man's naturally shifty. And he's afraid of the police. If he was under the impression that we knew nothing of that affair in Cape Town, it would account for a good deal. By the way, he sent that secretary of his for the pendant first thing this morning. I've a fancy he didn't dare risk leaving it with us too long! Well, sir, you go your way and I'll go mine. I'm not talking through my hat when I say that I hope yours will prove the right one. I sent a man down to Somerset House. What do you make of that will?"

"It didn't surprise me altogether," answered Constantine blandly, "though I shouldn't have credited Mrs, Miller with an uncle called Isidor Marks! That peroxide hair was misleading, though."

"Marks seems to have left a tidy sum of money. That he should have made Miller Mrs. Marks' trustee seems natural enough. After all, Miller was his niece's husband. You don't suspect any irregularity there, do you?"

Television being still in its infancy Constantine's smile was lost on Arkwright. His voice betrayed nothing.

"None," he answered blandly. "He probably looks after the old lady's property admirably, though I admit I wouldn't trust him with sixpence of my own. It's interesting, all the same."

"It would interest me more to see the inside of your mind. I've an inkling that you've got ahead of us somewhere, but I can't, for the life of me, make out where. Where is the catch, sir?"

"There isn't one," answered Constantine, "if I seem secretive it's because I don't see my way clearly yet. For your comfort, I may tell you that I'm asking myself two questions, How and why? And I haven't got the answers yet to either of them. Did you look up that firm of decorators?"

"Yes, and drew a blank. They're prepared to vouch for all their men."

Constantine gave Davenport time to reach his consulting rooms, then rang him up.

"I won't keep you a moment," he said. "Can you tell me, in language adapted to the intelligence of the layman, precisely what was the matter with Mrs. Miller's denture?"

"Easily," answered the dentist. "It was quite simple and the damage was not great, though the job required skilled handling. The denture consisted of six front teeth, kept in place by two gold bars which ran behind her own back teeth. One of these bars had become so bent that it was impossible for her to adjust the denture, much less wear it. Gold being a soft metal, it was easy enough to bend it back into position, but it needed careful adjustment. Is that clear?"

"Quite. To remedy this you would have to have recourse to the moulds you had taken of the patient's mouth, I imagine?"

"Naturally, though, if the moulds had been broken or mislaid, it would have been possible to do the work, using the patient's mouth as a model. It would have been a slower and more troublesome business, though. Fortunately, in this case, the plaster mould had been taken recently and was reliable. Plaster shrinks, you know, after a time."

"Any dentist, having the moulds, would have used them?"

"Undoubtedly."

"How was the damage done, do you suppose? Could it have happened when she was wearing the teeth?"

"Impossible. My own theory is that she either used too much pressure in cleaning them, which is unlikely, as the force used would have to be considerable, or she dropped them and stepped on them. She assured me that she had done neither of these things, but, as you know, she was an excitable woman and not very exact in her statements."

"If she kept them in a drawer and had caught them in it in shutting it, would the effect have been the same?" enquired Constantine guilelessly.

Davenport swallowed the red herring whole.

"That explanation hadn't occurred to me, but it would account for it admirably. Have you any reason to think it happened in that way?" he enquired with interest.

"It's not impossible," Constantine assured him, then thanked him and rang off.

His next act was to ring for Manners, to whom he gave the note he had doctored in Arkwright's room at Scotland Yard, together with certain instructions which sent that imperturbable person forth, dignified calm personified, but with adventure in his heart. After he had gone, his master settled himself by the fire, filled his pipe and, with curiously mixed feelings, gave his mind to the progress he had made during the last twenty-four hours.

The laws of coincidence are admittedly amazing, but Constantine refused to believe that the injury to Mrs. Miller's denture, an injury that would oblige the dentist to leave her alone in the consulting room while he supervised his mechanic's work, was due to an accident. Assuming that the damage was done intentionally, it placed the murderer definitely as a member of Miller's household, someone who was conversant with Mrs. Miller's habits and who had easy access to the bathroom in which she kept the teeth at night. This knowledge must also have extended to Davenport's house and it seemed safe to argue that the murderer was or had been, at one time, a patient of Davenport's. Whether he had made use of the empty house next door as a means of escape was still open to question, but it seemed significant, to say the least of it that this house should turn out to be the property of Mrs. Marks, whose affairs were in Miller's hands. The property had been bought as an investment and there seemed little doubt that the purchase had been made by Miller on her behalf. Constantine had a shrewd suspicion that the keys of that house were probably in the possession of her trustee at the moment. And, finally, Vera Abramoff was on her way to Miller's house when she died. Miller, it would seem, was the centre to which every path in that bewildering maze led, and yet Miller had been on the other side of London at the time of his wife's death and at work in his library when Vera Abramoff was killed. There had been little love lost between him and his wife, it was true, but Arkwright, in the course of his investigations, had been unable to trace any entanglement with any other woman. Miller was too rich a man to be seriously embarrassed by Mrs. Miller's expenditure, which, after all, owing to her penchant for precious stones, would, in the jeweller's eyes, savour more of investment than extravagance. On the face of it he stood to gain little by his wife's death and still less by that of an obscure Russian actress, whom, according to his own account, he had never even set eyes on. There remained, it is true, those lost years between Miller's departure from the Cape and his appearance in England, spent, so he had declared, in Switzerland, that hot-bed of secret agents during the war. It was certainly suggestive that he should have disappeared from Cape Town in nineteen fourteen, shortly before the outbreak of hostilities, and not unlikely that he had run across Vera Abramoff in Switzerland, in which case the motive for the murder might date from something that had passed between them there. But, even if this were true, it was difficult to fit Mrs. Miller into the picture, for she had been pursuing her rather dubious stage career in the Provinces during this period and was unlikely to have met her husband, whom she married in nineteen twenty-seven, until his appearance in England in nineteen twenty-six.

Constantine knocked the ash out of his pipe and rose to his feet, irritably aware that this was getting him nowhere. The knowledge that Arkwright, with his dogged persistence, and the immense resources of New Scotland Yard at his call, was working against him, oppressed him with the sense of his own futility. He had purposely exaggerated the seriousness of the position in his interview with Richard Pomfrey and he knew that, as matters stood, Arkwright would hardly dare to risk an arrest, but circumstantial evidence is a dangerous thing and, at any moment, the police might unearth some fact that would enable them to move.

Constantine's restless walk had brought him to the writing table, a massive Buhl affair out of keeping with the room, but which he had retained for old associations' sake. He unlocked a drawer and took out the notebook in which he had jotted down the salient facts connected with the case. That it opened of its own accord at the page that dealt with Miller's alibis was silent testimony to the amount of time he had wasted on them. Sitting down he bent over the book and ran, once more, through the evidence collected by the police and, later, amplified by Manners in the course of his investigations. Unless the whole of Miller's office staff was lying, he had, undoubtedly, been in his office at the time of his wife's death. With an exasperated shrug of his shoulders Constantine passed on to the evening of November the fourteenth. According to the police estimate, the murder of Vera Abramoff had taken place sometime between seven thirty and eight. At seven twenty-five the footman, going to the library to make up the fire, had found Miller writing at his table, and the butler had stated that he was still at work there when he went in at seven forty-five to enquire about the wine for dinner. He had been seen by the butler again at eight, coming from the secretary's room. Bloomfield, who had been working in his room had stated that he had taken letters into the library for Miller's signature several times in the course of the evening and on each occasion had found him there. It was physically impossible for Miller to have been in Eccleston Square at the time of the second murder.

Constantine leaned back in his chair, his hands clasped behind his head, and stared at the ceiling, and, as his eyes mechanically took note of certain dusty patches on the cornice, and one side of his brain registered the determination to have the room done up in the spring, the other side, still groping uncertainly among the dark issues of the Miller problem, was illumined by a sudden ray of light.

With an exclamation he straightened himself and, snatching up the notebook gave his mind once more to the time schedule of the night of the Abramoff murder. From there he turned back to the morning of the same day. Then, thrusting the book into the drawer, he rose and, with a new lightness in his step, hurried from the room, shrugged himself into his overcoat and, seizing his hat, ran down the stairs with a briskness that belied his years. He went on foot to his destination, for he needed time to sort his thoughts. Someone, if his theory were correct, had gone from Miller's house to Illbeck Street on the morning of Mrs. Miller's murder and had covered the distance in the quickest possible time. Arkwright, he knew, had circularised the cab ranks, but had been unable to trace any fare to Illbeck Street that could not be satisfactorily accounted for. Miller's car, after taking him to his office, had returned to the house, and the chauffeur had waited in the basement, in conversation with the servants, until it was time to drive his mistress to the dentist's, and had had his eye on the car practically all the time. It was while he was waiting for a break in the traffic at Piccadilly that Constantine had his inspiration.

As a result, the decrepit old Army pensioner, whose duty it was to keep an eye on the cars parked at the north end of the square onto which Miller's house looked, hobbling painfully back to the upturned box on which he was accustomed to rest his aged limbs, found an alert elderly gentleman with a little pointed white beard waiting for him.

"You haven't seen my man, I suppose?" he asked, with a singularly charming smile. "He was to wait for me here. Wearing a dark green livery and driving a Humber."

The old man shook his head.

"There ain't been no one of that description," he said, "I'd a noticed 'im all right."

The gentleman shrugged his shoulders.

"I'm before my time, I think," he remarked. "There's nothing for it but to wait."

He drew out a cigarette case and offered it to his companion.

"Not a very exciting job, yours," he went on, "unless someone takes it into his head to borrow a car. Have you had any trouble with car thieves?"

The old fellow squared his shoulders.

"They wouldn't have much chance 'ere," he declared "I've got my eye on the cars, I 'ave, and there's a policeman on point duty at the corner there. I'd only 'ave to blow me whistle, and they know it. Never 'ad a car stolen yet, which is more than some can say."

The gentleman looked thoughtfully across the Square. From where he stood the upper windows of Miller's house could be seen through a gap in the trees.

"It's all right on a day like this," he remarked, "but in foggy weather it must be difficult to keep an eye on a whole string of cars. It's a good deal to expect of one man."

The gentleman had a way with him and no mistake. Later, as he stumped off duty, the old man wondered at the unaccustomed looseness of his own tongue. There had been no call to tell a stranger how he'd got the push from that night watchman's job through him going to sleep and omitting to punch the clock, nor yet about Captain Walker and the fuss he'd made because he declared someone had used his car while he was calling on his mother at number twenty-seven. Said he knew by the speedometer. Probably made a mistake in the mileage though. Anyway, as he'd told him, he was only human and, with a fog like there was that morning, he couldn't be expected to keep an eye on a car right at the end of the line. But there hadn't been no sense in telling the gentleman about it. Silly to give himself away like that, just because anyone smiled pleasant and seemed to enjoy a bit of a chat. Couldn't remember when he'd done such a thing before. Captain Walker wouldn't make no fuss, he was a good sort, he was, but this gentleman, a stranger and all! Might as like as not cost him his job. Mumbling and grumbling the old man turned in at his favourite pub, to derive what comfort he could from the new ten shilling note that was burning his pocket.

Meanwhile, had he known it, the ten shilling note was doing double duty, for the gentleman who had beguiled him into indiscretion had been enjoying his money's worth in his own way. Five minutes in the nearest post office, with the help of the London and Telephone Directories, had given him the number of Captain Walker's mother, another five minutes in the telephone booth, with her butler at the other end had supplied him with Captain Walker's address and, less than half an hour later, he was interviewing that gentleman in his rooms in Duke Street. Captain Walker had heard of Constantine though he had never met him, and, when his visitor, with the most charming courtesy begged for details as to the suspected use of his car on a certain foggy morning, he was quite ready to oblige him.

"Though what he was after, I don't know," he said afterwards. "Said he'd got a pal at Scotland Yard and that this might have some bearing on a case he was interested in. My old Uncle Bill, who painted the town red with him in the year dot, told me he'd taken to that sort of thing in his old age. Anyway, he wasn't giving anything away and he looked as deep as they make 'em."

Captain Walker's story amounted to this. On the morning of November the fourteenth, he had called on his mother, leaving his car under the care of old Higgs, who, incidentally, was a protege of his mother's and a very decent, conscientious old chap. He was engaged with his mother from, roughly, eleven o'clock till twelve forty-five, when he came out of the house and collected his car. When he got into it the first thing that struck him was that his gloves and newspaper which he'd left on the driver's seat had gone. He found them on the floor in the body of the car. Being certain that he had not put them there himself he had a look at the speedometer and found that, whereas it had registered just under twenty-six miles when he left it, it now stood at over twenty-eight. He could speak positively as to this as he had been testing the speedometer the day before and was keeping a careful account of the mileage registered. He had spoken to Higgs about it, but, as no damage was done to the car, he had let him off lightly.

"What with the fog and the old chap's game leg, one couldn't exactly blame him, but I'll stake my oath that someone had been joy riding," he finished. "This won't let Higgs in for anything, will it?"

Constantine reassured him on this point and departed. When he got home Manners was waiting for him. His magisterial calm seemed unruffled, but it was a significant fact that he plunged into his recital before even helping his master off with his coat.

"It worked all right, sir," he announced, his diction slightly more hurried than usual. "I called round at Mr. Miller's to say that I'd got the evening off and to ask how early Roper could meet me. When we'd fixed it up I asked him if he could change a note as I wanted some coppers for my fare home. He spotted the note as soon as I took it out. Said that if that was the one he thought it was it would be a funny coincidence it's getting back to him so soon. He'd had one loose in his pocket and the billiard chalk had come off on it and marked it just like that. Of course he wanted to know where I'd got it and I told him, at a tobacconist's in Piccadilly. Then we started to work out how it could have got from him to me and, by the time we'd finished, I had the whole story, without having to ask a single question."

Manners, his bowler hat pressed to his middle, leaned forward impressively.

"If that stained note they've got at the Yard is the one Roper's been talking about, it was handed by him to Mr. Miller on the morning of Mrs. Miller's murder. I'm sure there's no mistake there."

Constantine's hand fell on Manners' shoulder.

"Manners, you're a marvel!" he exclaimed. "Have you got any details?"

"All that are necessary, I think, sir," answered Manners, blushing faintly with gratification. "Mr. Miller was in the habit of going to Roper when he was short of ready cash and Roper informs me that he made a point of keeping a certain sum in hand for the purpose. Shortly after breakfast on the morning of the murder Mr. Miller rang for him and told him he wanted five pounds. Roper fetched the money, which included the stained note he had been carrying in his pocket. He saw Mr. Miller put the notes on the writing table in the library and place a paper weight on them. What he did with them after that he cannot say."

Constantine's eyes narrowed.

"Put them on the table, did he?" he exclaimed. "You're sure he didn't stow them in a note case, or whatever it is he carries? Or simply put them in his pocket?"

"Roper was quite definite about it, sir. The last he saw of them they were under the weight on the table."

His eyes fell on Constantine's overcoat and, with a shock, he came back to a realisation of his duties.

"Excuse me, sir," he murmured, as he helped him off with it, then, with it hanging, neatly folded, on his arm, he reverted to his role of amateur detective. "As regards the identity of the note, sir, I think we can settle that to your satisfaction. Roper tells me that he got it in settlement from a bookmaker two days before. He mentioned the name in passing and I made a note of it. He says it was one of a batch and that he noticed they were all new notes. If the bookmaker got them from his bank it may be possible to trace the numbers."

Constantine nodded.

"It's worth trying, anyway," he said. "Your job or mine, Manners?"

Manners coughed.

"If you'll excuse me, yours, I think, sir," he submitted. "An enquiry from you would, er, carry more weight."

Constantine glanced at the clock.

"Lunch time," he said. "We shan't catch him now."

Before turning to go to his room, he faced Manners squarely, his hands in his pockets, a whimsical smile on his face. He looked as if a load had fallen from his shoulders.

"We're going to win this trick, Manners," he said softly.

The prim line of Manners' lips relaxed. For a moment he resembled a cat that has been licking cream.

"I was beginning to form that opinion myself, sir," he murmured deferentially.

In his interview with the bookmaker Constantine made shameless use of Sir Richard Pomfrey's name, but he did not mention Roper. According to his story, Sir Richard was anxious to trace certain notes that, he believed, had been paid out by the bookmaker on November the twelfth. As he had foreseen, Sir Richard's name proved an Open Sesame in that quarter and when he went on to drop a discreet hint that the enquiry dealt with a leakage of stable information, the bookmaker was only too anxious to convince him that, if one of his clients had been lucky enough to pitch on a vulnerable stable boy, he, at least, had had no hand in the business. He professed himself as entirely at Sir Richard's disposal, but, unfortunately, was not in a position to help as, very naturally, he kept no record of notes for small denominations that passed through his hands. He was ready enough to give the name of his bank and agreed that, if the notes were part of a new issue, the series might be traceable through his bankers.

This being a task the police were better able to deal with than himself, Constantine rang up Arkwright on his return to his flat. He gave him the name of the bank and the data supplied by the bookmaker and asked him to put the enquiry through as early as possible next day.

Arkwright, fresh from a protracted and unsatisfactory conference with his superiors, was not in the best of tempers. Superintendent Thurston had, as usual, spoken little but to the point and Arkwright had had to endure in silence a reprimand which should, by rights, have fallen to one of his subordinates. Only his genuine regard for the old man prevented him from flatly turning down his request.

"It would be easier if we weren't working in the dark," he grumbled. "I'll do what I can, but banks are jealous of their privileges and we have to move carefully. Couldn't you be a little more explicit, sir?"

Constantine ignored the plea. He realised, with some amusement, that Arkwright had not recognised the serial number he had given him and had failed to identify the note with the one he had got from the garage proprietor.

"Can you lay your hands on Greeve?" he demanded.

Arkwright with difficulty resisted the temptation to jam the receiver back onto its hook.

"We can pull him in again, of course," he answered shortly, "but we must have some excuse to do it."

"Get him to Scotland Yard tomorrow afternoon and I'll provide the excuse and what's more, I'll undertake to make him talk," declared Constantine, ringing off before Arkwright could question him further.

CHAPTER SIXTEEN

MONSIEUR KARAMIEV had risen late according to his custom and was sitting over his coffee when Constantine was shown in by the waiter. The fat little Russian prided himself on never forgetting a face and this friend of the English Inspector's not only possessed personality, but a name as easy to pronounce as it was to remember.

He sprang to his feet with outstretched hands.

"'Ow do you do, Monsieur Constantine," he chanted. "I am enchanted that we meet again under happier circumstances. There is something I can do for you, yes?"

Constantine endured an elaborate process of hand squeezing and shoulder patting with an equanimity Arkwright Would never have achieved.

"I am ashamed to trouble you again," he said, "but I have been trying in vain to get some light on Madame Abramoff's past life. I know you did all in your power to help the police, but I am wondering whether, perhaps, in the interval, something further might have occurred to you? Memory is a tricky business. A chance word spoken by one of your company might remind you of something else said by Madame Abramoff herself in the past. You know how these things happen."

The Russian nodded vigorously.

"Yes, indeed, it has come to all of us, myself included. But, alas, as regards poor Madame, there was no memory to awaken. She never spoke much of her affairs. All that was in my poor head I emptied out before your friend, the Inspector. As regards my artistes ..."

He paused, his eyes closed in reflection. Then, opening them suddenly, he dug Constantine hard in the chest with a plump, white finger.

"It is an idea!" he announced. "Madame Varsov, who recommended this poor Vera to my notice, is with us now. Only yesterday she joined us from Paris. As was natural, we discussed this tragedy at our meeting last night. There is nothing she has said to me that I did not know already, but she is the only one of us that knew Vera Abramoff before she joined our company. You would care to see her, yes?"

"If she would be so kind as to spare me a moment I should be deeply grateful," declared Constantine elaborately.

Karamiev departed, with bows and apologies, and returned a few minutes later with a big, handsome woman in the early forties, whose magnificent dark eyes were alive with intelligent interest.

"Madame Varsov knows well English, but she lacks confidence," explained Karamiev. "If Monsieur le Docteur would speak French?"

"But certainly," agreed Constantine, who claimed the gift of tongues as his birthright. "Monsieur has perhaps explained to Madame why I am here?"

Madame bowed.

"I am afraid there is very little I can tell you," she said, in the deep, veiled voice that is the happy possession of some singers. "The poor Vera never dwelt on her past. She would speak sometimes of her life in England, but, like we others, there were certain things she wanted only to forget. When I first met her she was absolutely destitute and too ill, as the result of suffering and want of food, to work."

"And Madame, of her goodness, no doubt took pity on her," interpolated Constantine quickly.

"I did my best," she answered simply. "It was not easy. Times were hard for all of us then. When she was better I was able to find her work as dresser to an actress of my acquaintance. She had held such a post before with a ballet dancer in the early days of the revolution, so it was not difficult. Then later, I introduced her to Monsieur Karamiev and she has been with him ever since."

"This dancer she worked for. Could you tell me her name?" asked Constantine, grasping at any straw connected with the murdered woman's past.

Madame Varsov's good-humoured face hardened.

"She called herself Ivanovna, Monsieur. She was one of the many figures of the Revolution, and though she worked always behind the scenes, she was powerful. Vera said little of her life while she was in her service, but sometimes she let drop a word that gave me, who have lived through that time, some hint of her suffering."

"Do you know if Madame Abramoff was in Switzerland at any time?" asked Constantine.

"I doubt it, Monsieur, though I can say nothing for certain. She told me that she left the stage here, in England, when she married, and went at once to Russia with her husband. I know that they lived for a time in Riga, where he held an important post, before they moved to Petrograd. After the revolution she was unable to leave Russia."

"She could not have been in Switzerland during the first years of the war, you think?"

"I should consider it most unlikely. She spoke of nursing in a military hospital in Riga and afterwards in Petrograd, before her husband was killed. I have the impression that she was in Russia all through the war."

"Did she ever speak of a man named Miller?"

"This man whose wife she was going to stay with in London? No, Monsieur. But of this I am quite sure. She did not know this man. Mrs. Miller she had known well long ago when they had acted together, but that was before Mrs. Miller's marriage. More than once she told me she was curious to see her friend's husband. I understood from her that Mrs. Miller had been a little difficult in the past and she had her doubts about the success of such a *ménage.*"

"Do you know at all when she first renewed her acquaintance with Mrs. Miller?"

"About six weeks ago, I believe. We were playing in Paris then, and Mrs. Miller, it would seem, saw her name in some theatrical journal. Vera had altered her English Christian name of Cora to one more suitable to her Russian surname, and Mrs. Miller wrote to her at the company's agent's address, thinking she was perhaps some relation of the Abramoff who had married her friend, asking for news of her. In that way their correspondence began."

Constantine thanked her and took his leave. In the hall of the hotel Karamiev, who had discreetly effaced himself during the interview, joined him. He held an envelope in his hand.

"Will Monsieur, perhaps, be seeing his friend the Inspector?" he asked. "These letters have arrived for Madame Abramoff, forwarded from Paris. I am at a loss to know what to do with them."

"I shall be going to Scotland Yard this afternoon," answered Constantine, "and will give them to Inspector Arkwright myself. As none of her relatives have put in an appearance the police had better take charge of them."

He put the letters in his pocket and, with some ceremony, the two men parted. On his return to his flat Constantine found a note from Arkwright awaiting him.

"You were right," he wrote, "though I do not see how you arrived at it. The serial number you gave me corresponds with that of a batch of new notes issued to the bank on November the eleventh. They were all paid out in the course of the next two days and your man undoubtedly cashed a cheque on November the twelfth. That is as much as the manager can say, but it sounds good enough. My head was full of other things when you telephoned or I should have recognised the number you gave me. I'm sorry, sir, but you'll have to put your cards on the table now. We hold that note and any information you may have about it belongs to us. What about it? Greeve has been instructed to report here at three this afternoon. Shall I expect you?"

Constantine's eyes twinkled as he read the letter. Arkwright's patience was giving out at last and he did not blame him. After a hasty lunch at the Club he drove to Scotland Yard, arriving there a good hour before he was expected. Arkwright raised a harassed face from his papers to greet him.

"Look here, sir," he began at once, "about that note. I know you've got your own way of doing things and I'm not saying it isn't successful, but I'm afraid I'll have to ask you to come forward now. I've got my report to consider."

Constantine nodded.

"I can appreciate your feelings," he admitted, "and I'm here to make amends. All I ask is that we deal with Greeve first."

He took a sheet of paper from his pocket and handed it to Arkwright.

"I want you to tackle him on these lines," he said. "If I'm right, I believe he'll talk. It's a gamble, I admit. As you'll hear later, I've unearthed some very curious facts and I've managed to string them into some kind of order. If Greeve fails us, I will hand them over to you and you must deal with them as best you can."

Arkwright, who had been running his eye over the list of suggestions he had given him, looked up quickly.

"I say, sir," he exclaimed, "have you any foundation for these? If the thing comes off, all well and good, but if Greeve calls our bluff, where are we?"

"No worse off than we were before," retorted Constantine. "Do you honestly believe that Greeve wasn't blackmailing Miller?"

"I'm morally certain that he was," answered Arkwright, "but I can't act on that alone. Can you give me nothing more to go on?"

Constantine eyed him with amusement.

"Nothing that you wouldn't throw back in my face," he said frankly. "Are you going to try it?"

Arkwright nodded. He looked anything but happy.

"I've sent for the man so we may as well go through with it, but I'm not too hopeful. Will you wait, sir?"

"No, I've got one more bit of business to do before you tackle Greeve. Will you give me a letter to your Alien's Department? The Special Branch, isn't it?"

Arkwright scribbled a note and handed it to him.

"If it's Miller you're interested in I've been over that ground already," he said. "They've no information whatever, I've even tried the War Office, but, if our suspicions as to the way he spent those lost twelve years are correct his activities would seem to have escaped the eye of the authorities there."

"I think I know where those mysterious twelve years were spent," replied Constantine. "When I see you again I shall be certain. The whole of my house of cards, which, I may tell you, is singularly full of loopholes, stands or falls by what happens this afternoon."

With that he was gone, leaving a very worried and doubtful police official behind him.

When Greeve arrived Arkwright left him to cool his heels until Constantine rejoined him. The man had been very sure of himself at their last interview and he must have known when he was so abruptly released that things had turned out precisely as he expected. If this abrupt summons had shaken his confidence, the longer he was left to his own reflections in the rather grim environment of the Yard the better.

When Constantine returned he bore under his arm a folder, the nature of which Arkwright recognised at a glance.

He raised his eyebrows.

"Good hunting?" he queried.

Constantine sank into a chair, deposited his burden on the table and placed his elbow on it.

"If the afternoon ends as well as it has begun, the answer is in the affirmative," he announced complacently. "Got your man?"

"He's been awaiting your arrival," answered Arkwright, with an amused glance at the folder. This was Constantine at his best and, unless he was woefully mistaken, Constantine successful and about to lay his winning card on the table with that dramatic gesture he never could resist. The elation in the old man's eyes was infectious and Arkwright, in spite of himself, found himself joining in the game. The official mantle was slipping from his shoulders as it had slipped before when, sitting over the fire in Constantine's flat, he had discussed his work with him, occasionally very much to his own profit. To the old chess player, the unmasking of delinquents was a game and he played it with a zest that took his companion back to the days when he had been in love with his job and still an undisillusioned enthusiast. To Arkwright, who knew his own limitations, Constantine's elastic, but always logical brain, backed by his immense experience of both men and things, was such a source of envy and admiration that even now, with the menacing shadow of the Commissioner lurking at his elbow, he was prepared to humour the old man and let him go about the business in his own way.

He ran his eye hastily once more over the suggestions he had given him and sent for Greeve.

The man's demeanour was as cool and detached as it had been at their former interview, but Arkwright caught the glance, half suspicious, half defiant, that he shot at Constantine and knew that the suspense and uncertainty had born fruit.

"Sit down," he said, his voice ominously terse. "You've been calling yourself Parker. That your real name?"

"No."

The man's voice was lifeless and constrained.

"You were known in Cape Town as Ernest Greeve?"

"Yes."

"You were convicted under that name for receiving stolen goods in nineteen fourteen. Any other convictions?"

"No."

"When did you first meet Mr. Miller?"

Greeves hesitated, his confidence obviously shaken, then, in view of the knowledge Arkwright appeared to possess, he wisely decided to tell the truth.

"In nineteen eight," he answered sullenly.

"Was that the date at which you entered his service?"

"Yes."

"After you were arrested in nineteen fourteen did you see him again?"

"At the trial, yes."

"After that did you meet him again?"

"Yes."

"When?"

It was here that Arkwright received his first surprise.

"Two days ago, in this room."

"Mr. Miller gave us to understand that you called on him some time ago."

"I called on him, but he was out. I saw his secretary."

"Did you never see Mr. Miller?"

"No."

"What was your business with Mr. Miller?"

"I offered him a piece of jewellery that I thought might interest him."

"Had you any reason to believe that, after what had happened in Cape Town, Mr. Miller would wish to deal with you?"

"He did deal with me. That speaks for itself, doesn't it?"

Arkwright ignored the insolence of his tone.

"Can you describe this piece of jewellery?"

"A gold and enamel pendant representing Apollo and set with precious stones."

"Can you name the stones?"

"Diamonds, emeralds, rubies and pearls."

"Could you draw the pendant?"

"I could make a rough sketch, yes."

"Have you seen Mr. Miller since you were confronted with him in this room?"

"No."

"Or his secretary?"

"No."

The answer came almost too quickly. Arkwright's eyes dropped for a second to the paper in front of him, then he leaned forward impressively.

"When I tell you that we know that Mr. Bloomfield saw you yesterday, do you still persist in that statement?"

For a second blank surprise showed in Greeve's eyes. Arkwright could read his mind. A moment ago he had not known how he stood with the police, now he found himself in the same dilemma as regards Bloomfield.

"Mr. Bloomfield couldn't have said that," he temporised, at last.

"Told you to hold your tongue about it, did he, and then gave you away?" retorted Arkwright contemptuously. "When he showed you that pendant you've just described so accurately, he didn't mention that he was coming to the Yard this morning, I suppose?"

Greeve's face flamed suddenly. If he had been doubtful of how he stood with Bloomfield, he knew now.

"I can't help what Mr. Bloomfield may have told you," he began, obviously feeling his way as he went. "Once I'd delivered the pendant, my job was finished."

"Suppose we drop the pendant," snapped Arkwright. "It's served its purpose and, by this time, Mr. Miller has no doubt put it back where it came from. We'll have the true story of your dealings with Miller for a change and it may help your memory if I tell you that I'm in a position to check every word you say."

"If Bloomfield ..." mumbled Greeve, obviously in desperation.

Arkwright cut him short.

"It's your story, not Bloomfield's, I'm concerned with. We've sufficient evidence to charge you with blackmailing Mr. Miller, so spinning the tale won't help you."

He paused, let his eyes rest for a moment on Constantine's inscrutable face, then, with an inward prayer that the old man was not mistaken, played his trump card.

"What interests us," he went on slowly, "is how you came by the knowledge you have been holding over Mr. Miller. If you can account for your movements on the night of November the fourteenth I should advise you to do so."

There was the crash of an overturned chair. Greeve was on his feet, his face working convulsively.

"So that's his game!" he cried. "The swine! The filthy swine! He sends his dirty little toady of a secretary to do his dirty work for him and then ..."

The realisation of his danger came home to him and he mastered himself with an effort that left him white and shaking.

"I wasn't anywhere near Eccleston Square that night," he gasped, leaning over the table, his stricken face within an inch of Arkwright's. "I can prove it. I found the car where he'd left it near Grosvenor Place. I came on it by accident. Ask the barmaid in that pub opposite the station. I don't know its name, but she'll remember. She must remember. I was carrying a bag and we talked about South Africa. She told me she'd got a brother out there. Tell her that. She won't have forgotten. I asked her the way to Soho and she chipped me because I didn't know the London streets. I was there for all of half an hour and we were talking, on and off, all the time."

His earnestness carried conviction. Arkwright pointed to the fallen chair.

"Sit down," he said. "I'll take your statement and when we've got onto your barmaid friend we'll see what she's got to say. What brought you into the affair?"

"Miller," answered Greeve simply. "He shopped me in Cape Town. He was the principal in that receiving business, had been at it for years, long before I joined him. I wish to God I'd never seen him. He'd covered himself so cleverly that I couldn't prove a thing, but I swore I'd get even with him, if it took me a lifetime. After I was discharged I tried to find him, but he'd left

Cape Town. If it hadn't been for that Russian woman that was murdered, I'd never have got on his track again."

"Where did you come across her?" demanded Arkwright.

"In the boat train from Dover. She was in my carriage with a crowd of foreigners, Russians, I suppose. Anyway they were talking French and I was sitting listening to their conversation when I heard Miller's name. There are plenty of Millers knocking about the world, and even then I didn't tumble to him till she said he was a jeweller. Then I began to wonder. I'd lived in Paris when I was a boy so the language was no difficulty, and when I heard her say that she was going to stay with Mrs. Isaac Miller and was being met at Victoria I made up my mind to hang around on the chance of the husband being my man."

"Did Miller meet her?"

"I don't know. I lost her in the crowd going through the Customs and, though I kept a sharp look-out, I didn't spot her again till I was outside the station and she drove past me in a car. I couldn't see who was with her, but I got the number of the car and made up my mind to try and trace it later, just on the chance that it was old Miller she was staying with. I hadn't any special plans, just meant to bide my time on the chance of getting my own back. Then I dropped into the pub, as I said. I was there over half an hour, I should think, and it must have been while I was in there that he did it."

"How do you know that?" rapped out Arkwright.

Greeve's eyes met his, triumphant and utterly relentless.

"Because there was blood in the car when I found it. I got my hand smeared with it when I took the bag."

"Where was that?"

"In a mews near Grosvenor Place. I don't know the name of it, but I took a short cut down it on my way from Victoria. A chap in Paris had given me an address in Soho if I wanted a cheap hotel and, when I left the pub, I started to walk there. The barmaid had given me so many directions that I got muddled and didn't discover I was on the wrong track till I got to Hyde Park Corner. When I was some way down the mews I recognised the car. I saw the number first and glanced into it as I went past to see if I could spot Miller. When I realised it was empty I had a look inside and there was a lady's bag lying on the seat. There was nobody about and, on a sudden impulse, I put my hand in and took it. It wasn't money I was after. I got an idea that I could return the bag later. Say I'd found it lying somewhere and have a look at the people the woman was staying with. Also, there was a chance there might be a letter or something in it that would give me a line on Miller. It was a rotten silly thing to do and I knew it when I caught sight of my own hand a moment later in the light of gas lamp and discovered that not only had there been blood on the cushions of the car but that there were smears that were still wet on the bag I was holding. Even then the idea of murder never occurred to me. I merely thought there'd been an accident of some kind and that was why Miller had abandoned the car. At Hyde Park Corner I bought an evening paper and wrapped the bag in it, then I went over to the Public Lavatory and washed my hands. Next day I saw the account of the murder in the paper. The description of the woman and the time at which she'd been found seemed to fit in, so I went to the mortuary."

He paused, his eyes grim and hard.

"Then I knew I'd got Miller where I wanted him," he finished slowly.

"Why didn't you report to the police?" demanded Arkwright. "According to your account you were out to get even with Miller and you'd got the means in your hands."

Greeve's haggard face flushed a dull red and Constantine, watching him, realised that the man had reason enough to hate Miller. Probably before he entered the jeweller's service he had been honest and self-respecting. Even now he had the grace to be ashamed.

"I suppose the money tempted me," he confessed, meeting Arkwright's eyes frankly, "but it wasn't only that. Miller loves money better than his life and I wanted to bleed him white and see his face while I did it. And I wanted to make certain that he got what was coming to him. What sort of story had I got to take to the police? I hadn't even seen the man in the car, though I was morally certain it was Miller. Time enough to go to the police later. My object was to make him pay for what he'd done to me and, if he was guilty, I could do that off my own bat."

"Added to which you'd got a theft on your conscience," put in Arkwright drily. "What have you done with the bag?"

"I made a parcel of it and deposited it in the cloakroom at Leicester Square Tube Station," said Greeves sullenly.

"And the cloak-room ticket?"

"Can I take off my collar?"

For a moment Arkwright thought the man was ill, then he understood. With a grim smile he watched him remove his collar and tie.

"You were taking no risks," he remarked, as Greeve slipped the ticket from inside the fold of his collar and handed it to him.

"It meant a lot to me," was all he said. Now that his first consternation was over he seemed to have relapsed into a mood of dull resentment.

"When did you approach Miller?" asked Arkwright.

"The evening of the day after the murder. I slipped the letter into his letter box myself."

"How did you know his address?"

"It was in a letter from his wife that was in the bag. It's there now, tucked away in a pocket behind the mirror, where I found it."

"Have you taken anything out of the bag?"

"Nothing," answered Greeve apathetically. "Not even the money. You'll find it all there. I didn't count it, but it's all in French notes and cash. There was no English money."

"What passed between you and Miller?"

"He answered my letter ..."

"Where to?" interrupted Arkwright.

"The Soho address. I'd given it when I wrote to him. I knew that, if I was right, he wouldn't dare go to the police. In his first letter he simply wrote asking me to go and see him."

"Did you go?"

"I called at the time he said, but I only saw the secretary. By then I'd had time to think things over and I'd begun to get cold feet. Though I knew Miller was a skunk, I'd never thought of him as a killer, but now I began to see myself going the way of the Russian woman. I'd no friends in England and no one would miss me. The secretary told me that Miller was out, but he had orders to settle with me. He asked me to go in but I wouldn't. I said what I'd got to say on the doorstep. Then I left."

"You made demands, I suppose. What were they?"

"I asked for a thousand down, in notes. I don't know how much the secretary knew. The woman was never mentioned between us and we might have been discussing any business deal. Even Miller wasn't aware of how I'd got my information. In my letter I'd simply stated that I knew who killed the woman and held the proofs in my possession. I fancy the secretary believed that I'd unearthed something that had happened in South Africa. Anyway, he said he'd report to his master."

"What happened next?"

Greeve's lips twitched.

"I did a bunk. I went back to the room in Soho, in case the fellow was following me. Later I slipped out and moved over to Battersea. Next day I wrote again, saying I would send a messenger for the answer. I posted that letter in Soho. And the following day I got Hoover to go up there. He brought a letter from Miller trying to beat me down. The next day I sent another letter by Hoover, saying I'd take eight hundred and arranging for him to call for it the following day. I was ready to let him off easy the first time. I hadn't finished with him by a long way. When Hoover called for the money, you took him. If I'd known Miller was going to try to turn the tables on me like this I'd have been across the Channel by now. As it was, I was beginning to realise I was carrying my life in my hands. If he'd got my address out of Hoover I'd have been for it."

Arkwright eyed him dispassionately.

"You're not out of the wood yet," he said coldly. "If you can prove you were in that bar on the night of the fourteenth all well and good. Meantime, you're held pending enquiries. Have you got those letters of Miller's?"

Greeve shook his head.

"I burnt them. They were no good to me. The wily devil had typed them. There wasn't even a signature. They'd have done me more harm than good if they'd been found."

Arkwright rang the bell and had him removed. He watched the door close behind him, then, with a sigh of relief, turned to Constantine.

"Well, I'm jiggered!" he ejaculated. "It worked like a dream. Congratulate you, sir. The question is, where are we now?"

"Rather in the position of the man who fished for a whale and caught a minnow," suggested Constantine sardonically.

Arkwright nodded.

"We've got Greeve for blackmail on his own confession, but, unless there's something pretty conclusive in that bag he stole, we're very much where we were before. His word against Miller's won't go far and Miller's alibi still holds. And Greeve never even saw him. So long as Miller and that secretary of his hang together and keep their mouths shut, we can't move."

He thrust back his chair and sat staring at the table. Then, with a frown, he straightened himself.

"Better have a look at that bag, anyway," he grunted.

Constantine waited while he arranged to have the bag fetched from the Tube cloak-room. When the messenger had left the room he picked up the folder he had got from the Special Branch.

"What about my little exhibit?" he asked mildly.

CHAPTER SEVENTEEN

ARKWRIGHT BENT forward and switched on the desk lamp, tilting it so that the light fell on the report Constantine had taken from the folder. It appeared to consist of a couple of typewritten pages, to the outer of which was attached an unmounted photograph.

"Not much to go on there, is there?" he observed disparagingly.

"What there is is to the point," answered Constantine, "though it only deals with the gentleman's activities in his own country. He was traced to Switzerland and your people were warned, both by the Swiss and Russian authorities, that he might try to land here. He's in trouble with his own government and would get short shrift if he were compelled to go home. Hence this little biography."

"Would it be indiscreet to ask what connection he has with this case?" enquired Arkwright, drily.

Constantine smiled.

"It would," he said, "at this juncture. Let me get my facts together in my own way. Did you follow up my suggestion as to the lettering on those two knives?"

Arkwright opened a drawer and produced a photograph.

"I did," he answered. "It didn't get us far. My knowledge of Greek is nil, but I gather that the letters, rough as they are, are easily decipherable. But the word is meaningless. Our man suggested that it might be Russian. This is what he made of it."

He pushed the photograph over to Constantine. It was a print of the inscriptions on the Chinese knives and underneath it was written the word *Malin* in Greek and English lettering.

"The chances seemed to point towards Malin being the name of the owner of the knives." he continued. "I'm beginning to see sense in all this. Is Malin the name at the head of your report?"

Constantine nodded.

"Peter Malin," he said. "We have both been misled by the fact that the knives were undoubtedly of Chinese origin, but I had less excuse, as I recognised, the first time I saw them, that the lettering might very well be a rough attempt at the Russian alphabet. What I ought to have remembered was the fact that Chinese executioners were imported by the Russians in the early days of the revolution. When it did occur to me I had no difficulty in fitting Vera Abramoff into the story."

He turned to the report.

"The Special Branch had the information we wanted all the time," he went on. "According to them, Peter Malin first came to the fore in nineteen nineteen, when he worked with the Chinese *Che-Ka* at Kiev. Later he became an executioner and has a long list of victims to his name. I think we may take it that the numerals written under his name on the knives represent the tally of the executions he performed. The clothes and jewels of his victims were his perquisites and he is believed to have lined his pockets well before leaving Russia. In nineteen twenty-one he was accused of stealing government property and seems to have got so badly into the black books of the authorities that he barely escaped from Russia with his life. Both our own agents and the Soviet Government marked him down as a dangerous man and, according to your own people he would be repatriated promptly if he were discovered in this country. And he wouldn't stand a dog's chance once he set foot in Russia. The Chinese had taught him how to use those knives and, with his record, he would not hesitate to adopt the easiest way to stop the mouth of anyone likely to inform against him."

"Presuming he were in England."

"He settled in England some time ago, built up a prosperous business and had every reason to consider himself secure. When one thinks of what discovery meant to him; the enforced return to his own country where, at best, he would have to face the confiscation of his money, at worst, a long term of imprisonment or, more likely, execution, it isn't difficult to see where the motive for the murder of Vera Abramoff lay."

Arkwright stared at him.

"You are referring to Miller, of course," he said. "We've no proof that there had ever been any earlier connection between him and Vera Abramoff."

"How about this?" retorted Constantine. "The report runs: 'Is believed to have gone to Switzerland on leaving Russia and to have passed there under the name of Miller. May be accompanied by a dancer named Ivanovna, with whom he was associated in Russia.' Now, according to a member of Karamiev's company, Madame Abramoff acted at one time as dresser to a dancer of the name of Ivanovna. It would hardly be stretching a point to assume that Vera Abramoff had seen Malin in Petrograd and would be in a position to recognise him. If he could have discovered any way of preventing her from coming to England she would no doubt be alive now."

"And Mrs. Miller? She'd never had any connection with Russia. Your motive doesn't hold good there."

"I admit I'm working in the dark as regards Mrs. Miller, but I suspect that her renewal of her old acquaintance with Vera Abramoff was the beginning of the end, as far as she was concerned. How Madame Abramoff came to suspect Malin's whereabouts, I don't know, but she probably communicated her suspicions to Mrs. Miller. There are a dozen ways in which Malin may have discovered what had passed between the two women. In a fit of temper Mrs. Miller may even have twitted him with her knowledge of his identity. From the moment she did that, her fate was sealed."

Arkwright frowned.

"Miller has been living openly in this country for five years," he said. "Our people were warned. They even knew of his change of name. Why didn't they get onto him when he first turned up here? There's been bad staff work somewhere."

Constantine's lips twitched. If Arkwright had not been absorbed in following his own train of thought he would have taken warning from the mischievous gleam in the old man's eyes.

"Don't be too hard on them," he said. "They had every excuse. Miller, according to his passport, was born in Riga in eighteen eighty-one. The date of Malin's birth is given as nineteen hundred and he is reported to have been working as an errand boy in Moscow at the time of Miller's trial in Cape Town. I understand that a certain amount of attention was paid to Miller when he first landed here, but it is a common enough name and it would not take long to convince them that he was not their man."

Arkwright's jaw dropped. He ran a frenzied hand through his hair and glared at Constantine.

"Then who, in the name of Heaven ..." he began.

Then, as the truth dawned on him, the words died on his lips.

"Bloomfield," he whispered. "Good Lord, I ought to have seen it. The egregiously efficient secretary! I knew he was too good a man for that job, but I put him down as marking time and picking his employer's brains in the process. How did he get his hold over Miller, do you suppose?"

"I fancy there's a relationship somewhere, but he may have simply terrorised the older man. In any case, I think we may take it that those lost years of Miller's were spent in Russia. There's no mention of him in the Malin report, but he hailed from Riga, remember, and the probability is that, after the Cape Town debacle, he went back to his own people. The mere fact that he came out of the revolution unscathed and fairly prosperous points to his having thrown in his lot with the Bolshevists, and Malin's adoption of the name 'Miller' suggests that there may have been some relationship between them. They would seem to have been in Switzerland at the same time and were probably together there. My own theory is that while they were there Malin discovered that the Soviet agents were on his heels and made his escape, changing his name to Bloomfield."

Arkwright nodded.

"Miller volunteered the information that he had brought Bloomfield with him from South Africa. By going from Switzerland to Cape Town he no doubt succeeded in covering his tracks. I'll get onto the Home Office and have a look at his passport. Not that that's anything to go by, nowadays. You're sure of your facts, I suppose, sir?"

Constantine unclipped the photograph from the report and threw it over to Arkwright.

"That proves his identity, I think," he said. "He wore a beard in those days, but the upper part of the face is unmistakable. As regards the two murders, there should be no difficulty in bringing Madame Abramoff's death home to him. The fact that he used a beard to disguise himself may prove his undoing. He was seen, not only by the garage proprietor and the porter, but by several members of Karamiev's company, who were naturally interested in Madame Abramoff's friend. I should suggest trying them first with the photograph. The difference in a photographic print between a grey beard and a black one is not so very great. The Miller murder is a more difficult problem, as it rests purely on circumstantial evidence."

"And we're still up against those alibis," Arkwright reminded him. "Bloomfield's just as well covered as Miller."

Constantine raised his eyebrows.

"Is he? I'll deal with those alibis in a moment. Meanwhile, I'd better give you the points against him as I made them. I started out on the assumption that the Miller murder, at any rate, was committed by some member of the Miller household. My object originally was to break Miller's alibi. I put Manners on the job and he failed, but, as you know, he succeeded in tracing the notes paid for the hire of the car, to Miller. I'd already discovered that the empty house next door to Davenport's was part of certain property bought by Miller on behalf of a Mrs. Marks and it seemed safe to conclude that he had access to it. Finding that Miller's alibi held good I turned my attention to the other members of his household and realised almost immediately that Bloomfield, when he took the dog into the Square on the morning of Mrs. Miller's murder, could, if he had passed straight through the Square and out at the opposite gate, have got to Illbeck Street, committed the murder and come back in time to pick up the dog and return to the house at the time he was seen by the butler."

Arkwright's eyes narrowed.

"Wait a minute," he exclaimed. "Bloomfield was actually seen in the Square by a child who played with the dog and also by the child's nurse."

"I'm not so sure. The butler's account to Manners was that the child and the nurse saw him cross the Square and that the child played with the dog for over half an hour. It was a foggy day, remember, and they naturally took it for granted, as they saw him both arrive and leave, that he was in the Square all the time. Manners has been trying to get in touch with that nurse and, knowing him, I have no doubt he'll succeed in the end. I've given him instructions to ring me up here if he manages to bring it off this afternoon, but I've no doubt as to what his report will be when it comes. My main difficulty has been to discover how Bloomfield managed to cover the ground between the Square and Illbeck Street in the time. No taxi has been traced and we know he did not use the Miller car. It wasn't till I turned my attention to the car parked on the opposite side of the Square that I arrived at a possible solution. I think you will find that Bloomfield walked straight across the Square, and, taking advantage of the fog, stepped through the opposite gate into a car standing at the rear of the rank, drove to Illbeck Street, and returned the same way, leaving the car where he had found it. If it had not been for the fact that the owner of the car had turned his speedometer back to zero the evening before no one would have jumped to the fact that the car had been borrowed. As it is he will be ready to come forward when the time arrives."

Arkwright leaned forward eagerly.

"Given that your theory is right, what about the evening? We have the butler's evidence that Bloomfield was working in his room at the time of the Abramoff murder."

"Bloomfield was ostensibly working in his room," corrected Constantine. "He was heard typing by the servants both at seven thirty and seven fifty, and we have his own statement and Miller's that he took letters to the library for his employer's signature several times in the course of the evening. I should imagine that that statement is hardly worth the paper it is written on! As regards the evidence of the servants, Miller was seen coming *from* the secretary's room at eight o'clock. Does that suggest nothing to you? Bloomfield was heard typing at seven fifty, remember."

There was a dull thud as Arkwright's fist struck the table.

"By Jove, they *could* have faked it between them!" he exclaimed. "If Miller was responsible for the typing!"

"Exactly. Miller was backwards and forwards between the library and the secretary's room all the evening. No one actually saw Bloomfield except Miller during that period. Bloomfield no doubt had a latch-key and could have let himself in and out of the house without attracting attention. Greeve assumed that the driver of the car was Miller, but he never saw him. I fancy that it's about the only time in history that a blackmailer has actually levied toll on his victim under the impression that he was dealing with a third person. Greeve was undoubtedly genuine in his belief that Miller was the murderer."

"It hangs together all right!" admitted Arkwright, "but I wish we'd got more to go on. If those people can identify him, all well and good. If they can't, I can see the Public Prosecutor pointing out some of the weak lines in the evidence! There are plenty of them!"

"We've traced the notes," Constantine reminded him.

"To Miller, not to Bloomfield," Arkwright objected. "And Miller's a slippery customer. He's safeguarded by his alibi and he can easily deny having given them to Bloomfield."

"That he did give them to him, I feel sure. According to the butler he placed them under a weight on his table when he received them instead of putting them in his pocket. I fancy we shall find that Miller was merely a dummy and entirely under Bloomfield's thumb. If Bloomfield isn't the real head of the firm I shall be surprised."

"How do you suppose he discovered Vera Abramoff's intentions? If Mrs. Miller suspected him she would hardly be likely to give the show away."

"He had the run of Miller's correspondence and Madame Abramoff's visit must have been discussed openly beforehand. If he recognised the name that would be enough to bring his danger home to him. In addition to which Miller presumably knew who he was and would have warned him. The most interesting problem to me is Miller himself. That he was an accessory after the fact is obvious, but how far he was implicated in the actual murders is an open question."

He was interrupted by the entrance of the detective who had been sent to fetch Vera Abramoff's bag from the station cloak-room. Arkwright stripped the paper off it and shook the contents out onto the table. As Greeve had said, it contained nothing but the murdered woman's passport, money, powder box and lip-stick. Tucked away behind the mirror was a letter from Mrs. Miller, but it consisted only of a blurred scrawl saying that, if she were not at the station to meet her, Madame Abramoff was to take a taxi and drive straight to the house.

"Precious little there to help us," grumbled Arkwright, as he rose stiffly to his feet. "Well, there's nothing for it but to act. We can't afford to let him slip through our fingers now. We've got a case, but a clever counsel can play Old Harry with it."

He picked up the report.

"I must see the Superintendent about this. Will you hang on, sir, and await results?"

"We may as well add one link to the chain, if possible," said Constantine. "Manners should be back by now. May I use your telephone?"

Manners had returned and, judging by his voice, was in a state of restrained jubilation.

"I was about to ring you up, sir," he explained. "I had no difficulty in obtaining a few words with the little girl's nurse. It is as you thought, sir. After Mr. Miller's secretary had passed her with the little dog she did not see him again until he called the dog and went back to the house with it. When the dog came running towards them they naturally took it for granted that the secretary was still walking in the Square. It was very foggy just then, the nurse says, and she was in two minds whether to take the child home. The little girl was playing close to her all the time and she is sure that she did not see the gentleman either."

"I told Mr. Arkwright you'd pull it off!" exclaimed Constantine. "As a matter of curiosity, I wish you'd tell me how you did it."

"It came about very naturally, sir. I watched the nurse go into the Square and then dropped in on Roper for a friendly call. Finding him occupied I offered to take the little dog for a run in the Square. Very unpopular with the household, the little dog is, on account of its constant barking, and they were glad to get him out of the way. If I might make a suggestion, sir."

"Yes?"

"I worded my enquiries as carefully as I could, but the nurse is the kind of woman that puts two and two together, as they say. She is also of a chatty nature. If steps are to be taken it might be advisable to take them at once, sir."

"I quite agree with you, Manners. You've done magnificently."

Arkwright, who had been availing himself of the second earphone, grinned.

"Manners deserves a presentation watch and he shall have it if this comes off," he said. "Anything else you can suggest?"

"Nothing, I'm afraid," answered Constantine. "Karamiev gave me these for you, by the way. They were forwarded to Madame Abramoff from Paris. Evidently arrived too late to catch her before she started."

He handed Arkwright the letters the manager had given him. Arkwright ripped open the envelope and ran through them.

Three of them were circulars, the fourth was a long letter, in a handwriting which made him glance swiftly at the signature.

"From Mrs. Miller," he exclaimed, as he turned back to the first page. Constantine bent over the table and they read it together. It opened abruptly and had evidently been scrawled hastily on the spur of the moment.

"This is just a line to say for God's sake do not breathe a word to Charles of what you told me about Julius Bloomfield. I told you how potty he was about him. He might be his son instead of his nephew from the way he behaves, but I did not think he had got it in him to behave like he did today. After I wrote to you this morning I had a beast of a row with Charles. The same old thing, a couple of bills he could have paid without noticing. It is Julius who makes all the trouble, you would think the money belonged to him instead of Charles. He would be all right if it was not for Julius. Anyway, Charles said things to me and I went further than I meant and told him I could tell him a thing or two about his precious Julius and his goings on before he joined him in Switzerland. I thought Charles would have a fit, but he had got me started and I went on spilling the beans. And in the middle of it in walked Julius. He did not say much, but you should have seen his face. If he could have killed me then and there he would have. I tell you, he frightened me. He can do what he likes with Charles and he will get his own back through him. I never breathed your name, but he may have guessed. But, for goodness sake, keep quiet when you come about what you told me. I am certain now he is the fellow you knew in Russia, but you said he might not remember you. Anyhow I have burnt your letters. We can talk it over when you come, but do not say a word till you have seen me. Yours with love, Lottie."

Arkwright looked at the envelope.

"Written on the twelfth," he said. "He got his own back all right, two days later. This must have just missed her. It went to her lodgings and from there to the Theatrical Agent's. They forwarded it, hence the delay. You weren't far wrong, sir."

Constantine had picked up the letter and was re-reading it carefully.

"Those two women literally held Bloomfield's life in their hands and never realised it," he said. "If they had they would have been more careful. Mrs. Miller evidently detested him and she must have jumped at the chance of poisoning her husband's mind against him. Then, when it was too late, she got frightened. Well, I'm afraid that's the whole of our case against him. No one saw him on the occasion of the Miller murder except Cattistock and his was only a fleeting glimpse."

"There's that pendant of Mrs. Miller's," Arkwright said thoughtfully. "Bloomfield took it as a blind, of course. We may come on it among his things. We've failed to trace the surgeon's coat and gloves, but he may very well have bought those abroad. He was in Paris on business about ten days before the murder."

"There's one problem that still confronts us," observed Constantine. "Madame Abramoff's letter to Miller."

"I'm beginning to see light there," answered Arkwright. "We've admitted all along the possibility that it might be a forgery. Unfortunately there were no very adequate specimens of her writing available for comparison, apart from the signatures we got from Karamiev. Bloomfield, on the contrary, could have laid his hands on any of her letters to Mrs. Miller. He may have written the letter and posted it just before leaving Paris ten days before the murder. He would deal with it with the rest of

Miller's correspondence on his return. It would then merely be a question of altering the date on the postmark, an easy enough job if you know how to do it. There's a sure test for that, however cleverly it's worked."

"Photography?"

Arkwright nodded.

"The photo-micrographic camera. If there's been any fancy work done on that envelope we shall know it. I'll be off now. See you later, sir."

"If you're still there to see me," observed Constantine mildly. "Judging from that report I can hardly imagine a less pleasant job than that of arresting Malin."

CHAPTER EIGHTEEN

As THE TWO MEN parted outside New Scotland Yard Constantine placed a hand on the detective's arm.

"You're dealing with a desperate man, Arkwright," he said.

Arkwright, realising the old man's anxiety, felt oddly touched. Outside his work he was a person of few ties and his friendship with Constantine was a very real factor in his life.

"Not for the first time, sir," was all he said, but he determined to get in touch with him and set his mind at rest at the earliest opportunity.

He had already rung up Miller's office and been told that the jeweller and his secretary had left over an hour ago. Accompanied by three plain-clothes detectives he drove straight to Miller's house. Roper opened the door.

"Mr. Bloomfield in?" demanded Arkwright.

"He's with Mr. Miller in the library, sir," answered the butler, turning in the direction of the library door.

Arkwright barred his way with an arm like a rod of iron. At a sign from him one of the men ran down the steps and descended into the area. Followed by the other two Arkwright brushed past the open-mouthed butler into the hall. A second later the three men were in the library, with the door closed behind them.

Miller was seated at the big writing table facing them. On the blotter in front of him was a pearl necklace and, behind him, stood Bloomfield, holding a list from which he had evidently been checking the pearls.

Before either of the men had time to move Arkwright was on the other side of the table and had one hand on Bloomfield's shoulder, the other inside the cuff of his coat.

"I have to arrest you, Julius Bloomfield, alias Peter Malin, and you, Charles Miller, for being concerned in the murder of Vera Abramoff on the night of Monday, November the fourteenth, and to warn you that anything you say may be used in evidence against you," he said rapidly.

He felt Bloomfield stiffen under his hand. Beyond that first, involuntary movement the secretary made no sign, but remained rigid, his eyes fixed on the cowering figure of his employer.

Miller, his face ashen and distorted, twisted half round in his chair, saw the second detective at his elbow and went to pieces completely.

"You cannot arrest me," he shrieked. "I know nothing, nothing, I tell you. Julius, tell them I know nothing ..."

His voice snapped like a thread. His body that, a second before had been writhing in an agony of apprehension, seemed to freeze into stillness. And, above him, silent and menacing, towered the figure of Bloomfield.

Then Arkwright spoke.

"Coming, Bloomfield?" he demanded. "Or have I got to take you?"

As he uttered the words he moved a step towards the door, drawing his prisoner with him. Bloomfield made no show of resistance, but his eyes never wavered from the figure of Miller, who still sat, crouched and motionless in his chair, his hands gripping the edge of the table. With a jerk of his head Arkwright motioned to the detective to take him and the man laid a hand on his arm. The contact seemed to galvanise Miller into action. He wrenched himself to his feet and made a frenzied attempt to get past the detective, who tightened his grip and held him in spite of his futile efforts to break free.

"Let me go," he sobbed, his face riven and distorted with terror. "Don't you see? Julius, he will ..."

He flung his arm in the direction of Bloomfield.

He was too late. The detective on guard at the door, with a yell of: "Look out, sir!" hurled himself forward, but Bloomfield's right hand was already out of his pocket. The revolver it held spoke once and Miller, with a little sigh, slipped down onto the carpet and lay still.

Bloomfield only spoke once on his way to the station.

"For a crime committed in this country there is no extradition?" he demanded.

"You will be tried at the Old Bailey," Arkwright told him.

With a deep breath Bloomfield sank back in his seat.

Arkwright rang up Constantine and, late that evening, called upon him at his flat.

"Carling thought he was doing a bunk and grabbed him and held him bang in the line of fire," he said, at the end of his recital. "The poor beggar was trying to take cover! He won't live through the night. He was conscious when they got him to the hospital and he made a statement. Bloomfield's his nephew, by the way. Miller was with him all through that time in Russia and declares he wouldn't have lived a week if he'd gone back there. They want him badly, apparently, and he seems to have got the idea that if his uncle had told us all he knew, we should have let them have him. He was wrong, of course, but the mistake cost Miller his life."

"Was Miller party to his wife's murder?" asked Constantine.

"I think not. He declares it came as an appalling shock to him. He never dreamed that Bloomfield would go to such lengths. His version is that if Bloomfield had not overheard Mrs. Miller's threats against him he would never have known that she suspected his identity. Miller knows he is dying and no doubt believes he is speaking the truth, but he was so entirely in Bloomfield's hands that it's difficult to believe that he wouldn't have told him about the scene with his wife."

"What do you make of his feeling for Bloomfield? Was he merely terrorised, do you think?" asked Constantine.

Arkwright shook his head.

"It was far more complicated than that. He was under no delusions about the man. He'd been his jackal, as it were, all through those days in Russia. Towards the end of his statement, when his grip on things was beginning to weaken, he spoke almost with admiration of him and there seems no doubt that he was completely dominated by him."

"Bloomfield had all the qualities that Miller lacked," said Constantine, "and Miller probably realised it. It is easy to guess what he and his people may have suffered under the old regime. His mind had probably been irretrievably warped by things he had seen in Russia as a child. No doubt Bloomfield, in his eyes, was all that he would have wished to be himself if he hadn't been born a weakling and a coward. Miller would no doubt have shrunk from the idea of murder. He might even have dared to oppose Bloomfield, but it would have been because he was afraid of the consequences, not from any inherent sense of decency."

"He certainly didn't instigate the murders," agreed Arkwright. "According to his statement he knew nothing till he was confronted with his wife's body. He recognised the knife, of course, and, from then on, lived in an agony of terror. He was afraid of us and what we might find out, but, I think, still more terrified of Bloomfield. He declared to me that he had no suspicion that the Abramoff letter was a forgery and went to the station fully expecting to meet her there. When she did not come he still suspected nothing, being convinced that that was the train she had meant to travel by. I questioned him as to Bloomfield's whereabouts that evening and he admitted that he was not in the house at the time of Madame Abramoff's death. It was Miller, of course, who was heard typing in the secretary's room, but I'm inclined to believe his story, which is that Bloomfield told him that he had to go out on urgent business connected with the Miller murder and that he wished him to cover the fact of his absence. One must remember that he had been on tenterhooks ever since he had seen his wife's body that morning and was probably prepared to follow any suggestion of Bloomfield s blindly. Bloomfield told him late that evening what he had done. I gather that they both omitted to foresee that Miller might be called upon to identify the corpse of Madame Abramoff. Miller was in consequence unprepared and, in his panic, made the fatal mistake of concealing the fact that he had never seen her."

"Bloomfield could hardly have been saddled with a worse accomplice," said Constantine. "I should imagine that he simply did not dare confide in him. Did you get anything out of Miller concerning the business of Greeve?"

"Yes. Bloomfield intercepted the whole of that correspondence and the first Miller heard of it was when Bloomfield rang him up at his office after receiving our telephone call announcing Greeve's arrest and asking him to call at the Yard; Bloomfield primed Miller then as to the story he was to tell. The enamel pendant was, of course, one that they already had in stock and Miller brought it with him from Hatton Garden that afternoon, so as to have it in readiness if it were needed to corroborate his story. By the way, a messenger did deliver a parcel at Miller's office on the day he declared to us that Greeve had brought the pendant. We have failed to trace him and the head clerk is unable to describe him, but he certainly was not Greeve, who was playing darts in the Goat and Horns at the time. Bloomfield was certainly an adept at using the material he had to hand. He saw Greeve, as you suspected, after his release, and put him wise to the yarn about the pendant."

"Talking of pendants, did he tell you what had become of his wife's emerald?"

"No. He was getting very feeble towards the end and I did not press him. He was only too ready to talk, seemed to have a sort of craving to get it all off his chest. He must have been through Hell since his wife died. His fear of Bloomfield was the only thing that prevented him from giving the show away earlier, I imagine. He was shot through the spine, by the way, and the lower half of his body is completely paralysed, but his brain is quite clear. He literally talked himself into a state of collapse. If the hospital people hadn't considered his case absolutely hopeless, I shouldn't have been allowed to interview him."

Constantine rose and pulled a small inlaid table up to the fire. Placing a box of Halva at Arkwright's elbow, he began to set out the chessmen.

"I'm glad it's over," he said, "and that I'm free to cultivate my garden. Yours is a nasty job, Arkwright, and, for the future, you can prosecute it without any interference from me."

Arkwright, who was mixing himself a whiskey and soda, turned to him, a shrewd twinkle in his eyes.

"To the next time, sir," he retorted, raising his glass.

A few minutes later the Miller case and all its ramifications had become a thing of the past. They were playing chess.

The mystery of Mrs. Miller's pendant was not cleared up until after her husband's death in hospital, when his business was being valued for probate. The emerald was identified in a tray of unset stones. Miller had broken up the setting and added the gem to his stock. If he had lived long enough to draw the insurance money and dispose of the emerald he would have realised on its value twice over and made a very pretty profit on his wife's death.

THE END

Made in United States
North Haven, CT
22 February 2023

33006928R00117